KILLER
HEELS

Sheryl J. Anderson

KILLER
HEELS

 St. Martin's Minotaur
New York

www.minotaurbooks.com

ISBN 0-312-31946-0

10 9 8 7 6 5 4 3 2

To Lisa Seidman, the truest of friends, who made it possible

Acknowledgments

I am delighted to have this opportunity to acknowledge and thank my amazing husband, Mark Parrott, my partner in all things, including the writing of this book; our splendid children, Sara and Sean, who were willing to watch a little extra television so the first draft could be turned in on time; my parents, Alden and June Anderson, whose love, support, and proofreading are always invaluable; Mark's parents, Bob and Iva Parrott, who demonstrated their love and support by racing each other through the first draft; our siblings and siblings-in-law—Eric and Allison Anderson, Chip and Karen Parrott, Kathy Parrott and David Wechtaluk—for their love and encouragement; Louis E. Catron, Grant Tinker, and Rob Kaplan, who taught me about writing and much more; our book agent, Andy Zack, who made it seem simple; our editor, Kelley Ragland, who made it seem painless; her assistants, Benjamin Sevier and Carly Einstein, who kept it all on track; and all our friends who so thoughtfully remembered to ask, "How's the book coming?"

1

I always knew I'd make my mark on the world. I just didn't expect it to be one of those chalk outlines they draw around dead bodies. Of course, the chalk came later. It started with the blood. But that's the price you pay for wearing open-toed shoes in Manhattan. You never know what you're going to step in.

It's actually Cassady's fault that we went by my office when we did, and I'm not above using that to guilt her into buying me a new pair to replace the ones that soaked up all the blood. But then, Cassady Lynch is a lawyer and she's got a much stricter view of liability than I do. So I suppose the shoes will just turn into another one of those debit/credit things you pile up with girlfriends over the years—sweaters that got stretched out, cars that got dented, boyfriends that got stolen. But shoes that got trashed at a murder scene—brand-new Jimmy Choos, mind you, the Cat 85mm's with that gorgeous blue striped fabric and fabulous heel that cost me more than I can bear to think—probably demand a whole budget line item all their own.

I suppose I could have told Cassady no. But that's pretty much a superhuman feat and it's not successful very often, for me or anyone else, so it's not surprising that I caved.

What started the whole deal was I was trying to describe this hideous piece of art The Publisher had just installed in our offices and Cassady said it couldn't possibly be as awful as I was making it out to be. Granted, there were several *mojitos* fueling the fires of art criticism, but I stood my ground. It was one of the uglier pieces I had ever seen. Cassady insisted that I take her to see it right away. She said she wasn't going to be able to concentrate on dinner with the images of this abomination dancing in her head.

Cassady took some art classes when we were in college, but then she tried to submit her boyfriend for a midterm exam. She'd stripped him—remember, it's very hard to say no to her—and painted this *Guernica*-like mural all over his body, leaving only his genitals unpainted because, as we all remember from *Goldfinger*, he would have suffocated otherwise. Cassady said it was a political statement. I contend that she was bored and looking to get kicked out of the class. They were going to give her an incomplete, but she threatened to launch a whole freedom-of-expression brouhaha and walked away from it all with a B. She's amazing that way.

Small wonder she persuaded me to leave Django and walk over to the office. I work for *Zeitgeist* magazine, which is right down Lexington Avenue. You can find us wedged between *Marie Claire* and *Cosmo* at your finer newsstands and markets. We do the whole lifestyle thing, but we like to think we have more of a sense of humor than the competition. God knows it takes a sense of humor to survive in our business, and I mean both the magazine business and the business of being a single woman in New York City. And those are both big businesses. In fact, they may support every other one. Single women drive the economy of this city and the magazines report on it.

Everything else is just an offshoot, a subcontractor. The restaurants, the bars, the shops, the shrinks, the florists, the designers, the garment and jewelry districts, the theaters, the gyms, the hotels . . . Detect a pattern? If they don't exist because of the needs and wants of single women, they exist to employ the men that single women need and want, which accounts for the lawyers, doctors, and stockbrokers. And the whole subset of baby stuff and nannies and houses in Connecticut is there to inspire the single women to put up with the single men. It's a delicate economic model, but it seems to be working.

I have to admit, it was my idea not to turn on the light right away. I wanted to go for a sort of "tah-dah" moment and snap the light on to reveal the grotesquery in all its glory in a blaze of track lighting. There was a fair amount of outside light bouncing in through the windows and off all the chrome and acrylic in the bullpen, that vast middle ground where those not deemed office-worthy sit at desks with nothing to protect them from learning way too much about their colleagues. There aren't even glorified bulletin boards masquerading as cubicle walls to give people the illusion of their own space. Everything's out in the open—desks, filing cabinets, sexual preferences, dating disasters. The overheard phone conversations are the most colorful things in the bullpen.

So while we favor a lush, vibrant palette in print, we're just this side of institutional in our office design. The Publisher believes comfortable people don't work fast enough. He must believe the same thing about rich people, because he's not turning any of us into them. The press calls him a business genius. I guess "miser" is too old-fashioned.

I know my way around the office well enough that I

wasn't concerned about tripping over anything. The assistants' desks are laid out in diagonals—on the bias, as Caitlin, the fashion editor, likes to point out—to keep the floor plan from looking too much like an insurance company, but it's still simple to navigate. I just didn't expect Teddy to be lying on the floor with a knife in his throat. One moment, I was leading Cassady through the darkened bullpen and the next, I was aware of my foot squooshing. I knew immediately that I had stepped in something that was not going to be good for my shoes, but I was thinking more along the lines of yogurt someone had somehow spilled and neglected to clean up. I stopped suddenly, my toes curling up like cocktail shrimp.

"What?" Cassady said impatiently.

"I stepped in something."

"If it's on the floor at this hour of the night, it's disgusting. Don't touch it. Where's the light switch?" Cassady started to feel her way toward the wall.

"I'll get it."

"No, stay put. You don't want to track it around or grind it into your new shoes, whatever it is."

As Cassady groped for the switch, I bent over to see what I could see in the dark. All I could tell was that there was a large pool of something dark on the carpet and a big pile of something against one of the desks. Then Cassady found the light switch and I realized that the darkness on the carpet was blood and the big pile was Teddy Reynolds, advertising director for *Zeitgeist*. I think I already mentioned the knife.

Now, I believe I deserve points for not fainting, puking, or even screaming. I only made a delicate sound of concern. Of course, Cassady later described it to Tricia as "the sound a Yorkshire terrier would make if you threw it against the wall. Hard." Cassady came running back over, took a look, and said, "Holy shit." But then, it was a different experience for her. She didn't know Teddy.

"You know him?" For some reason, she was whispering. I nodded as she helped me up, noting my right foot planted firmly in the pool of blood. The red was already soaking in and discoloring the blues in the fabric. "That's never going to come out."

"Isn't it shallow to be thinking that way at a moment like this?"

Cassady shrugged. "People handle grief in different ways." She grabbed the phone on the nearest desk.

"Call Tricia on her cell. She has an event tonight." Good times, bad times, you call your girlfriends first.

Cassady squinted. "You're kidding, right?"

Actually, I wasn't. "Who else?"

"I thought I'd start with the police." Cassady dialed 911. You can always count on her to have the logical reaction, even in times of extreme stress. Granted, she doesn't always follow through with the logical reaction, especially when a man is involved, but at least it occurs to her. Not all of us have that particular gift.

So the police came and the building security guys had a fit because Cassady hadn't bothered to clue them in and they looked pretty bad when the cops came stomping into the lobby. The cops didn't let them hang around too long before banishing them back down to the lobby to get security tapes and all that sort of stuff. They also got to place the call to Yvonne Hamilton, our editor, informing her that there was a "problem" at the office and asking her to come in. Poor guys. But at least they could feel useful. I felt like a complete and utter idiot. As a journalist, I pride myself on being observant and insightful. But in the clutch,

I found myself transforming into a total bobblehead. I couldn't remember Teddy's wife's name right away or how long he'd worked at the magazine or if he'd been in his office when I left that night. Cassady said it was probably a form of shock. I guess I'll take that over useless.

It was also really hard to concentrate with poor Teddy lying there on the floor. Especially with the knife in his throat. Teddy was a big man who, until now, had always been in motion. It fascinated me that a guy who could not sit still could not burn calories more efficiently. He'd actually been trying to diet lately, a compulsion that's hard to duck when you work at a women's magazine, but I think his idea of dieting was to add some fresh fruit to his expansive caloric intake. He was always pacing and chewing on something while chewing out someone. Not that he was a bad guy, he was just very difficult to please. He went through assistants like J.Lo goes through men and I'm sure at least half the desks in the office contained voodoo dolls in his likeness. But he was great at his job and he could be very sweet when it suited him, so I realized the staff was actually going to miss him. At least the rest of the staff was going to get to remember him rumbling around the office with a sheen of sweat on his face and a bagel in his hand. From now on, I was always going to see him in a crumpled mass on the floor with a knife in his throat.

The first thing I wanted to do when the police arrived was get away from the body. Cassady had insisted that I not move until they came, to minimize the damage to the crime scene. So when the uniformed officers showed, I asked if I could sit down before we started answering questions. They were really impressed that Cassady had tried to preserve the scene. They were also really impressed with

Cassady period, but they were young male officers, so that was no surprise. Cassady's incredibly smart, but she's also all legs and has this incredible head of auburn curls that a lesser woman would envy. I just admire them. And then there are the green eyes and the bonded teeth and her fondness for push-up bras. So they were leaning in pretty closely as she filled them in on how we happened to find Teddy, and I had to interrupt.

"Could I sit down or at least move over there?" I asked as non-shrilly as possible. I could feel shrill trying to work itself into my voice and I was determined to get through this with some grace. "Grace under pressure" has always struck me as a very admirable trait and I'd always imagined that I possessed it to some degree, but this was a new level of pressure and I wasn't coming up with sufficient amounts of grace in a timely fashion.

The officers looked down at my feet, still planted in Teddy's blood. "We're going to need you to leave the shoes there," the blond one, Officer Jankowski, said. The uniforms and all the stuff these guys wear on their belts tend to make NYPD officers look chunky, but not this one. He was tall, with broad shoulders and slim hips—a swimmer's build. He held his hand out like he was helping me out of a cab and I slipped out of my shoes, stepped over the blood, and grabbed a chair two desks away with as much grace as I could muster. Officer Jankowski followed me and pulled up another chair. I guess he was going for the whole eye-to-eye thing. They must teach them that at the academy. His partner, Officer Hendryx, stayed with Cassady. Hendryx was a ruddy brunette. He wasn't quite as tall as Jankowski and had a thicker build, but I could tell it was all muscle. I could see his biceps working under his sleeves. I'm sure Cassady could, too.

"I know this is very difficult, Ms. Forrester, but I need you to tell me everything you can about what happened here tonight." He flipped open his notebook with a flick of his wrist. I think he learned that from *Law and Order*, not the academy. "Did you know the victim?"

That's when the bobblehead problem started. I nodded and I felt like I kept nodding for about ten minutes. Officer Jankowski watched me with a very patient smile, then gently asked, "What's his name?"

"Oh, right. Teddy Reynolds. Our advertising director. That's his office right behind him."

"Is he married?"

I bobbled again until I came up with Helen's name. The minute I pictured Helen, the reality of what had happened knocked the wind out of me. Up until then, I'd been able to look at Teddy's body like The Publisher's new sculpture—some incredibly ugly piece of art that had somehow found its way into our offices. It wasn't real. It couldn't be real. But it was. And someone was going to have to tell Helen, and she was going to have to tell her parents and Teddy's parents and all their friends. I made another delicate sound of concern. Cassady and Officer Hendryx came rushing over and Officer Jankowski grabbed my hand. His hand was warmer than I'd expected and felt really good. "Are you going to be sick? It's okay, it happens all the time."

I knew I wasn't going to be sick, but I did think about fainting for a couple of seconds. Then somehow, without even deciding to, I opted for crying. Pretty gently, all things considered. Usually, I go for the heaving sobs and my face gets all blotchy and it's not a pretty sight. This time, the tears started rolling down my face and I couldn't do anything about it. Maybe that was shock, too. Cassady snagged the box of Kleenex off Gretchen Plotnick's desk and eased it into my lap. Well, at least my crying had grace.

There was noise behind us and Officer Hendryx excused himself to go meet the other police personnel who were arriving. They turned on every light they could find, which made it even harder to avoid looking at Teddy and all the blood. Officer Jankowski explained that the new people were going to secure the crime scene, start gathering forensic evidence, all that CSI stuff. I just wanted them to cover up Teddy. I had this wild thought that he was getting cold, even though Teddy was one of those guys who could sweat in a snowstorm.

The new arrivals, all in NYPD windbreakers, started setting up equipment. It seemed very routine to them and I found that incredibly sad. There was a woman with a camera and a couple of guys with what looked like great big toolboxes. They unloaded evidence bags and tweezers and brushes and I started to be fascinated; then they pulled on rubber gloves. There was something about the sound of the gloves snapping closed against their wrists that made me consider fainting again. I wasn't fascinated anymore. I did my best to focus on Officer Jankowski's questions and keep the bobblehead at bay. But then he asked me, "Can you think of anyone who would want to hurt Mr. Reynolds?"

I don't want to speak ill of the dead, but Teddy had plenty of enemies. Not murder-level enemies, but it did give me pause to think of the number of people I knew he'd pissed off. There were bound to be more. I work at home a lot, so I don't see all the drama that goes down in a day at *Zeitgeist*. But these were all business enemies, unhappy advertisers or agencies or layout people.

"Nothing worth killing over," I told him.

"You'd be surprised," Officer Jankowski replied. "Murder's rarely a rational act."

I bobbled again, considering that, and Officer Hendryx came back to tap Officer Jankowski on the shoulder. "They're here."

"Excuse me, ma'am." Officer Jankowski gave me a polite smile and stood up to follow Officer Hendryx. Cassady, leaning against the desk behind me, moaned.

"What?" I asked her, trying not to watch the technicians examining Teddy.

"Definitely not your night. You just got ma'am-ed."

"I'm sure he learned it at the academy. Or on TV."

"He learned it from his mother. He's a baby, Molly, showing respect to his elders."

"Don't start trying to make me feel old because your little boy in blue wasn't handing over his phone number."

Cassady waggled a business card in front of me. I caught a glimpse of the NYPD seal. "Would that be his office phone or his cell phone that he wasn't handing over?"

"But did you get a home phone?"

"I appreciate a man who likes to go slow."

"Only once you get him home."

Cassady was about to say something devastating in return, but something across the room caught her eye. I turned to look, too. The man who had just entered was middle-aged, tall and powerful, African-American, somewhere between imposing and intimidating. I glanced over at Cassady in surprise. He wasn't really her type: She's currently in a young-and-malleable phase.

But then I looked back at the policemen again and saw the second guy and realized why Cassady's antennae were up. He couldn't have looked better if he were backlit and walking in slow motion. It was a chain-store suit and his shoes were a couple of years old, but he was breathtaking. Square jaw, tousled hair that got that way honestly and not because of seventy-five bucks worth of product, and amazing blue eyes. The little clarity I'd been able to summon threatened to evaporate, but I took a deep breath. Cassady also gave me a firm jab in the ribs, which is always good for focus. "Dibs."

"This is a murder scene, not a nightclub."

"The story will delight my grandchildren." Cassady flashed me a quick smile, then quickly turned back to watch the two new arrivals come across the room to us. Officers Jankowski and Hendryx were obviously filling them in on the situation and their attention was focused on poor Teddy. In fact, the older man peeled off to go look at Teddy and the young hunk came straight to us. How nice.

"Ms. Forrester, Ms. Lynch, I'm Detective Edwards, Homicide." Cassady and I stuck our hands out like two debutantes in a receiving line. Detective Edwards missed half a beat, which increased his desirability quotient considerably. He then shook my hand first, which got him even more points. Cassady sniffed loud enough for me to hear.

"My partner, Detective Lipscomb, and I will be handling this case. The officers tell us you two found the body." He looked us both over carefully, but in a forensic, not a foreplay, sense. He stopped when he got to our feet. More precisely, to my feet. "You came into the office barefoot?"

"No, but I stepped in the blood and they asked me to leave my shoes there." I tried to sound businesslike, but the almost-shrill thing was happening again. I could've sworn I'd be better than this in a traumatic situation.

Detective Edwards glanced at the officers for affirmation,

then over at Teddy. "I know you've already been inter-viewed, but we'd like to talk to you after we look around. You don't mind waiting, do you?"

Cassady sat, pulling me back down into my chair while she was at it. "Not at all, Detective. Anything we can do to help."

Detective Edwards looked us over again, a little less fo-rensically this time, and went over to his partner and Teddy. Officers Jankowski and Hendryx trailed along behind.

"Have you ever been at a murder scene before?" I asked Cassady. We've known each other since freshman year of college, but we didn't get to be best friends until we both came to the city after graduation, so I don't know every-thing about her. Besides, she's a girl who knows how to keep her secrets.

"No. They don't come up very often in my kind of law." Cassady isn't a criminal lawyer, though I've always thought she'd be great at it. Besides the fact that she looks awesome in those Ally McBeal suits. Instead, she's counsel for the Coalition for Creative Expression and Enterprise, also known as C^2E^2. They're this wonderful, funky public-interest group that's into all sorts of issues where creative expression and business crash into each other—stuff like Internet privacy and intellectual copyrights. They try to get the two sides to work together to find mutually beneficial solutions, but sometimes Cassady has to take people to court to get their attention. "Why?" she asked suspiciously.

"Because I would think you'd find it fascinating."

"I do."

"No, you're bored."

"What makes you say that?"

"Because you have one cop's phone number in your pocket and you're already salivating on another one."

"You're projecting. You're a little more emotionally involved here than I am, but that's a function of circumstance and nothing I need to be punished for." All of which I would have taken more to heart if she'd said any of it looking at me, instead of staring at Detective Edwards the whole time.

But I had to admit—to myself, not to her—that I was having a harder time with this than she was. I realized that it was mainly because I knew Teddy and she didn't, but there was a little professional angst going on, too. As wholly inappropriate as it might have been, part of my brain was whining because I was in the middle of what could have been a great story if I were working for the *New York Times* and not *Zeitgeist*. Not that I don't love my job at the magazine, but it's not exactly where I intended to wind up.

See, I'm a news junkie. Blame my parents. My father couldn't eat dinner without Walter Cronkite intoning in the background because it was every American's responsibility to stay informed. My mother put my playpen in front of the Watergate hearings because she thought it would be stimulating for me. I guess it was, but I also get this really weird, tingly feeling whenever I see a man with big, bushy eyebrows. I haven't brought that up in therapy. Yet.

Anyway, you can see why I thought the whole news gig would be pretty cool. But I realized it wasn't all style, it was substance, too. So I did the well-rounded liberal arts deal, then marched out into the world of journalism to seek my slot. I was going to offer insightful commentary on the events that shape our world, enlighten the populace, and make the world a better place. And I sort of do. But not as much as I'd like to.

"You're the advice columnist?" The detectives had returned from their inspection of Teddy and were questioning Cassady and me. Detective Lipscomb said it in a completely non-judgmental way, but it still stung a little. Especially since I was sitting next to my drop-dead gorgeous public-interest lawyer best friend. Put me in bunny slippers and a quilted bathrobe: I'm the advice columnist. It's not a field that the Pulitzer Committee is paying a whole lot of attention to. This year. But I don't plan to be doing this until I drop in my tracks, God bless the dear departed Ann Landers. I'm barely over thirty (no need for specific numbers) and I'm always looking for the opportunity that's going to take me closer to real news.

And this is actually a sweet setup: I do a lot of my work at home, so I get paid to sit in my pajamas and tell people how they're screwing up their lives and what I would do were I in their situation, which I am so eternally glad I am not. I enjoy it most of the time, though some of the letters make me fear for the future of the human race. I mean, my God. Write to me about delicate shadings of ethics and etiquette, but think for yourself occasionally! How can you focus long enough to type *Dear Molly, I've been sleeping with my brother-in-law for the last six months and the sex is great, but I'm starting to feel guilty* and still feel the need to ask, *Should I come clean with my sister?* Like any reasonably intelligent, self-respecting woman who survived high school doesn't know that given a choice between keeping a secret and sharing the truth, you lock up that diary and throw away the key.

"Oh, man," Officer Hendryx blurted. "I shoulda known. Molly Forrester. 'You Can Tell Me.' " He grinned at me the way I thought guys only grinned at professional athletes.

Cassady arched an eyebrow at him. "You read Molly's column?"

"Not really," Officer Hendryx confessed. "My girlfriend basically reads it to me. It's her favorite part of the magazine, and she's always saying, 'Ohmigod, Davey, you gotta listen to this!' She's gonna be so amazed I met you."

"We're all very happy for you, Officer," Detective Edwards said, just firmly enough for Officer Hendryx to straighten up and shut up. Detective Edwards swung those very impressive blue eyes back over to me. "And why are you and your lawyer here after hours, Ms. Forrester?"

"She's not my lawyer. She's a lawyer, but not my lawyer."

"She's also in the room," Cassady pointed out. "We're friends. We were having drinks and Molly said there was a hideous piece of art here in the office that I had to see."

"Is it still here?" Detective Edwards looked around.

"Ohmigod, you don't think Teddy interrupted some sort of art theft?" It came out before I'd really thought it through and they all looked at me in varying degrees of surprise.

Detective Lipscomb tried to sound patient, but he made sure the effort showed. "We have to consider all the possibilities at this stage."

"Not that one. Teddy wasn't exactly the heroic type. If someone came in to steal the monstrosity, I bet Teddy would've held the door open for them. Not that Teddy would have been in on it or anything . . ." Maybe if I kept talking long enough, my brain would catch up with my mouth. But right now, my mouth had quite a good lead. Maybe it was time to go back to bobbling.

The detectives exchanged a look, then Detective Edwards put his hand on my arm. I'm sure it was meant to calm me, but it didn't. "Can you show me this piece of art?" I nodded and started to walk past Teddy and all his new companions, then stopped, very conscious of my bare feet. I looked down and so did Detective Edwards. He nodded sympathetically. "I'm sorry about the shoes, but we're going to have to keep them for a while."

"Not like the blood's going to come out of them," Cassady muttered behind us. I looked around, surprised that she was following us. "The statue's the whole reason I'm here," she explained. "I'm damn well gonna see it, if it's not gone."

It wasn't. It was still squatting on its pedestal outside The Publisher's office. It was called *Muse 47*. According to The Publisher, the artist said it was the embodiment of the urge to create. To me, it looked like a disfigured gnome straining to pass a kidney stone. Detective Edwards looked at it for a few minutes, taking in the statue itself, then examined The Publisher's reception area, even checking the carpet for footprints and other trace evidence. The carpet and furnishings in this part of the office are just as bland as the ones in our part of the office, but you can tell they cost more. The chrome shines more brightly or something. Detective Edwards didn't seem particularly impressed by any of it. I stood as quietly as possible, watching his every move. Cassady frowned at the sculpture. "Modern art's such a joke."

"Pretty sweeping statement," Detective Edwards countered, continuing his inspection.

"Unless the law has changed since I left my office, I'm entitled to my opinion." It's always an education to watch Cassady sizing up an opponent, deciding whether he can be consumed in one bite or two.

"Y'know, we tried really hard to take away everybody's civil liberties today, but we couldn't work it in, what with the murder rate climbing and all. So yes, you can have an opinion for another day or two." He stopped inspecting and looked at us, waiting for a reaction.

Cassady was expressionless, hanging tough, so I seized the moment. "I happen to love Jasper Johns."

Cassady rolled her eyes. Detective Edwards grimaced a little, so I could tell we weren't going to bond on this one. But I could also tell he knew I was trying to help and that he appreciated it. Lord knows, I get tired of all the whining and shrieking that I have to listen to in the course of my job, and it's all on paper or a computer screen. Imagine the stuff a homicide detective in New York City has to put up with in the course of a day, and I'm not counting having to actually solve the crimes. The least I could do was deflect a little of Cassady's scorn. And I do like Jasper Johns.

"This area seems untouched, but I'll have the forensic guys check it out. Thank you," Detective Edwards said, gesturing us back to the bullpen. Cassady led the way and I hung back a little, not anxious to see Teddy again. Detective Edwards walked beside me, but he looked like he was concentrating, so I figured I should stay quiet. Especially since I couldn't think of anything helpful to say. You gotta figure "How could this happen?" is something a homicide cop gets sick of hearing pretty early in the work week and I couldn't push my bobblehead much past that.

Detective Lipscomb was waiting for us. Detective Edwards shook his head. Detective Lipscomb nodded. "No sign of struggle in the office. Blood spatter looks like it all happened out here. Wallet and watch are gone."

Detective Edwards' frown deepened. "Odd place for a robbery. Lots of locked doors between here and the street."

"Security guys are pulling the records. We'll see what that points to. Not much here otherwise." Detective Lipscomb held up an evidence bag with the knife from Teddy's throat in it. The inside of the bag was streaked with blood and did this weird stained-glass-window thing when Detective Lipscomb held it up to the light. "Kitchen knife."

"It's Teddy's. He was trying to lose weight and ate a lot of fruit in the afternoon. Liked to slice the apples and said the knives in the kitchen weren't sharp enough, so he kept that one in his desk."

Detective Lipscomb glanced over to Teddy, who was being placed in a body bag. "Guess this one was sharp enough."

Detective Edwards winced. "You're buying breakfast."

Detective Lipscomb was highly offended for some reason. "I am not."

Detective Edwards shook his head at his partner and turned to us to explain. "If somebody starts to sound like a wisecracking TV cop, he has to buy breakfast."

"You punish him?" I asked, not sure I saw the logic.

"Best way to break a bad habit," Detective Edwards explained.

Detective Lipscomb wasn't enjoying this and held the knife bag up again, refocusing everyone. "You're sure this is his?"

"Yes. I borrowed it a couple of times. It really is better than anything we have in the kitchen."

Detective Lipscomb walked over to stand in Teddy's office doorway, bag still in his hand. "So he's working late, hears a strange noise, grabs the knife to arm himself, walks out and . . ." We all looked down at the blood on the carpet and filled in the rest for ourselves. In my version, Teddy wrestled with a shadowy intruder twice his size, the intruder wrenched the knife away, and suddenly Teddy was on the floor, bleeding. I imagined the detectives' version was a little less *noir* than that. And probably, given Teddy, closer to the truth.

Cassady's face was expressionless. I think she'd had enough.

"Ms. Forrester, did Mr. Reynolds have enemies?" Detective Edwards asked after the silence had stretched on a little too long.

"Oh, sure."

Detective Jankowski gave me a perturbed look. "Ma'am, you told me no."

"You asked me if I knew anyone who'd want to hurt him. He asked me about enemies."

Officer Jankowski opened his mouth to protest, but Cassady was quicker. "Definitely two different lists in my life. There's a big difference between someone you'd like to see dead in the business sense and someone you're willing to hurt literally."

"Teddy could be nice, but he could also be really difficult," I admitted. "All depending on what you wanted from him. You could probably split his Rolodex in half between the people who'd vote 'sweetheart' and the ones who'd go for 'bastard.' But I can't imagine a single one of them doing this."

Detective Lipscomb rubbed his forehead. "We'll take that into account." He turned to Jankowski and Hendryx. "Go get with the security guys. Make sure you get the full rundown on cleaning crews, night messengers, standard traffic." The officers nodded to us and hurried out. Cassady waved Officer Hendryx's business card at him in farewell.

"You think it was a stranger, an intruder?" I pressed. Cassady shot me a warning look.

"We see a lot of this. Somebody comes into the building

on so-called legitimate business, then takes advantage of a situation."

I was trying to picture the world in which killing someone was taking advantage of a situation. "So you think this was a robbery or something?"

"No, I think it was a murder," Detective Lipscomb said quietly and Detective Edwards shot him a warning look. There was no breakfast at stake here. Detective Lipscomb was getting angry.

I plunged in anyway. "It's just . . . the knife is so personal. You'd have to get close to him . . ." I wasn't sure where I was going with this, but I got the sense that the detectives were about to veer off in a direction that wasn't going to help Teddy much.

Detective Edwards took a step forward to distract me from his glowering partner. "We appreciate your input. I'm sure this is overwhelming for you and we don't mean to keep you any longer than absolutely necessary." He pressed his business card into my hand.

I had more to say, but Cassady grabbed my arm and almost bolted for the door. "I know an exit cue when I hear one. Thank you very much, gentlemen. You know where to reach us if you have any more questions."

I leaned back, like a toddler resisting her mother's efforts to put her to bed. "Wait."

"No, Molly," Cassady insisted, "it's time to go." She managed to walk me past where Teddy was being loaded onto a gurney for his trip to the morgue.

"But I want to help." I hated how my voice sounded, all thick and unstable, but it stopped Cassady.

She gave me a pained smile and let go of my arm. "I know you do, Moll, but we should leave it to the professionals. You've done everything you can here."

"No, I haven't. I've been emotional and vague and made a miserable impression. I always thought that if I ever found myself in this sort of situation, I'd rise to the occasion, be brilliant and insightful. Maybe even get a feature article out of it."

She dug her phone out of her purse and started dialing. "Even if you have been daydreaming about something like this, which is a whole separate problem, the reality is obviously very different. Trying to look at this as some sort of career opportunity is just your way of ignoring the pain of losing a colleague."

Since I couldn't think of a proper comeback, I asked, "Who are you calling?"

"Now I'm calling Tricia. I think we should meet her for many drinks. Don't you?"

"I'm not sure I can."

Wary that she was missing a joke, Cassady proceeded carefully. "Why? What else do you have to do tonight?"

"I need to solve this murder."

2

"*I come bearing shoes.*" Tricia slid a shopping bag onto the table and me into her arms in one elegant move. Being momentarily engulfed in blue merino can be quite soothing. She smelled great, too. Chanel No. 5 since she was twelve years old. Tricia goes for the classics and makes them work.

"Oh, honey, honey, I am so sorry this happened to you," she whispered in my ear. I squeezed her shoulder in thanks and she stood back. She blew a kiss at Cassady that was acknowledged with a twitch of the nose, then turned back to me, prepared to assess. I seemed to meet with her approval, at least given the circumstances, though I suddenly had an urge to brush my hair. But those sorts of urges come over you frequently when you spend time with Tricia. She's one of those women who is always perfectly put together—hair, outfit, accessories. All the outside stuff, anyway. But with Tricia, it's impressive rather than irritating, mainly because she doesn't make a big deal about it. It comes naturally.

And she's channeling that into her job with great success. Tricia Vincent's an event designer. Have a good cause? She'll design you a party that will fill your treasury and boost your media coverage. She started off doing events for her parents' causes, but her reputation has been spreading and her client base is broadening. She still does a lot of Old Guard stuff, but she's done some really cool political groups lately. Stuff we were actually interested in crashing.

Tricia pushed a strand of hair back from my face and seemed pleased with the result. Maybe I didn't need a brush after all.

"How are you feeling? What can we do for you?"

I faltered because I honestly didn't know what to say. Cassady stepped into the breach. "You brought shoes. A crucial first step."

Tricia reached into the bag and pulled out a glorious pair of Giuseppe Zanottis, corset-laced sandals I had only coveted since the now-ruined Choos had blown my shoe budget for several months. "I forgot to ask Cassady what you were wearing and these go with anything," she said, pitching her voice a little louder as a group behind us started guffawing. Cassady had decided backtracking through our evening might give us a sense of comfort, so we were huddled at a table in Django. They have literally millions of pink beads strung like curtains and there's something very soothing about them, but the crowd was a little too perky. We should have gone to a jazz club. They mute everything. Nothing against Django. It's a wonderful hunting ground, but I didn't feel like hunting.

"Put them on," Cassady suggested. "You'll feel better."

I took the shoes and held them in my lap while I tried to discreetly remove the plastic sandals Cassady had purchased for me at the 24-hour Rite Aid our cabbie found. She had insisted that I sit in the cab and wait, listing with a certain relish the number of diseases to which I had already exposed myself by walking from the office to the cab barefoot.

When we first stepped out of the office building, I was struck by the beautiful simplicity of fresh air. Not that I normally think of the air on Lexington Avenue as being fresh, even in October, but in contrast to what we'd been breathing for the last hour, this was like a morning breeze blowing across acres of newly mown hay. Not that I've actually ever smelled newly mown hay, being a city girl, but I can appreciate the contrast nonetheless. I breathed in as deeply as I could, as often as I could, until Cassady grabbed my arm in concern.

"Are you hyperventilating?" She didn't seem to approve.

"Would it help?" I was feeling a little lightheaded, but I actually welcomed the new sensation.

"Help what?"

"This." I rubbed at a spot on my chest, right in the center of my breastbone, that was so tight I figured she could see it pulsing. Coming down in the elevator, it had felt like some malevolent little creature had crawled into my chest and was gnawing at the spot, making itself a nest. Now it felt like the little wretch was trying to claw its way back out. Somehow, I'd become Sigourney Weaver in *Alien*, dreaming of monsters exploding out of my chest. Thinking about the movie for a minute actually distracted me from the pain. That, and imagining myself with Sigourney Weaver's cheekbones. But it only helped for a minute.

"Scream," Cassady suggested.

"Excuse me?"

"Scream. A great, big, deep one. From your toes." I hesitated and Cassady gestured around us. "Come on. This is Manhattan. Unless you scream more than once or scream 'Fire,' you're not going to bother anyone. And you'll feel much better afterwards."

The nasty creature was about to rupture my sternum from the inside out, so I decided to give it a shot. I took a deep breath, rocked up on my stockinged toes a bit, and screamed. The force of the scream ripped that little sucker right out of his nest and blew him about two blocks away. It was raw and uncomfortable where he'd been digging, but Cassady was right. I did feel better.

I wasn't sure about Cassady, though. She was looking at me with this odd mixture of respect and fear. I think she'd been expecting something a little closer to my mild sound of concern from upstairs. "Wow," she said finally and stepped to the curb to hail a cab. "Want to call your therapist now or wait till morning?"

"I'm better. I'm okay." I really was better and the okay thing was going to be a matter of time. I knew that. There was still a disconnected quality to everything that had happened and it was going to be a while before I got it all sorted out. But then again, I'm not sure I want to be the kind of person who can see a dead body and take it in stride.

Now, in the bar with Cassady and Tricia, the creature was trying to worm its way back into its nest. I thought about screaming again and decided it would draw a little more attention in this setting. I settled for another deep breath, trying to get my glass to my mouth without spilling, while picturing great cheekbones.

"Cassady, how are you doing? You experienced this horror, too." Tricia moved her stool so it was directly between Cassady and me.

"Thanks, but this is Molly's deal. She's the one who

knew him and she's the one who lost the shoes."

"Still." Tricia climbed up onto her stool. Tricia's the small, delicate one in our trio. Too tall for gymnastics, too short to model, was her mournful cry in college. Not that she was really committed to either field. She's always been a behind-the-scenes type, and her impulse for orchestrating people's lives keeps the two of us on our toes. Tricia's quiet, but she's cunning, and you can find yourself talked into anything from a blind date to a charity pledge before you realize what she's done to you.

"What are you drinking?" Tricia asked me, more like a nurse taking a medical history than a friend trying to decide what to have herself.

"A lemon drop."

"I ordered champagne. You know that'll make her sleep," Cassady said.

Tricia snapped her head in a tight little move that made her chestnut hair skate on her shoulders. "Where's the waitress?"

"Why?" Cassady asked, sensing dissent.

"She needs a brandy alexander."

"Why?" Cassady repeated, this time sounding a little offended.

"Because they don't serve Häagen-Dazs here."

"You think she should have ice cream? She found a body, she didn't have her tonsils out, Tricia."

Usually, at this point in a conversation about me, I would try to speak up for myself, but I found, at the moment, that I had neither the energy nor the desire to do so. I was grateful that I had such good friends who were willing to debate the best way to get me back on my feet. Or get me falling-down drunk, whichever would be more beneficial in the long run. I just needed to be sure that I had gotten

Tricia's shoes on and successfully navigated all the little straps before I got too buzzed.

"She needs fats and carbs," Tricia replied crisply.

"When did those become good things?" Cassady didn't look too impressed with Tricia's edict, but I had to admit, it sounded great.

"It's a basic, chemical stress reaction. Adrenaline makes the body crave fats and carbs. Lest she dive face-first into a pizza or inhale raw cookie dough, we'll allow her this drink." Tricia glanced over at me. "Okay?"

I shrugged in acceptance. Besides, pizza-stuffed cheeks would defeat the effect of my Sigourney cheekbones. Tricia flashed Cassady a small smile of triumph. She loves taking control of a situation—any situation but her own life, that is. It's kind of in her blood: Her dad runs political campaigns and her mom's a compulsive volunteer. The whole family's a little tightly wrapped, but they're New England Republicans for a hundred generations, so what else can you expect? I mean, Tricia was named after Tricia Nixon, for crying out loud. She doesn't like anybody to know that, but she won't let anybody call her Trish either. She's a very precise person, but she'll do anything for someone she cares about.

The waitress came back with the champagne and Tricia ordered the brandy alexander. "Does that mean I don't get any champagne?" I asked as the waitress withdrew and Cassady started pouring. Cassady made a point of sliding the first glass over to me.

Tricia didn't take offense. "Drink whatever makes you feel better, sweetie. How do you feel?"

I groped for a moment, then settled on, "Surreal."

Cassady raised her glass and we followed her lead. "To Molly the Surreal."

"To Teddy," I responded. They hesitated, but I went ahead and took a sip. I meant it. May he rest in peace. But I only took one sip, because the idea of the brandy alexander was sounding better and better and I didn't want to press my luck by mixing my cocktails too freely.

"She thinks she's doing well," Cassady told Tricia, "but she's still in shock. She says she's going to play Nancy Drew."

"That's not what I said," I protested.

"You said you want to solve this crime."

Tricia looked horrified. "Molly, what are you thinking?" she asked, sounding a little too maternal for comfort.

"I want to help," I said and it came out a little weaker than I had intended. Maybe the nasty little creature in my chest was pressing against my voice box now, too. Small price to pay for good cheekbones. "Teddy was a friend of mine and I want to make sure he gets the attention he deserves."

"So plan his memorial service," Tricia suggested. "Don't turn vigilante." She turned to Cassady so I couldn't protest. "What did the police say?"

Cassady picked up her cue. "Robbery gone wrong."

"They know what they're talking about, Molly," Tricia cautioned.

"Yeah, but they don't know Teddy. He would've given a robber anything he asked for, plus a little something extra to go away quickly."

"That's not always enough," Cassady said quietly. "Sometimes people get killed because the robber's crazy, not because they put up a fight."

"I understand that. There's just something about this . . ." I wasn't in any shape to debate this with them. It was a feeling I had that I couldn't fully articulate yet. "I could have an insight on this that the police don't."

"Because of your close, personal relationship with Teddy," Cassady muttered.

"Okay, we weren't best friends, but I did know him. They don't."

"But they get paid to figure him out. And to figure the crime out," she continued with a hint of impatience. "But you—" She stopped as a new thought pinched her on the bottom. "I get it," she said slowly, then turned to Tricia as though she were about to recite the alphabet for a preschooler who would struggle to keep up with her. "Molly wants to solve the crime. Molly wants to be a real journalist when she grows up."

"Thanks for the support, Madame Supreme Court Justice," I sniped back. Cassady being right was beside the point. She didn't have to be so bitchy about it.

"Wait a minute." Tricia was working to catch the train. "Molly, you're going to use your friend's death as a stepping stone in your career?"

"That's not why," I protested.

"You're such a Good Samaritan that you're going to thrust yourself, completely inexperienced and unwelcome, into the middle of a murder investigation," Cassady said. "And get a feature article out of it along the way."

To hear Cassady say it, out loud and with that special tartness of hers, didn't help. I could feel my resolve slipping. It probably was silly of me to think that I could help New York's Finest solve a murder. And if Detective Lipscomb thought it was a robbery gone wrong, he was speaking from experience and, chances are, he was right. Just because I have this little flair for the dramatic and I'm always looking for a big story-behind-the-story doesn't mean that there was really more to Teddy's murder than met the eye.

I took a deep breath and let it out slowly, a holdover from a dalliance with yoga last year. It didn't help. I could feel my new cheekbones dissolving. Tricia reached across the table and put her hand gently on mine. Tricia has these delicate little hands that are always cool and dry. They'd be perfect, except she picks at her cuticles and can't wear nail polish for more than about three hours before she starts chipping it off with whatever's handy. We used to go get our nails done every Saturday morning, but Yooni, the salon manager, told Tricia she couldn't come back until she started respecting their artistry and stopped chipping the polish. "You need to do what you think is right, Molly." She left her hand on mine and smiled reassuringly. Leave it to Tricia to make it about doing the right thing.

Cassady leaned in, making a big deal about giving me an appraising look. I should have known trouble was coming. "This isn't about helping or about a big break. This is about an incredibly handsome homicide detective."

That wasn't it, but I still couldn't articulate my reasons. Besides, when I saw how Tricia brightened, I decided to let it go. "How incredibly handsome?" Tricia asked, and I could see from the set of her mouth she was willing me to follow this new, lighter path of conversation.

I actually found myself starting to smile. "Moderately incredible."

"What's his name?" Tricia looked like she was about to start taking notes.

"Detective Edwards."

"Does he have a first name?"

Cassady and I looked at each other, each expecting the

other to come up with it. "Don't think he said," Cassady admitted.

"Cassady was too busy trying to bed the babyface in uniform, so she wasn't paying much attention." I patted my pockets and found Detective Edwards' business card. "Kyle," I read.

"Great name," Tricia nodded approvingly. "Single?"

"No ring," I answered.

"You looked," Cassady said triumphantly. "I knew you liked him."

"Looking isn't a sign of liking, it's a sign of being alive," I countered.

"Still, you liked him."

"Swear to God, I haven't thought about it." Back in the office, with Teddy on the floor, it had seemed wrong to think about it. I had appreciated Detective Edwards—all the cops—on an instinctive aesthetic level. Anything beyond that, though, would have been inappropriate, like hitting on someone at a funeral. It seems wrong to look for action in a setting where the guest of honor can't possibly get lucky. Of course, Cassady once did pick up a guy at her uncle's funeral and had sex with him in the back of the florist's truck, but that's Cassady. And even she will tell you she threw her neck out, the relationship went nowhere, and she can no longer stand the smell of lilies.

But now that I did stop and think about it, "He might have potential, if I'm remembering correctly." I glanced at Cassady for confirmation.

Cassady nodded enthusiastically. "A lot there to work with, no doubt about it." She smiled lasciviously and Tricia laughed approvingly.

"So are you going to wait and see if he calls to ask if you've remembered anything helpful, or are you going to call him and offer new information?" Tricia asked. She's a natural planner. No matter what the situation, she's always the first one mapping out angles, options, plans of attack.

I shrugged. "I don't have new information."

"You're a clever girl," Tricia prodded. "Come up with something."

"But see, that's my whole point. I really think I could come up with something they aren't going to see. I want to do something."

"So do the detective and leave the rest to the rest," Cassady said. "This isn't something you want to play around with, especially if it turns out to be more than a robbery gone wrong. God knows, we don't want to be here a week from now, toasting you in absentia because you're in jail or the hospital or worse."

"Which would be worse, jail or hospital?" Tricia asked, trying to keep the conversation from running up onto the rocks.

"The morgue trumps them all," Cassady persisted.

"Point made," Tricia assured her.

"Then smack her on the head or something, you're sitting closer." Cassady set her drink down in frustration. "You've got such a good heart, Molly, and always have great reasons for the things you do, but that doesn't mean you should push your luck. Promise us."

I knew she was right, they were right, but I couldn't let go of the notion of helping, especially now that it was coupled with the notion of getting to know Detective Edwards better. That was even more attractive than the feature article, which I knew was a long shot. The waitress arrived with the brandy alexander, allowing me to take a moment without being accused of stalling. I took a sip and decided to let Tricia prescribe the drinks for all my traumas from now on. This was the perfect concoction for my situation and I was going to enjoy it.

The drink, that is, because the situation was about to become, believe it or not, even more uncomfortable than it already was. I was letting the second sip slide down my throat in a frosty trickle when a square, firm hand came to rest—a little too heavily—on my shoulder. Startled, I gagged slightly and had to cough before I could turn around and look. By then, my girlfriends had already looked and I could tell from their expressions that I didn't want to hurry in turning around.

I thought about the weight of the hand as I turned and was reasonably sure whom I was about to see. And because the evening hadn't been complicated enough, I was right. Nothing like a current boyfriend showing up just as you're contemplating the possibilities of a new man.

"Hey, Peter." I tried to strike the proper tone of surprise. Of course, my bigger surprise was feeling somehow guilty about thinking of Detective Edwards in less than professional terms only moments before.

"Moll," he said as he leaned in for a kiss. I pressed my lips against his with moderate firmness, not perfunctory, just not sloppy or suggestive. He gave the other two a mock salute. "Good evening, ladies."

Peter Mulcahey is one of those golden boys that Robert Redford talks about in *The Way We Were*, an All-American in looks, breeding, and attitude to whom things come easily. Not that he didn't have to work to get me, but I did get a little caught up in the whole Ivy League mythos. That's just not my normal playground. So when he made it clear it was his desire to sweep me off my feet, I allowed myself to be swept. It was great at first, very heady stuff. He knows how to play the romance, I'll give him that. But the last couple of weeks, I'd been unable to shake the feeling that that's all he was doing. Playing. The random moments of insincerity were accumulating and the complex interior I had been convinced lay beneath the golden exterior didn't seem to exist after all.

Cassady said he had intimacy issues and I needed to go to the mountains for the weekend with him and see what happened. Tricia said he wasn't Mr. Right, but asked me not to dump him until he bought a table at the Jazz at Lincoln Center Anniversary Dinner. I didn't know what to do. I knew I wasn't in love, but we had a pretty good time. And the Lincoln Center party was bound to be a blast. So I'd been dragging my feet about making a move and he'd very considerately gone out of town for some family function, but I hadn't used the time wisely and still didn't know what to do about our relationship. He knew something was off, but it either didn't bother him or he was trying to reach a decision of his own. All in all, not an emotional tar pit I needed on top of everything else that had already happened.

"When did you get back?" I asked, realizing that he still had his hand on my shoulder. Was it possessiveness or laziness? I couldn't tell. Like I couldn't tell how much of our daily contact before he left had been passion and how much had been habit. Another distressing thought. I wasn't sure I could handle many more.

"Just got in. Ran out of cousins to get drunk with. I left a message on your machine, but I guess you haven't been home in a while."

"No, it's been kind of a wild night," I said carefully, not sure I wanted to share what had happened with him right now.

So, of course, Tricia announced, "Molly found a dead body."

Now, I'm pretty certain Emily Post doesn't have a chapter on how to deal with the whole dead-colleague-on-the-floor scenario, but I still was disappointed that Tricia was the one who blurted it out. I hadn't finished sorting everything out for myself and I was not prepared to have Peter in the mix, either as my boyfriend of indeterminate status or as a rival journalist.

Yes, Peter's a journalist, too, but his Pulitzer chances don't look a whole lot better than mine. He writes for *Jazzed*, a men's magazine that tries to hide its obsession with starlets with new boob jobs and overpriced electronic gizmos only a boy could love with the occasional article on world politics or business ethics. Tricia calls it *Jerked*, referring to both the way the cover girls are posed and the way the average male reacts when passing an issue on the newsstand. Cassady calls it something more obscene that we suspect was their publisher's original idea for a title. I can't say it, but I like to imagine it on their front cover when I'm feeling competitive with Peter.

Peter and I met at a birthday party for Julie McLeod, a photography editor who'd moved from my magazine to his, and bonded over our common frustration with trying to get ahead in the writing world. He had made it clear from the outset that he considered himself a few steps further down the path than I am, based on *Jazzed*'s larger circulation. I endeavored to point out that most men buy two copies of each issue, one to read on the subway and one to keep at home. And in both places, they read it with one hand. He didn't find that nearly as funny as I thought it was. And yet, somehow, we still wound up going out. If I have instincts like that about dating, what on earth had possessed me to think I could track down a killer?

"A body?" Peter squeezed my shoulder gently, reacting to the nervous bands of steel that had formed there. "What'd you do, walk through the Park?"

"I don't really want to—"

"In her office, on the floor. A colleague. Most godawful thing I've ever seen," Cassady chimed in. I tried to give her the "shut up or change the subject" look, but she was turned to face Peter. I slid her champagne glass rather forcefully into her hand, but all she did was grab it and keep talking. "Even if I drink this stuff all night, I'm still not going to be able to sleep." Cassady took a healthy swallow of her champagne as I watched, bewildered. She had seemed so together in the office. Was the impact of what had happened hitting her belatedly? Or was she just making it a better story, especially for the male audience?

Peter kept his reaction bland. His fingertips started kneading the back of my neck. "Jesus. You okay, Molly? You can stay with me tonight." I might have bought that as a gesture of real concern, but I was distracted by the perfunctory quality of his neck kneading. Usually, Peter's kneading is really firm and soothing; he played guitar growing up and has nice, long, supple fingers. But now, he was more or less drumming his fingertips on the back of my neck. I was tempted to shrug his hand away, but I didn't want to let him know I was onto him. Not until I figured out what had him so distracted. And I was forming a pretty good guess.

I turned on my stool to face him and his hand fell from my neck. "I appreciate the invitation, but I think I'd rather be alone tonight."

"But you must want to talk," he started, revving up to present his case.

"That's what we're doing," Tricia pointed out.

"I can only imagine what you must be feeling, what you must be going through," Peter continued, undeterred. The girlfriends glanced at me. His method was becoming obvious, but his goal was still unclear to them. I gave a little toss of the head, meant to convey inexpressible angst, and Peter reached out to caress my cheek. Now I knew he was full of shit. He is not a cheek caresser. "Who's the detective on your case?"

My teeth clenched, but I managed to flash him a smile. Oh, baby, you are so busted. It's bad enough that I'm considering exploiting my friend's death, but to have you thinking about doing it secondhand? It's cheap, it's underhanded, and it's one more reason we need to have a serious discussion about the course of our relationship.

Of course, that's what I thought. What I said was, "I don't remember, I have it written down somewhere." I gestured vaguely, confident that my co-conspirators would see that I was being deliberately evasive and not rush in to supply Peter with the name.

Peter tried one more time. "It must be a fascinating story."

I shook my head. "Just a robbery gone wrong. I'm sure there are better stories in the naked city tonight."

"I don't know, sounds like a pretty compelling one to me. Not that I want to diminish your pain in any way," he tacked on hurriedly. "A brush with mortality is something we all respond to so strongly, yet so differently. It could be an illuminating microcosm of how we relate to personal tragedy in the wake of 9/11."

Now the girlfriends were catching on. And how could they not, when Peter was basically practicing the pitch he'd use on an editor if I were dim enough to tell him *my* story and let him turn it into *his* article. Tricia was staring at him in open amazement, but Cassady became very interested in her champagne glass, mouth pursed to hold back the laughter. When a man does something that confirms her belief in the inborn stupidity of the gender, Cassady finds it highly amusing. Peter was about to send her into gales of giggles without even trying.

"That's very true," I said, working to keep my voice light and sincere, "and that's why I hope you'll understand that I just want to have a drink with my girlfriends and then go home and put the whole thing behind me." I pulled him in close enough to kiss him and made sure it was just moist and open enough to distract him for a moment. "I'll call you tomorrow, okay?"

"Maybe you'll feel like talking then," he said, trying to sound supportive, but clearly still fishing.

"Maybe. 'Night." I turned back to the table, trusting that his male ego would force him to leave at that point, lest he be seen as in any way more interested in me than I was in him.

" 'Night, ladies," he said, and made his exit. You take your life in your hands any time you try to predict what a man is going to do, but sometimes you have to throw the dice and, wonder of wonders, every now and then they surprise you in a positive way. Men are experts on negative surprises, of course. But in all honesty, most of the times I've gotten bad surprises, when I looked back later—with the benefit of time and a good, stiff drink—I've realized that it wasn't so much that the man surprised me as I wasn't paying close enough attention. The boyfriend who cheats— it's not really a surprise that he cheats, it's a surprise that I didn't realize it was happening. The boyfriend who bolts— it's not that he left, it's that I should be able to spot intimacy issues at ten paces at this point. The boyfriend who lies—who doesn't?

"Well, that was pleasant," Cassady said, toasting Peter's departing back. "How over is it?"

"If it wasn't before, it is now," I said. I lifted my brandy alexander to Tricia. "Thanks, Tricia, I may get hooked on these."

"Oh, that wasn't my intent at all." Tricia eased my hand back down to the table. "Fat and carbs, like all else, in moderation."

"My imagination, or was he trying to scoop your story?" Cassady asked.

"Over my and Teddy's dead bodies," I replied.

"So it is all about the story," Cassady sneered.

"No." I wished I sounded a little more convincing, so I continued, "Not completely. It's about making sure Teddy doesn't get lost in the shuffle. It's about a hunch I have that the cops are going down the wrong path."

"And *then* it's about the story," Tricia finished for me.

"Plus the handsome detective," Cassady contributed.

I turned to Cassady, surprised at her stance. "You saw him. Teddy, I mean. Don't you get it?"

"I guess, but . . ." Cassady shook her head. "Hey, if you're going to be an idiot, be an idiot for really good reasons. And a gorgeous guy and a possible strong career move qualify."

"But I'm still an idiot."

"Only if you wind up dead. So please, prove us wrong."

"Yeah, well, if I do wind up dead, make sure someone other than Peter gets the story." We clinked glasses on that one, a nice warm moment shattered by the trill of my cell phone. Mine's the one that plays "Satin Doll."

I reached for it and Tricia grimaced. "Who could it possibly be that's more interesting and/or important than we are?"

Cassady grinned. "The fine young detective."

It wasn't. It was my editor, Yvonne. "Oh. My. God. Molly. Are you . . . all right?" Yvonne's very sparing with punctuation in the magazine's prose, but she uses it freely in her conversation.

"Yvonne, where are you?"

"Where do you think? In the office! Ankle-deep in blood! Strange people in dark uniforms—I'm beside myself. Molly. I can only imagine. How you must . . . feel."

I couldn't find a nice way to tell her that I'd been feeling better until she called. "I'll be fine, Yvonne. I'm sorry you got dragged into this."

"You? Sorry for me? I didn't even see his body. Much less trip over it. In the dark! You. Poor. Dear."

I sighed and propped my head up with my hand. Once Yvonne got rolling, it was hard to tell how long a conversation was going to last, though it would probably not be much longer than the average article in *Zeitgeist*. Cassady rolled her eyes supportively and filled the champagne glasses. "Helen's the one we should be worried about, Yvonne," I said. "Maybe you should talk to her in the morning."

"No. I'm going. Out there now."

"Are you sure that's a good idea?" My heart, already broken for Helen, shattered further at the thought of Helen having to deal with Yvonne and her big mouth and cotton candy hair in the middle of the night.

"What? Molly? You think she should get the news—the worst news she's ever going to get—from these cold strangers?" I could only assume that she was talking about Detectives Edwards and Lipscomb and could only pray that they were out of earshot. "She'll need. A friend! Someone to comfort her."

"I'll go with you." It was out of my mouth before I'd really thought it through. Something I'm getting a little too prone to do. But I'd been able to contain my own grief by not considering Helen's at all. Now that Yvonne had pried the lid off that well, I could not stomach the thought of Yvonne unleashed on Helen in her darkest hour. The others looked at me curiously, wondering no doubt what could be luring me from their company in my hour of semi-darkness.

"Well. I hadn't . . . Let me ask the detectives."

I waited as Yvonne put her hand over her phone and went in search of the detectives. I thought she'd called with the intent of inviting me, but now she sounded like I was raining on her parade. I put my hand over my phone to explain. "Yvonne's going with the detectives to tell Helen."

"Molly, you have to go. And if you can possibly gag that fiend and put her in the trunk before you arrive, even better," Cassady urged.

Tricia nodded in agreement as a voice issued from my phone. "Ms. Forrester?"

I nearly swallowed my phone in my eagerness to answer. "Detective Edwards?"

Cassady raised her glass. "Detective Edwards," she whispered to Tricia and they clinked glasses, laughing.

"Ms. Hamilton says you'd like to come with us to notify Mrs. Reynolds," Detective Edwards said, with no hint in his voice as to whether he thought it was a good idea.

"It seemed the right thing to do."

"It would definitely be a help," he answered and I knew that was more of a slam on Yvonne than it was a compliment to me. "Where are you? We'll pick you up."

"I'm at Django. I thought a drink with friends might help me sleep," I added, feeling a sudden need to justify my location and activity.

"I understand. We'll be outside in ten minutes."

"It's a date," I blurted, then wished I really could swallow my phone. "Sorry, I mean—I don't know what I was thinking."

"Too bad," he said, and the quality of his voice warmed just a little. "Thought it might be a Freudian slip."

"Wow," I breathed. "Detectives don't miss much, do they?"

There was a long enough pause that I could feel him debating with himself. "Ten minutes," was the reply that won.

"Ten minutes," I echoed and hung up. I dropped my phone back in my bag and stood up. "Ladies . . ."

"She's ditching us." Tricia cut to the chase.

"It's the right thing to do," I defended.

"I've seen him. It's the right thing to do," Cassady assured Tricia. She turned back to me for a hug and a kiss. "Call us in the morning. Me first or I'll be hurt."

"Don't wreck my shoes," Tricia warned. "And stay out of trouble."

I should have listened to Tricia, parked my butt back down, and finished my brandy alexander. But no, I had to do the right thing. That'll teach me.

3

Dear Molly, I recently had to break some really bad news to a friend and another friend insisted on coming along with me. Okay, I'm a wimp—I should have told her to stay home. But still, was it wrong for me to imagine throwing my friend from the moving police car because she wouldn't shut up about how horrible this was for her when it wasn't her tragedy in any way, shape, or form? Signed, Vivid Imagination

It's a habit I've developed in the two years I've been writing the column. When I'm in a stressful situation, it helps me to imagine a reader sending in a letter about said stress and asking my advice. I like to think of it as a creative way of gaining perspective on a problem. I'm sure my therapist would say that I'm emotionally distancing myself from the issue at hand, but I haven't discussed it with her yet. There are bigger fish to fry.

So that's why I was sitting in the back seat of the police car, trying not to watch Yvonne wail for the benefit of the detectives in the front seat, writing letters in my head. I was torn between the aforementioned desire to chuck her out the window and to tell Detective Lipscomb to stop at the first available corner so we could drop her off without actually injuring her. That was the more polite option, but it lacked the necessary emotional satisfaction element.

To listen to her, you'd think Yvonne had lost the love of her life, rather than a colleague with whom she rarely socialized and frequently argued. Both Yvonne and Teddy were on the hothead end of the spectrum and they disagreed loudly and often, over everything from the magazine business to movie reviews. A couple of times, I thought Teddy was trying to get fired, but eventually I realized they both loved a good shouting match, so it really wasn't a problem for the two of them. Even though it drove those of us who had to listen to it crazy.

Sort of the way Yvonne was driving me bonkers now. "Oh. Poor. Helen."

"Yes, Yvonne," I said automatically.

"What will we say?!" Yvonne sobbed a little more and I literally bit my lip. *We?* God help us. In my column, I've had to give people some pretty harsh news: He's cheating on you, leave him; she's lying to you, dump her; he's in denial, run very, very fast. But there was nothing in my archives to prepare me for breaking the news of Teddy's death to Helen. And there wasn't even a very long ride to give me time to practice what I was going to say. But I was absolutely going to find a way to stop Yvonne from saying it first. And I had less than ten minutes in a speeding police car to figure out how.

I have to admit, it was kind of cool having the detectives pick me up. I was standing on the sidewalk, gulping outside air, willing my Sigourney cheekbones into full being, when the car screeched up. Detective Lipscomb was driving a very clean but very plain Oldsmobile and he laid on the ocean liner–size horn and cut off two taxis and a BMW to pull to the curb. The other drivers started screaming and flipping him off, then Detective Lipscomb got out and

flashed his shield at them. The taxi drivers stopped screaming and went away. The BMW guy kept screaming, but he
drove away, too.

Detective Edwards got out and opened the back passen-
ger door for me. I could tell that everyone on the sidewalk
was watching and I figured, the way the night had been
going, that I'd trip and fall flat on my face three feet from
the car. I was wearing unfamiliar shoes, after all, and slender
heels at that. But I imagined *les* cheekbones buoying me
aloft and I walked with what I hoped was grace and poise
to the car. Detective Edwards stayed at the door so it was
clear to all the onlookers that I wasn't being arrested. I'm
sure there was a lot of speculation going on as to what my
story was and it was kind of cool to be the object of speculation, since I'm usually the speculator.

I mean, don't you see things in passing that make you
wonder, "What's that all about?" A couple quarreling in a
restaurant, a man running down a crowded sidewalk, a
woman weeping as she hails a cab—we see all these fragments of other people's life stories as we pursue our own.
And I often get sidetracked by those fragments and try to
fill them in, imagine what led to that moment and what
might happen next. Maybe it's the journalist in me. Maybe
it's because it's easier than attending to my own fragments.

I got up to the car and looked Detective Edwards right
in the dazzling blue eyes. "Thank you," I said, trying to
make it sound layered with many meanings.

"No, thank you," he replied with a wry smile as Yvonne
popped her head out from the back seat.

"Molly! Thank. God." She held her arms out to me, but
there was no graceful way to embrace her without getting
in the car first. So there was this uncomfortable tangle of
arms and legs that I hoped the speculators on the sidewalk

missed and somehow, I was in the back seat with Yvonne. Detective Edwards closed the door behind me, got in front with his partner, and we screeched away.

"Ms. Forrester," Detective Lipscomb growled in greeting.

"Detective Lipscomb," I returned as pleasantly as I could, given that Yvonne was twisting my hands into pulp.

"Oh. Molly." Yvonne has bleached her hair so many times that it has acquired a faint lavender undertone and an odd scent not found in nature. She hugged me to her and I had to twist my neck as far as possible to keep my nose from being buried in the platinum Brillo pad on top of her head.

I struggled to sit up. Why was everything making it so hard to breathe tonight? "Yvonne, I know you're upset, but it's not going to help Helen if you show up hysterical."

"You're right! So right!" Yvonne was still wringing my hands and I had to pull them out of her grasp while the skin was still attached. "So glad you're here!"

I glanced up at the detectives to see if either of them seemed glad I was there. Detective Lipscomb was concentrating on his driving, but Detective Edwards was looking back at us. More precisely, he was looking at Yvonne, and it was clear from his expression that he was growing less fond of her by the moment. His eyes slid over to meet mine for just a moment and a hint of a smile played across his face. Then he turned back around and I was left to consider the possible implications of the smile.

"I want you to come in tomorrow morning. This morning. Whatever," Yvonne raced on. "Help me tell everyone! Need to plan a service. Write an appreciation."

"Yvonne, let's take this one painful step at a time. Let's talk to Helen and see what we can do for her. Then we'll figure out what we need to do for the magazine."

"Yes!" Yvonne leaned forward and poked Detective Edwards in the shoulder. "Told you! Best advice columnist there is. Didn't I?!"

"Yes, ma'am," Detective Edwards replied.

I considered advising her to be more careful about poking armed homicide detectives, but I decided to let it go. There were no doubt going to be plenty of opportunities to correct Yvonne as the night progressed and I would have to conserve my strength and choose my battles.

We reached Helen and Teddy's building way too quickly. They owned a condo on West 82nd and Detective Lipscomb must have made every green light between Django and there. It was an older building with a crumbling grace to the sandstone exterior. I had no idea what I was going to say or do and was, in fact, beginning to have grave doubts about Yvonne's and my being there at all. But the detectives assured us that it was helpful to have a familiar face on hand when they broke the news, so we followed them as they showed their shields to the doorman. He was an older man, with deep smile lines at the corners of his mouth. He wasn't interested in giving the cops any attitude and he figured things out pretty quickly when Detective Lipscomb said we needed to see Helen Reynolds.

"How bad's Mr. Reynolds?" he asked as he ushered us into the lobby. It was heavy on the dark wood paneling and someone had overcompensated with an area rug with way too much orange in it, just this side of painful. When no one answered him right away, the doorman knew exactly what that meant. He picked up the house phone and, as he dialed, asked, "Who should I say wants to see her?"

"Molly Forrester," I blurted, wanting to give Helen the extra few minutes it would take us to get up to her apartment before she found out she was a widow. And I was determined to keep Yvonne as quiet as possible.

The doorman announced me to Helen, then held out the phone to me. "She wants to talk to you."

I took the phone and was amazed that my hands weren't shaking more visibly than they were. "Helen?"

"Molly," she said groggily, "it's almost two o'clock."

"I know and I wouldn't be coming by at this hour if it weren't important. I'm so sorry, but I need to come up."

"Teddy's not here, Molly."

"I know."

I could feel the quality of silence at the other end of the phone change. "Okay," was all she said. The line went dead.

I handed the phone back to the doorman. He replaced it gently in the cradle, then called the elevator for us. We stood together in uneasy silence until the elevator doors opened. "Mr. Reynolds was a good man," the doorman said as we filed past him. We all nodded in agreement.

Upstairs, Helen was standing in the doorway, watching the elevator. I got off first and she glared at me, her mouth compressed into a thin, white line. Then Yvonne and the detectives got off the elevator, too, and Helen's look of anger collapsed into confusion. I grabbed Yvonne's sleeve to keep her from sprinting down the hall and engulfing Helen. The hallway suddenly seemed very long and yet somehow, not long enough.

Yvonne started to sniffle. I yanked on her sleeve as inconspicuously as possible as we drew within reach of Helen. I started to say something, I'm not sure what, but Helen cut me off, pointing to the detectives. "Who are they?"

"Mrs. Reynolds, I'm Detective Edwards—"

Helen screamed. That made Yvonne scream. I grabbed Helen, Detective Edwards grabbed Yvonne, and Detective Lipscomb herded us all into the apartment. No need to wake the neighbors; Helen had enough to deal with for the moment.

We got Helen to the couch in the living room. She had clearly had a free hand in decorating the apartment. Everything was soft floral prints and rounded corners and highly polished woods. All the furniture had plump cushions topped with firm throw pillows. Laura Ashley without the benefit of English restraint. I wondered if we were going to be able to sit down or if we would just slide off the shiny rounded surfaces and land with a soft thud on the plush patterned carpet. I was willing to bet that she made Teddy take his shoes off before he put his feet on the hassock, with its skirt of infinite pleats. I couldn't quite picture him being comfortable in such a room. His office was just this side of chaos and he seemed to revel in it. Was it a reaction to all this precision? It was becoming clear that I didn't know Teddy as well as I thought I did. Was I getting in over my head here?

"He's dead," Helen gasped as though she needed to say it before anyone else could. Was it any less awful that way? Or was she hoping someone would correct her?

Instead, Yvonne responded with, "Stabbed. Right in the—"

"For God's sake, Yvonne," I implored. Yvonne looked like she was about to take offense, so I sent her into the kitchen for a glass of water and a box of tissues. The detectives sat across from Helen, giving her a moment to collect herself. I was kind of amazed how they hadn't had to say anything and she knew why they were there. Who knew the angel of death wore such a cheap suit?

"When you called . . . from downstairs . . . I thought . . ."
Helen struggled to get the words out between the tears.
Her face already had a light gloss to it, probably night mois-
turizer. It smelled like Oil of Olay. I'd seen Teddy and
Helen's wedding picture a million times—it sat on Teddy's
credenza, facing out the door of his office. And even
though I'd seen Helen countless times, I'd never compared
her to the young woman in the picture. Since they'd gotten
married almost twenty years ago, Teddy had filled out and
Helen had contracted. The angles in her small, pale face
were sharper, her brown hair had gone from a cap of curls
to a severe bob, and she seemed almost bony. Was this
maturity or had something deeper taken its toll?

Yvonne came back with the tissues and water and we
let Helen help herself. Yvonne plopped herself on the other
side of Helen but, to her credit, wrung her own hands
instead of Helen's. Helen blew her nose and took a deep
breath. "You said you knew he wasn't home," she said
finally. "I thought you were coming to tell me you were
having an affair with him."

Me and Teddy? Never happen. That was my first
thought, but thank God I didn't blurt that one out—or
laugh. Though it did explain Helen glaring at me as I got
off the elevator. It was actually very moving to imagine
Helen thinking of Teddy having an affair, with me or anyone else. Poor rumpled, sweaty Teddy wasn't exactly a
poster boy for passion, especially with male models and
wannabes wandering through the office hallways all the
time. But I guess Helen figured we could all see in him
what she saw in him—whatever that was.

Maybe that's the sign of a good relationship, that you
see your partner as being as desirable to any other woman
as he is to you. I've never had a very good handle on the

whole jealousy issue, but I've heard the theory that if you're not a little jealous, you don't care enough. On the other hand, did a wife being jealous or suspicious ever stop a husband from messing around? A man who's going to stray is going to find a way, my grandmother used to say. I hope that didn't have any relevance to my grandfather, but who knows. My Grandmother Forrester was one of those women who whispered when she had to say "cancer" and arched her eyebrows instead of saying "sex" or "menstruation," so it's not like we got a lot of straight information from her. Not that we really wanted it. The only thing weirder than trying to imagine your parents having sex is trying to imagine your grandparents having sex. I think there's actually a rule against it in the Old Testament.

"You suspected your husband of having an affair?" Detective Lipscomb spoke gently. The transition from officer of the law to father confessor caught me by surprise.

"No, not really," Helen fumbled. "It was this bizarre thought, when Molly called, and I was half-asleep, I don't know what I was thinking . . ." She looked to me for reassurance and I gave her my sagest nod. But at the same time I found myself thinking: She's blurting. But not the way I'd been blurting all night. More the way a child will blurt out a story to explain how the lamp got broken or who ate the last piece of chocolate cake without asking. Had she actually suspected Teddy?

Could Teddy have been having an affair? I scanned my mental images of Teddy in the office, which was really the only place I ever saw him. Had his behavior changed? Had his routine changed? I thought as carefully as my jangled emotions would let me, but I really couldn't see anything that would point to an affair. Except the diet. Teddy had been a big guy and it had never seemed to bother him until the last month or two. He told everyone that he was dieting because his doctor had read him the riot act. But what if the motive was romantic, not medical? What if he figured there was no need to slim down for Helen because she loved him no matter what, but there was now someone in his life worth making the effort for? Someone who might not love him no matter what, someone he had to get buff for? Who was Teddy sleeping with? Or maybe even, trying to sleep with? Poor Helen.

"Were you home all evening, Mrs. Reynolds?" Detective Lipscomb continued.

"Just. One. Minute." Yvonne was working herself up into a fit of righteous indignation. She was fond of the grander emotions and the chance to defend a friend was as irresistible to her as a lingerie sale at Saks, I'm sure. But I snaked a hand behind Helen's back and nudged Yvonne as hard as I dared because I could see the detectives were in no mood for her theatrics. I was pretty done with them myself.

"Mrs. Reynolds?" Detective Lipscomb repeated, but his voice was gentler. Yvonne sat back a few inches, like a snake recoiling.

"I got home from work a little after eight. I ordered dinner from Costa del Sol and if they don't time code the orders, I paid with a credit card." Helen straightened up a little, her own brand of indignation distracting her from her sorrow. "Then I made some phone calls and spent some time online, both of which you can also check on. Unfortunately, I went to bed about eleven, so you'll just have to trust me from there."

Detective Lipscomb wasn't bothered in the least by Helen's mounting fury. I'm sure they saw this all the time—

a newly minted widow looking for some way and any reason to release the searing pain growing in her. "We have to ask the questions, ma'am," Detective Edwards explained quietly.

"Don't lecture her," Yvonne snapped. "The woman just lost her husband! For. God's. Sake."

Detective Lipscomb nodded in patient understanding and paused a moment before continuing. "Was it unusual for your husband not to be home by eleven, Mrs. Reynolds?"

"Not unusual, but not a regular thing. Every once in a while. He goes through these bouts of insomnia and he feels it's more productive to stay at the office and work if he has the energy, rather than pacing around here all night." Her voice faltered toward the end, as though she'd lost faith in the story as a result of saying it out loud. She was still referring to Teddy in the present tense, but it didn't seem like the sort of thing you correct. Helen tightened her grip on my right hand and I patted hers with my left, wishing I had cool, tiny hands like Tricia, even with the chipped polish. My hands were feeling pretty wrung out and clammy at this point and I was developing a very distracting urge to crack the knuckles in the hand Helen was squashing. And all I could think was, who was Teddy sleeping with?

"True, true!" Yvonne flung herself into the fray. "I'm a bit of a night owl myself! Teddy and I often bumped into each other. In the office. In the wee hours." Yvonne smiled broadly, as though she'd won the third grade spelling bee. She was actually handling this better than I had feared she might on the ride over. She wasn't trying to appropriate Helen's grief and she deserved a gold star for that.

"Did your husband call to say he'd be late?"

Helen folded her mouth back into that thin line. "Sometimes."

They let that hang in the air for a moment. Detective Lipscomb jotted something down and Detective Edwards just looked at Helen. He really had amazing eyes. Such a bright blue, and a direct, piercing quality without being cold or harsh. Helen looked back at him and the pressure on my hand eased up. She was relaxing as she gazed into Detective Edwards' eyes. Almost as though he were willing her to.

I nearly jumped as I realized what he was doing. He was seducing her. Okay, maybe that's a step too far, but he was definitely lulling her into a sense of comfort and safety. He knew he had great eyes and he was using them. He wanted her to trust him, be willing to say anything to him. Then he added the voice to the mix, gentle and rich and smooth. "But not tonight."

Helen's breath caught and my hand instinctively went to her shoulder. "We had an argument. I told him not to call. I told him . . ." A huge sob convulsed her. Yvonne retreated slightly in the face of so much genuine emotion and I drew Helen to me as best I could. The detectives leaned forward solicitously.

"Take your time," Detective Lipscomb said.

Helen couldn't hold it in. She straightened back up, pulling away from me. "I told him not to call. I told him I didn't care when he came home."

"What did you fight about?" Detective Edwards asked.

Helen laughed bitterly, even as she wiped her eyes with already sodden tissues. "About his working so late! And I said such . . ." She shook her head hard, trying to dislodge the memory of those last angry words. "It's stupid now, but it seemed important then."

Both detectives nodded. "This had been a problem for a while?" Detective Lipscomb proceeded gently. "I know my hours have bugged my wife since day one."

"No, it's just been the past several months. Maybe six." Helen looked down at the rug as though it would help her do the math. "Maybe a little longer."

"We had a big advertising slump after 9/11. Everyone did. Teddy's been working so hard to build us back up," Yvonne volunteered.

"Everything else has been okay?" Detective Edwards asked.

"Yes," Helen answered defiantly.

"Do you have children?" he continued.

"No," Helen answered, but the defiance wasn't there, just a slight hollowness that everyone could hear and tried not to react to.

"What do you do, Mrs. Reynolds?" Detective Lipscomb asked.

"I'm human resources director at Anderson and Wood. We're a law firm."

"Where are your offices?"

Helen sighed. "We're two doors down from the maga-zine." She waited for the detectives to make something out of that, but Detective Lipscomb just jotted it down and Detective Edwards kept gazing at her.

"Can you think of anyone who might want to hurt your husband?" Detective Edwards asked.

"What happened to the robbery gone wrong?" I said, a little too loudly. But it worked. They all looked at me, Helen most importantly. I couldn't—didn't want to—believe she had anything to do with this so I wanted her to be careful about what she said, especially to Big Blue Eyes. Of course, Big Blue Eyes was looking at me pretty intently now, too, but I could handle it. I hoped. This was certainly not the time for me to blurt any affair-related thoughts.

"We're looking at all the options," Detective Lipscomb said, his tone much more friendly than when he'd told me that back in the office. He was in sincerity mode and I wasn't going to shake him out of it. His eyes swung back to Helen, but Detective Edwards kept looking at me. He was trying to figure out what I was up to. So was I.

"Teddy doesn't have any enemies. Everybody loves—" Helen crumpled so suddenly that I was afraid she'd fainted. "Loved . . ." she corrected herself before she started sobbing. Yvonne grabbed her like she was going to perform some cockeyed Heimlich and started rocking with her. Helen hadn't let go of my hands yet, so I had no choice but to sit beside them and wait for the fury of Helen's acceptance to pass.

After a moment, Detective Edwards eased back in. "There aren't problems with debts or drugs or—"

"No," Helen snapped. She worked out of Yvonne's embrace and blew her nose loudly. "We were fine. We were happy and we were fine." The words had a surprisingly forced crispness. Helen wasn't telling the truth. What had gone wrong?

The detectives exchanged an unreadable look. Surely they heard the brick wall in her voice, too. Helen was done talking. She was wrapping herself in her myth of happiness and shutting the rest of us out.

Detective Lipscomb flipped his notebook closed. "Is there anyone we can call for you, someone who can come stay with you?"

"I want Molly." Helen grabbed at me, her hands still filled with wet tissues. I tried not to recoil from the tissues or the thought of staying with her all night.

"I can stay, too," Yvonne offered.

"Thank you, Yvonne," Helen said. Yvonne beamed. She was probably picturing some wonderful bonding experience that would make us all better people. I was picturing a lot of weeping and wailing and feeling useless, none of which I enjoy.

Detective Edwards held his business card out to Helen. "We will need you to come down and formally identify him, but you can wait until morning if you'd like."

Helen stopped, her hand withdrawing from the business card. "I have to see him—like that? Molly already told you it was him."

"If there's another family member—"

"Oh, my God. The family. His parents. Oh, my God." Helen sagged against Yvonne as a new wave of tears overtook her.

Detective Edwards turned back to me. I held his gaze as best I could, but it was hard. Helen's weeping was compelling and I could feel the urge to cry tickling the back of my throat. It overrode any chance of Big Blue Eyes lulling me into saying anything. He placed his business card on the glistening surface of the coffee table and stood. Detective Lipscomb slid forward in his chair. I thought he was going to reach out to comfort Helen, but then I saw he was easing himself to his feet.

"Mrs. Reynolds, call us if you think of anything or if you need anything," he said with surprising tenderness. He put his card next to Detective Edwards' and stood. Detective Edwards inclined his head toward the front door. Leaving Helen literally in Yvonne's hands, I followed them.

Detective Lipscomb paused long enough to say, "Good evening, Ms. Forrester," before he went out into the hallway. I stood just inside the doorway with Detective Edwards, still a little confused. Were they really done? What were they thinking? What happened next? Who *was* Teddy sleeping with? Who was Detective Edwards sleeping with and how serious was it?

Okay, so random thoughts sneak in at the most inopportune moments. But it had been quite a night, so I was entitled to a slight loss of control. As long as my mouth didn't blurt at the same time my mind was wandering. That could get complicated and/or embarrassing.

"Why didn't you tell me he was having an affair?" Detective Edwards asked quietly, not interested in Helen hearing this line of questioning.

"Because I didn't know. I mean, I'm not sure he was. Helen's not thinking clearly," I finished, each statement more feeble than the one before it.

"So he wasn't having an affair with you," Detective Edwards persisted.

"No," I answered, trying very hard to be mysterious. Let Detective Edwards wonder who *was* having an affair with me. And please, let him think of someone more exotic and challenging than Peter. He seemed pleased with the answer, but I wasn't sure if he was professionally or personally pleased. Just in case he was getting more personal, I tried to be more businesslike. Couldn't prove the girlfriends right too early in the process. This was about helping Teddy, not bedding Detective Edwards. Yet. "When will they do the autopsy?"

"Why?"

"If she has to see him, I want her to see him before that."

"So you two are close?"

"Not at all," I admitted. "But she's looking for someone to help her get through this and I'm trying to do the right thing."

"She's lucky to have you here." I shrugged off the compliment and tried to ignore how nice it felt. "We don't control the autopsy schedule. But the sooner she comes down, the better, across the board."

"I'll have her call you first thing, see if she can get some sleep first." I was certain Yvonne would have some sort of pharmaceuticals in her purse to make sure Helen passed out for at least a few hours, but it didn't seem the sort of information to share with a detective.

"Anybody you need to call, let them know you won't be coming home?"

I had the presence of mind to pause for a moment before answering. Didn't want to seem too eager to assure him that there was no competition on the live-in level. Or was it going to seem like I had to pause and think whether I'd left some boy toy draped across the four-poster when I went out this evening? "No," I answered and stopped there. This one-word-answer approach was very interesting. I might have to try it again.

"Okay." He seemed content with my answer.

I pressed my luck. "Your roommate must be used to the awful hours."

He nodded and my stomach fluttered in disappointment. "That's the great thing about fish. They're very understanding."

"Fish?" I tried not to sound too happy.

"A salt water tank. A childhood passion I haven't outgrown."

"Fascinating."

62

"Actually, it's pretty geeky, but I enjoy it."

I was trying to figure out how to invite myself to a fish viewing when Detective Lipscomb stepped back into the doorway. I felt like my father had flipped on the porch light while I was kissing Randy Gochenauer good night in ninth grade. Embarrassment doesn't get easier with age.

"You booked on a later elevator, Edwards?" Detective Lipscomb growled.

Detective Edwards took a step toward his non-smiling partner. "You have my card. Call us in the morning and we'll arrange to meet you at the morgue. Ten or eleven, maybe."

"I will. Thank you, Detective Lipscomb." I stuck my hand out instinctively. Detective Lipscomb shook it without comment. "Detective Edwards." I moved my hand to him and he shook it with a gentle pressure that made me want to leave my hand in his.

"Good night." Detective Lipscomb walked out of the doorway again, giving Detective Edwards his exit cue.

Detective Edwards released my hand slowly and started out after Detective Lipscomb. "Call me if you think of anything."

There was an invitation I could do something with. "Count on it." He was almost out of the doorway and I blurted one more time. "Too bad your partner's already buying you breakfast."

He vanished into the hallway and I wondered if maybe he hadn't heard me or worse, if he had heard me and decided that such a stupid line wasn't worthy of response, but a second later, he was leaning back into the doorway. "Lipscomb can wait."

"Carnegie Deli about eight?" I suggested. "Yvonne can stay with Helen. I think I could have some ideas for you by then, people you should talk to, that sort of thing. Official business."

Detective Edwards smiled. "Doesn't have to be official. But I'll be there." And he vanished from the doorway again. I closed the door behind him and waited there until I could wipe the stupid grin off my face. That was the last thing Helen needed now.

4

"What you need," Tricia advised, "is something business-like, with a hint of provocative softness."

Cassady grimaced. "Thank you, Melissa Rivers."

It was seven o'clock in the morning and I should have been standing there counting my blessings that I had two such good friends who were willing to be up, dressed, and in my apartment taking control of my life at that wretched hour. But I was not in the most altruistic of moods at that moment, so what I was doing was standing there, wrapping myself up in my bathrobe and hating the contents of my closet. Hating my waistline and thighs was next on the list, but that's such a natural progression it hardly needs mentioning.

My apartment's not bad by New York standards, but the bedroom was feeling a little small this morning with all three of us in there and my being cranky. I actually love my apartment. I'm in the West 40's, I get a little morning light, and the bathtub's not in the kitchen. I've been here three years, but I still haven't progressed past the framed movie posters and bookcases-wherever-possible level of decorating. I need to paint, but I keep changing my mind about how dramatic to be, so I keep putting it off. The apartment's in transition and so am I.

"It's breakfast," Cassady said.

"So, a moderately plunging neckline," Tricia suggested.

"I don't want him looking at my breasts," I muttered.

"Yeah, I can see that," Cassady nodded.

"Excuse me?" My less-than-perfect mood had the slam-sensors working overtime.

Cassady grimaced at me now. "I'm agreeing that it would be distracting. What did you think I meant?"

With a good night's sleep, I might not have thought she meant anything, but this comment combined with her question while we were strolling through the lingerie department at Saks a week ago—had I ever thought about a Wonderbra?—put a different spin on it. Clearly, she was trying to find a way to tell me, "You think my breasts are too small."

Cassady blinked slowly so I had time to appreciate how ridiculous a statement she thought that was. "I try very hard not to think about your breasts at all, but it's hard, given their sheer perfection and outright magnificence."

"Then why did you ask me about a Wonderbra last week?"

Cassady took a moment to dial back to our shopping trip, then shrugged. "Idle curiosity. Molly, I could ask you right now if you've ever had sex with two men at a time, but that doesn't mean it's something I think you should run out and do as soon as possible."

She was right. I was being overly sensitive. Tricia was being wide-eyed and quiet. "What?" I felt compelled to ask her.

"I was waiting for you to answer the question."

"About the men or the bra?" Cassady asked.

"Both, actually," Tricia replied.

"Ooookay. If you two would like to follow me, we'll be moving back over to the subject of my clothes." I put down my cup of coffee and gestured at my closet.

"I'd go for the purple Wonderbra and the white lawn blouse." Cassady doesn't let go of things easily—except men.

"You're not being very helpful," Tricia cooed with a little hint of warning thrown in.

"I don't think she wants my help," Cassady cooed back.

"Left to her own devices, she'll go in her bathrobe and we can't have that, can we?" Tricia sniffed. They really love each other. It can take people a while to realize that because they snipe at each other with the greatest of ease and come off like enemies. But it's really more like sisters.

"She works for a fashion magazine, she can always proclaim she's starting a trend. What're you wearing to bed these days, Moll?"

"An extra large Redskins T-shirt," I confessed, pulling a nice, classic pair of black slacks out of the closet. I wasn't sure whether Tricia's gasp was in response to the T-shirt confession or to the slacks. "Now that I live here, it's the only time I can wear it. I know better than to wear it out on the streets and invite bodily harm from Giants fans."

Tricia was, however, reacting to the slacks. She ripped the hanger out of my hand and jammed the slacks back into the closet. "No." Tricia is one of those potentially annoying women who is always perfectly accessorized, down to her color-coordinated underwear, no matter the occasion or lack thereof. Yes, I work for a fashion magazine—a lifestyle magazine with a large fashion section, that is—but I have been known to wear a pink bra with purple briefs. I even own white. But I know when to wear it—

basically, when I am absolutely certain that no one else is going to see it. And while Detective Edwards was unquestionably gorgeous, I was pretty much in a white cotton mood right now.

I like sleep. I enjoy sleep. More importantly, I need sleep. I try to keep myself properly caffeinated so the world doesn't have to experience me without sleep, but every once in a while, the timing's off. Like this morning. I'd just spent five hours with Helen and Yvonne, which would classify as a debilitating activity if it occurred on a sunny afternoon. The fact that it had transpired in the middle of the night only added to the difficulty.

Actually, while I was there, adrenaline did a lot of the work and I was able to keep any of us from jumping out windows, emptying medicine cabinets, or otherwise causing damage to self or companions. Though I thought about causing Yvonne some damage more than once. But now that I was home, I had that awful adrenaline hangover thing going, where your head feels like it's still vibrating because you just stopped screaming and your extremities start to fill with molten lead. Fortunately, I was ten ounces into a pot of Kenya Gold, so hope was in sight.

"You really need to get over the Redskin thing," Cassady suggested. We both grew up in the Virginia suburbs of Washington, DC; we discovered that during Contemporary American Literature freshman year of college, and the friendship was launched. Cassady doesn't have much use for professional sports, but I continue to spend sixteen Sundays a year hoping that this will be a Super Bowl year. I like to think of those Sundays as an indication of a hopeful, optimistic heart. Cassady considers them a waste of time. This from a woman who will date married men.

"This is a date," Tricia insisted, selecting a teal silk

blouse. It's a great blouse, with a top button that's in just the right place for a black, front-clasp bra but a bit too low for your basic white back-clasp.

"No, it's not," I insisted, guiding her hand back. Tricia and Cassady looked at each other and laughed. Warmly, but they still laughed. I gulped another two ounces of coffee. "He has date potential, but this is not a date. And I'm not going to dress like I think he's taking me out to dinner when I'm meeting him for breakfast to discuss my dead colleague."

It came out a little harsher than I meant it to, but then again, it should sound harsh to say "dead" and "colleague" together. Part of the adrenaline burning off was also the reality setting in. I'd had a really long night and I'd learned a lot. Many things I could have quite nicely continued living without knowing, but too late now.

Right after I found Teddy, I thought I understood how awful his death was. When we told Helen, I realized it was even more awful. And then when I sat with Helen and Yvonne at three o'clock in the morning while Helen tried to dial her parents' phone number so she could tell them, I thought I was going to shriek and not stop. Her agony was so palpable and I wanted so desperately to do something, even take it on myself, to relieve it for even a moment. And I couldn't. Because the only thing that could make it better for her would be to bring Teddy back from the dead and I know my limits. Most of the time.

I wasn't sure any of us were going to make it through the night. But once Helen had called Teddy's parents, her own parents, and her sister, she actually settled into this kind of dignified Zen deal which was pretty impressive to see. She started getting super-organized, making lists of who else to call, who to call right away and who to call once the sun came up, who would be offended if they heard after someone else. Maybe it was shock, maybe she just ran out of tears, but she kept going, she kept thinking, and I admired that. I would have scammed pharmaceuticals from my visitors, curled up in the fetal position, and moaned for at least three weeks.

Of course, when her sister Candy arrived from Queens at about five o'clock, Helen went to pieces again, but she was entitled. Especially since Yvonne had been hovering over her most of the damn night, despite my best efforts to get her to heel. When she wasn't suggesting that I write a series of articles for the magazine on how to deal with this kind of situation, Yvonne was grabbing Helen and telling her, "We all loved him so much." It wasn't helpful. I finally came up with the multi-purpose idea to send Yvonne out to an all-night pharmacy to get some Valerian and anything else she thought might be helpful (the pill case in her Prada handbag having proven to be deplorably empty). You'd think Eisenhower had asked her to take Omaha Beach all by herself. She seized upon the mission with frightening zeal, kissed us both about eight times before she left, and raced off.

The door was barely closed behind her when Helen asked me, "So what do you really think happened to my Teddy?"

The question threw me and so did the cool, clipped way she asked it. There was something in her tone that I couldn't quite place, but it made me uncomfortable. Still, I'd never been with someone who was going through what Helen was going through, so I figured I needed to let it go and answer the question. But how honestly did I want to answer it? "I'm not sure," I told us both.

"Whoever did it should burn in hell." She said it with that same tone and the unsettled feeling spread through my stomach. I semi-nodded and she gave me this tight little smile. The unsettled feeling turned to an ice cube and I thought—*she knows something.*

I actually wished, for the briefest moment, that Yvonne were still there. I had this odd sense of dislocation and I needed to orient myself to a third party to get steady again. I started to change the subject, for my own comfort, and then realized that if I was serious about solving this crime, I couldn't flinch at the first queasy moment. But I couldn't suddenly go all Phillip Marlowe on her either. Maybe I could ease into it and start with the classic table-turning that keeps a discussion with a boyfriend so entertaining. "What do you think happened, Helen?"

Her jaw locked and her expression cooled appreciably. I forced myself to meet her gaze and to not apologize, which I readily do in most awkward social situations, occasionally even when I know it's not my fault but I want the moment to pass. If she was offended, she was going to have to explain why. "I think my life is over," she finally answered, just a few degrees warmer.

Dear Molly, how do I keep going when the most important thing in my life has vanished? I get this question, in various permutations, way more often than I should when you figure most of my readers are in their twenties and should be able to take a few more kicks in the teeth from life before needing dentures.

"No, it's not," I said gently. "It's going to be hard, but you can do this."

"The question is, do I want to?" Her tone didn't get any warmer, but she started to tear up. I couldn't quite tell if they were tears of sorrow or anger, even when she continued, "I can't tell you what it feels like to be in this place and so full of regret."

"Regret about what?"

She looked at me really hard for a really long moment as she weighed some pros and cons. I'm pretty sure she was going to tell me, but the phone rang and made us both jump. I started to answer it for her, but she grabbed it, as eager to end our conversation as she was to start another one. It was Teddy's brother Charlie in Minneapolis. Helen began to bravely recite the facts as she knew them and I backed off.

I slipped into the kitchen, seeking a glass of water. What I really wanted to do was see what kind of ice cream Helen kept in the freezer or, better yet, what kind of wine Teddy kept in the fridge, but my good breeding prevented me from being a total pig. You wait for the wake to stuff your face. I did open the fridge in the hopes of finding cold bottled water and found myself staring at carryout containers from Costa del Sol. So she really had ordered in. That much of her alibi stood up.

The word "alibi" trailed a little flush of guilt in its wake. On a visceral level, I knew Helen had nothing to do with this, yet, here I was, sneaking a peek inside the bag. Had she ordered for one or for two? The crinkling of the plastic bag sounded like a tarp flapping in the wind as I listened with one ear to make sure Helen was still on the phone. Inside, there were two foil carryout dishes. I pried up the cardboard cover of the top one: it held a few beef medallions in Madeira and some stray slices of vegetables. Leftovers. I eased the dish up to inspect the one underneath, holding my breath as Helen seemed to stay silent too long, then breathing again as she sobbed anew into the phone.

The second dish was full. Paella, beautifully presented given that it was for takeout. Now, a woman who can't finish one entrée isn't going to order two. And you don't order something with shellfish in it a day ahead unless you like flirting with intestinal distress. Helen had ordered it for Teddy in the hopes that he'd be home early enough to eat it. She'd thought he was coming home. Whatever the regret was, she hadn't given up completely. She knew something, but she hadn't killed him.

Yvonne returned while Helen was finishing up with Charlie and then Candy arrived. I knew I was not going to get Helen back to confessional mode with her sister around. Candy has four kids under the age of nine, one of those expansive women who always smells of cookie dough and carries safety pins in her purse and mothers everybody. That's probably what Helen needed most right now, so it was a perfect time for Yvonne and me to get ourselves home.

Helen made me promise to meet her at the police station at ten to help her through the identification and all that stuff. Candy didn't leap in and tell me that it wasn't necessary, that she would take over from here, so I confirmed I'd meet the two of them at the station. Yvonne waited a moment to see if Helen would ask her to be there, too, but Helen hugged us both and thanked us for helping her through the worst night of her life. It actually choked me up, but it seemed to tick Yvonne off. She left her shopping bag with goodies on the coffee table and practically marched me to the elevator.

"So. What did she say? While I was gone?" Yvonne asked as we waited for a cab. The sun was uncomfortably bright and I was craving a toothbrush and a cup of coffee, so I was inclined to be snippy. Then I realized she wasn't being ghoulish, she was being worried. Good Lord. Did she know something, too? Here I was, vowing that I was going to solve this crime and I was apparently the only one I had talked to all night with no clue as to what might have happened.

I felt no compunction about being blunt with Yvonne. "Why, Yvonne? What do you know?"

"Oh. My. God. Like I could know a thing." She refused to look at me, keeping her eyes a little too wide and a little too intent on the stream of traffic.

"Save the coys for the boys, Yvonne. This is serious." She waggled her fingers at a taxi and it pulled over. She headed for it and I grabbed her arm, which she didn't appreciate. "You and Teddy go back a long way, right? Don't you want to make sure this gets solved, for his sake?"

Yvonne gave me a look of such malevolence that her mascara should have vaporized from the heat. "What does it matter? He's gone. Nothing can change that."

"It'll matter to Helen."

"I owe that bitch?"

I was so startled that her arm was out of my grasp and her butt was in the taxi before I took another breath. I started to scramble into the taxi beside her, but she stopped me. "Nine o'clock. You'll help me tell the staff." She slammed the door and the taxi slipped away.

Which is why I was less than playful with Cassady and Tricia and why I selected a charcoal wool crepe pencil skirt and white blouse for my breakfast . . . thing with Detective Edwards.

"Okay, it's not a date, but it's not a job interview either," Tricia protested as I changed. She held out the Zanottis from the night before.

I slipped them on, considered them, then took them off

and handed them back. "Thanks for the loan." I sighed as my Achilles tendons unknotted and my heels sank to the ground. There was a good chance that would be the extent of my workout for the day, so I wanted to relish it.

Cassady gave me one of her piercing lawyer looks. "It's not too late to cancel."

"On the breakfast?"

"On solving the murder. We all say things in the heat of the moment that we quickly come to regret and there's no shame in finding a graceful exit as long as you find it early."

Tricia scrunched her mouth into a little knot of disbelief. "And that's worked so well for you on how many occasions?"

"Advice is meant to be given, not followed," Cassady retorted.

"That adds meaning to my life," I said as I repacked my Achilles tendons into my Stuart Weitzman Babydolls. When in doubt, go with black pumps. Really sweet, really high black pumps.

Cassady had the grace to wince. "Sorry. I meant casual advice, not professional advice."

"No need to apologize for me. I'm well aware I make no meaningful contribution to society. That's why I'm going to solve this crime and turn things around." I grabbed my jacket and my purse. "You two are welcome to stay here and talk behind my back. Just make sure you lock up on your way out."

Tricia rocked up on her toes, unhappy. "Can't we all share a cab? We'll drop you at the deli."

"I love you both, but I need some quiet time. To pull together my thoughts."

I was still trying to do just that as I stared blankly at the menu at Carnegie Deli and secretly hoped that Detective

Edwards was about to stand me up. What was I going to tell him? Helen was innocent because there was food in her fridge? Because she seemed nice? Wanting to be helpful and being able to be helpful seemed to be drifting farther and farther apart at the moment. But before I could sort it all out, he was sliding into the seat across from me, looking better than I was prepared for. "Good morning. I was afraid you'd stand me up."

I tried a whimsical look, but it felt more like a twitch. "Why would I?"

"Better offer?"

"Didn't get one. But I haven't checked my messages in the last hour or so."

"Please don't." He smiled lazily and pushed the menu out of the way without looking at it. I put mine on top of his. He clearly knew what he wanted. I didn't have a clue, but I was developing a taste for figuring things out on the fly.

"How was Helen Reynolds when you left her?"

Oh, fine. Right to business. I actually felt a flicker of disappointment, but then again, I had been the one to insist that this was not a date. Served me right. "About the same. Her sister came in from Queens and that helped. You don't still suspect her?"

"I thought we were having breakfast so you could tell me what you know." He upped the wattage on his smile, but now there was a touch of warning to it, too.

"Helen didn't do it."

"What makes you so sure?"

I figured he'd scoff at the paella, so I went for a more psychological approach. "She wants vengeance on whoever did do it. And she wasn't faking."

"You know her that well?"

"No, I know real emotion when I see it."

His smile loosened a little and I waited for the smart response, but the waitress intruded. He ordered an everything bagel, toasted, and coffee. I thought about doing the same, then thought about the number of times poppyseeds wind up between your front teeth, even when you're being careful, and ordered a bowl of fruit and coffee. It seemed a shame to order so simply when the smells of steak and eggs and maple syrup and melting butter meandered through the whole place, but I wanted to make sure he understood that I understood that this was a working breakfast. And yes, I am also one of those girls who thinks twice about eating hearty in front of a guy in the early stages.

"Refresh my memory. How long had you known Teddy?" He was playing with his pen against his closed notebook, turning the pen end on end. He kept his eyes on mine, but I kept glancing down at the pen, less distracted than avoiding the Big Blues for a moment.

"Three years. I'd heard of him before that, but I came to the magazine three years ago."

"Heard of him?"

"An old friend of mine, Stephanie Glenn, worked with him at *Femme*. That's where he was before *Zeitgeist*. In fact, Yvonne worked there, too. They go way back, she's the one that brought him over to *Zeitgeist*. He had a great reputation, business-wise. It's his social skills that got mixed reviews."

"What'd your friend think of him?"

"She thought he was a hoot. But she didn't work *for* him, which is where you find most of the people who weren't big fans."

"Did she sleep with him?"

I almost laughed, imagining Stephanie with Teddy. "No way." Edwards arched an eyebrow. "She's gay."

"I see. Do you know who did sleep with him?"

"Why are you back on that?" It was fine for me to be obsessing about the possibility of Teddy's rancid romantic past, but I was doing it as a journalist and a student of human behavior. Edwards was doing it as a cop and that road could only lead back to, "You do still suspect Helen."

"At this stage, I suspect everyone. Statistically, the wife goes to the head of the class."

"You're wasting my time."

"So point me in another direction."

"I think it was someone he knew pretty well. Someone who knew he worked weird hours. Someone who was furious with him." Like his wife who had just discovered he was sleeping around on her, but not her. The thought clanked around noisily in my head, but I refused to say it and prepared myself for Edwards saying it.

Instead, he asked, "Why furious?"

This was a test, right? He knew the answer and wanted to see how keenly observant I was capable of being. Fine. I resisted the impulse to begin with "Well, duh," and said, "Because she left the knife in his throat."

Edwards stopped tapping his pen and looked at me oddly. Had I failed the test? Didn't it make perfect sense that you'd leave the knife behind only to make a statement? Sort of like signing a painting. "If you stabbed someone in a moment of anger or passion, don't you think you'd realize what you'd done and pull the knife back out, to clean or hide the knife if nothing else? To leave the knife in there—that's rage. The ultimate 'screw you, Teddy.' "

The pen started tapping again, but slowly and deliberately. "She?"

"What?" I'd hoped for an "exactly, my dear Forrester" or something a little more indicative of how well we were doing.

"You said '*she* left the knife.' Why?"

"Because Teddy was a bully, but a coward. He wouldn't have gotten close enough to an angry man for a man to stab him like that."

Edwards didn't react at all for a moment, then nodded. "Our analysis of the blood spatter indicates that Reynolds was in the doorway of his office, probably leaning against the frame, and was stabbed with an overhand thrust from a lower angle."

I raised my hand, trying to figure that one out. "So she's shorter than he was."

Edwards watched my hand. Keenly aware that my nails were a mess, I dropped my hand back into my lap. Edwards' eyes slid up to mine. "How tall are you?"

I almost told him, but for once, my brain worked faster than my mouth. "Excuse me?"

"How tall are you?"

"You've got to be kidding." He didn't shake his head, didn't smile, didn't look away. I felt like Carrie as the pig's blood hit the top of her head. Of course Detective Edwards didn't want to take me to the prom because I was cute. He thought I was guilty.

I tried to laugh derisively, but it came out as the mutant child of a sob and a hiccup. I could feel my cheeks reddening and realized I had transformed into some kind of scarlet frog, blurping and blushing madly. What would the detective make of that? Would he take it as a sign of guilt or would he be sharp enough to recognize that I really wanted to throttle him, but was restraining myself because

I knew it would be completely counterproductive at this point.

"I don't know what to say."

" 'I'm five-seven'?" he suggested.

"I'm five-eight in my bare feet, but I'll look taller as I stand to leave." I grabbed my purse and took a moment to arrange my feet beside my chair so I wouldn't trip as I got up for my grand exit.

Before I could stand, Edwards put his hand over mine, pressing it down into the table with a slight but undeniable pressure. "Please don't make a scene."

"I can't. I don't have any silverware."

He leaned in, his voice low and urgent. I leaned in to listen, hating it, but needing to hear what he had to say. "It's been my experience that when a civilian gets all gung-ho about helping to solve a crime, they have some invest-ment in the crime."

"He was my friend," I hissed.

"There's more to it." He leaned in closer. If this had happened two minutes earlier, I would have thought he was going to kiss me. Now, I felt like he was trying to smell Teddy's blood on me. "Tell me."

Dear Molly, I'm sitting in the middle of Carnegie Deli, hold-ing hands with this super-hot homicide detective and I have a choice. I can tell him I want to help on this case because it could further my career, in which case he'll think I'm a heartless bitch, or I can tell him I want to help because I think he's super-hot, in which case he'll think I'm throwing myself at him. Which has the greater potential for soul-shriveling embarrassment? Signed, Getting Madder by the Minute

"I want to write about this investigation from an inside perspective and use the article to further my journalism career." Let's face it. Appearing desperate to advance in your business life is showing good hustle. Appearing desperate to advance in your personal life is just—being desperate. And that we cannot be.

Edwards sank slowly back into his seat, his hand trailing off mine. He stared at me and I managed to stare back with what I hoped was the proper blend of hurt and disdain. I couldn't tell if he believed me or if he was playing me, but for the moment, I didn't care. I just wanted to get out of this with one shred of dignity, even if it was trailing behind me like toilet paper caught on the bottom of my shoe.

"Am I free to go?"

He nodded slowly, still staring at me. He wasn't sure if he believed me or not. His problem.

I stood and my legs were steadier than I had expected them to be. "I am glad you've abandoned the botched burglary theory."

He nodded, still turning something else over in his mind. Was he feeling bad about accusing me? Wouldn't that be nice. "We found his wallet in a dumpster outside the parking garage. Someone used his cardkey to get out through the garage, then tossed the wallet with the money and credit cards still inside."

Sometimes, not saying "I told you so" is even more fun that saying it. I started away, but the waitress appeared with our food and coffee. She looked at me, my purse in hand. "You're leaving?"

"Yes, I am."

"You need yours to go?"

I shook my head. "Leave mine with him. He knows what he can do with it." I gave Detective Edwards my most charming smile and walked out. And I didn't trip once.

5

On a purely mathematical level, the people you work with consume more of your time than your family ever gets a chance to, so it's no wonder that the workplace is filled with the same dysfunctional backstabbing, infighting, competition, and just plain lying that make family gatherings so much fun. But tragedy can bring together an office like it can reunite a family and, at the outset anyway, the *Zeitgeist* family rallied appropriately at the news of Teddy's death.

Yvonne was still a little icy with me when I arrived in her office at five minutes of nine, prepared for instructions on addressing the troops as she had commanded earlier. I stared at her mouth, marveling at how her upper lip had curled when she called Helen a bitch, while she prattled on about sensitivity and times of crisis and a bunch of other pabulum that I knew she'd wind up weaving into a "very special article" for the next issue. "Can you understand?" she sniffed.

"Everything except why you think Helen is a bitch," I sniffed back.

"Go forth!" She pointed out to the bullpen where the staff was gathering. I figured most of them already knew what had happened. Gossip is the only thing the building ventilation system moves properly and some of our staff early birds had apparently encountered police personnel just packing up and releasing the scene. Plus there was the huge field of brown paper the management company had duct taped to the floor, presumably to cover the bloodstains they hadn't had time to steam out of the carpet.

"Aren't you coming?"

"I need. A moment." She plopped down in her desk chair and moved a large box of tissues in front of her with a flourish. Funny, for all her sniffing, I couldn't see a single tear.

There were lots of big boo-hoos out in the bullpen. Most of the guys looked slightly ill and really uncomfortable. The women were evenly split between the badly shaken and the sobbing. The ringleader of the weepers was Gretchen Plotnick, Teddy's assistant. It made sense that she was taking this hardest, especially since she'd put up with him for longer than any other assistant in his entire career—eight whole months. Liz Isihara in Human Resources sent Gretchen a dozen roses when she hit the four-month mark and set a new record. It saved Liz so much time not having to hunt for a new assistant for Teddy every six weeks.

I tried to keep my remarks to the staff brief and to the point, especially when I realized that Gretchen was going to punctuate them with melodramatic wails every ten words or so. Besides, what more was there to say than Teddy was dead, that sucked? Oh, and first dibs on the article about uncovering the murderer who certainly was not Helen, but Yvonne better start cleaning up her act really quick? Okay, so that part remained unsaid.

"If you have any information that might be helpful to the police, I have the number of the detective assigned to the case," I added at the end of my lame little spiel. *Dear Molly, At least you thought you had his number. But seems he thinks you're a killer and not the good kind. Didn't see that coming, did you? Signed, Just Being Helpful*

I counted noses as the staff gathered around Gretchen as though she were the one to be consoled. Certainly, she was the one making the most noise about her grief. But Gretchen doesn't do much halfway. She dreams big, dresses big, talks big. Her hair is a shade of red approximating strawberry jam, her clothes are usually some bizarre conglomeration of current style and her "own special touches," and she can outtalk anyone in the office, Yvonne included. She was actually a great match for Teddy—every bit as large, loud, and bossy as he was. No wonder she'd been able to put up with him. She'd lost a kindred spirit.

Everyone on staff was present or accounted for: Yvonne's assistant Fred Hagstrom was out of town at his niece's wedding, assistant advertising director Brady Cooper was on an about-to-be truncated vacation in Maine, and Sophie Galliano in Accounting was still recovering from the removal of four impacted wisdom teeth, but everyone else was there. Of course, if you killed a colleague, you'd probably want to show up at work the next day to avoid the appearance of disappearance. Could it be someone on staff?

Yvonne entered from her office at that moment and again there was that flush of guilt—or was it adrenaline—as I watched her and considered suspects at the same time. Could it be Yvonne? But they'd been friends for so long. What could've gone wrong?

Yvonne knocked on top of Fred's computer to get everyone's attention. Or more precisely, to draw everyone's attention away from Gretchen. Yvonne loves her moments and it was pretty clear to me that she considered this one hers and not Gretchen's. It was the Battle of the Work Widows. "I want to take a moment. To remark upon Molly's remarks."

Yvonne tried to muster a smile, but made sure we could all see how difficult it was for her before she gave up. She rambled into some story about how much Teddy meant to her and to the magazine and the sort of stuff you'd expect to be said in this situation, but I had a hard time focusing. I was trying to remember where Yvonne said she was when the security guys called her and asked her to come in. She'd changed out of the gray Max Mara suit she'd worn to work when she and the detectives picked me up to go see Helen and was wearing a slightly ridiculous multicolored Versace sheath. Was that because there was blood on the Mara?

Unfortunately, any attempts at luring that information out of Yvonne were going to have to wait. I needed to get down to the precinct and meet Helen and Candy for the identification and all the horrors that might generate. I thought about trying to fake a coma so I didn't have to go, but then I worried that Yvonne might go in my place and I really didn't want Yvonne anywhere near Helen until I figured out what was going on.

Yvonne wound down her address to the troops with some trembling proclamation of Teddy's undying influence on us all, then thumped her chest with her fist like Celine Dion. For a terrifying moment, I thought she was going to launch into song, but she just dropped her head and spun away from the group, a diva move that was amusing by itself but a little pathetic in context. I reached to grab my purse but Yvonne grabbed me first.

"His reception. Has to be magnificent."

"I'm sure Helen will plan something lovely."

Her grip on my arm tightened like a falcon clamping down on a perch. Bruises tomorrow weren't going to surprise me at all. I winced, trying to ease my arm away, but she wasn't letting go. "I don't want Helen to worry about such a thing."

Yeah, and Louis XVI didn't want Marie Antoinette to worry her pretty little head about such things either and look where that pretty little head wound up. And his own head, for that matter. "What are you suggesting, Yvonne?"

"We'll pay for the reception."

I loved Teddy, but I knew my checking account balance. "Define 'we.' "

"The magazine." I waited, still suspicious. Yvonne slid her hand down my arm to grasp my hand. At least the blood was flowing in my arm again. "It should be big. As grand as he was. And Helen shouldn't have to pay."

What disturbed me was I could understand Yvonne's logic. If the reception turned into an industry event, which it would unless Helen restricted it to family only or something like that, it was going to get big. And Helen had enough to worry about without footing the bill for that. "I'm sure Helen will appreciate the offer, but—"

"Good. Talk to her."

Not exactly the point I'd been trying to make, but better me than Yvonne, I supposed. "All right."

"And your little friend Tricia."

"Excuse me?"

"She'll do it."

"Plan the reception? I don't know, Yvonne, it's not exactly her area of expertise."

"Money's no object." Now there's a powerful phrase. It can make you reconsider just about any decision, at least for a few moments. Funeral receptions weren't Tricia's game, but I had no doubt that she could put together a terrific one. And if Yvonne was going to unchoke the money flow, Tricia would be able to give Teddy a great send-off. No losers there.

"I'll talk to her."

"Both."

"Yes."

"Good. Go." Yvonne gestured with an imperial vagueness to somewhere other than where I was standing and retreated to her office. I gathered up my stuff and prepared to look death in the face.

The cab ride over to the morgue wasn't long enough to prepare myself, but a cruise around the world wouldn't have been either. The building itself is tough enough—cold, institutional and forbidding. It made me think of an old folk song about mining my dad used to sing on long car drives: "Dark as a dungeon and damp as the dew, where the danger is double and the pleasures are few . . ." My hat's off to anyone who feels called to this kind of work.

The identification process was horrific on two levels. Helen and Candy arrived looking pretty pulled together, considering, but Helen left resembling one of the bad guys at the end of *Raiders of the Lost Ark*—everything stripped away but the vibrant pain underneath. On the other level was the process itself—Lipscomb led Helen through it so smoothly, almost elegantly, that it drove home the unspoken point that homicide detectives go through this on a regular, if not daily, basis.

I did what I could for Helen, literally offering her a shoulder to cry on. When she seemed to be cried out for the moment, I tiptoed into delicate territory. "Have you thought about his service?"

I might as well have opened the floodgates myself. Helen

sobbed anew and Candy squinted at me, not happily. "It's all a little overwhelming."

"The magazine would like to host the reception."

Helen stopped crying so abruptly that she choked. Candy patted her on the back until she stopped coughing, then Helen looked at me with a fierce frown. "What?"

"If it's all right with you, the magazine would like to pay for the reception. As a tribute to Teddy."

Helen wiped uselessly at her eyes. "By 'magazine,' you mean Yvonne."

It was pretty clear that line of reasoning was going to take us to a dark place and I wasn't properly dressed. "No. All of us. Though Yvonne authorized it."

Helen struggled with something bitter, but Candy cut her off. "Let them foot the bill. It's the least they can do, all the hours he gave them. All the hours they took him away from you."

I hadn't thought of it that way at all. I'd just assumed that Yvonne was looking to show off. But it was a theory I felt comfortable nodding to support. Helen shifted her ravaged eyes between my encouraging nod and Candy's resolute face a couple of times. "I want to be part of planning it."

"Oh, of course," I assured her. Yvonne might not go for that, but Tricia would make sure Helen was included throughout. "A friend of mine will take care of everything and she'll consult you on all points."

Helen hesitated and Candy plopped her arm around her shoulders. "You've got enough to worry about, honey. Let them do this."

Helen's gaze shifted back to my eyes. She was looking for something but I couldn't tell what. Which made it a lot easier to play innocent, nod again, and muster up an encouraging smile. After a long moment, Helen nodded. "Okay."

"Good. My friend Tricia Vincent will call you." I made sure Candy had all my numbers and understood I was sincere about her or Helen calling if there was anything else I could do. I repeated that to Helen and wasn't sure she heard me until she whispered back, "His office."

I hadn't thought of it yet. Teddy's office needed to be packed up. "Want me to help you?"

"Could you just . . . do it?"

"Sure." I could certainly understand Helen not wanting to deal with the packing or having to see everyone—especially Yvonne—right now. Maybe it would be less creepy to pack his stuff without her there to tell me what personal significance each and every item had. Though there was also the possibility that there wouldn't be that much and that would be pretty sad, too. My friend Bill works in advertising and is constantly getting cut loose and rehired. He swears that you should never have more personal stuff in your office than can fit in one paper carton. That way, you only have to make one trip when you leave.

But if you're packing up at the end of a life, not at the end of a job, shouldn't there be lots of stuff? A proud collection of items that humanized your office and now stand as memorials to all the hours you spent, all the work you did, all the lives you touched? Shouldn't your life spill over into at least a second carton? For Helen's sake, I hoped I was going to pack up a rich trove that she could go through at her own pace and find some comfort in.

And, of course, I thought with another adrenaline surge, there was a chance I could find something in his office that might make this whole miserable thing make sense. "I'll take care of it this morning and call you about a good time to bring the boxes by."

She thanked me and hugged me. She felt lighter and more fragile than when I had left her apartment, and that provoked the tears I'd been fighting since Lipscomb had first come out to meet us. I patted her awkwardly on the back, detached myself, and turned around just in time to step on Detective Edwards' foot.

I wished it had been with my heel—the heel on these Weitzman pumps is pretty potent—but it was with my toe. He had been walking up behind me, should have zigged when I zagged, and *pow*. Neither of us was amused.

"Detective Edwards," I acknowledged and made a bee-line for the ladies room. I paced, I peed, I repaired my makeup as much as my blotchy cheeks and trembling hands would permit, and I checked my watch about three times before deciding that I could safely emerge. Surely he and Lipscomb were occupied with Helen or something else by now. But as I stepped back into the hall, Edwards was waiting for me.

There are times I wish I smoked. Lauren Bacall could always buy a moment to come up with the perfect scathing line by doing the whole cigarette case ritual—click, tap tap, long, soulful gaze as the match is struck, deep inhale, lazy exhale, withering line. I could've used one of Bacall's cigarettes just then. Better yet, I could've used one of Bacall's writers.

Edwards made the first move, which would have impressed me more if I hadn't been dismissing it as technique. "This morning didn't go the way I'd hoped."

"Bagel not fresh?" I asked, almost able to taste one of those little pieces of tobacco Bacall was always lifting off her tongue with a perfectly manicured nail.

"I deserve that." He smiled and it was pained enough to pass for sincere. "I misjudged you."

"Is this where I excuse you because you're only doing your job?" Even if it was sincere, the smile was not enough. Not by a long shot.

"That'd be great."

"I'm sure it would be. Have a nice day, Detective."

Touché, Leigh Brackett. I felt really good about leaving him that way. Until I told Cassady about it on the cell phone on the way back to the office. "You don't want to burn that bridge, Molly," she snapped.

"I'm not going to get involved with a guy who thinks I'm capable of murder. Or of sleeping with Teddy Reynolds," I said in an effort to defend myself.

"I'm talking about having access to the police department so you can solve this crime and become a world-famous journalist," she snapped even harder.

"You're so supportive. One of the many reasons I love you," I snapped back.

"I am being supportive!" she protested. "I'm thinking clearly for you since you apparently don't have time for that today."

Snap, snap, snap.

"What am I supposed to do, Cassady? Thank him for considering me a murder suspect?" One of the great things about Manhattan is that everybody has so much on their minds that they rarely care what's on yours. You could have sex in the middle of the sidewalk on Sixth Avenue and people would step around you without breaking stride. But I guess my voice got a little shrill on "murder suspect" because three different people looked directly at me—one with horror and two with interest. I turned up the collar on my coat, like that was going to muffle anything else I blurted, and kept walking.

"You're supposed to laugh off the ridiculous misunderstanding and start keeping notes in case you want me to sue him later on. Just don't slam the door. Keep it open. You may need it."

"You don't need it. The door, the aggravation, any of it," Tricia insisted when I called to get her point of view. "He's clearly an idiot when it comes to judging people, which leads me to believe he's not that good a detective. Therefore, he's of no use to you on a personal or professional level, so move on."

I didn't answer her right away. I was thinking about what she said, but I was also watching the people stream in and out of our building. I'd decided to hover outside to finish my conversation with Tricia because I didn't want anyone in the office to have the slightest inkling of the journalist angle to this whole mess. It would be unseemly. And might give someone ideas. I already had Peter to worry about on that front.

So I was watching the people come and go and realizing that Edwards had said the killer had used Teddy's cardkey to get out through the garage after killing him. But how had the killer gotten into the building? Everyone who had checked in must have checked out or Edwards would have a list of discrepancies. So how do you get into the building and not show up on the security system?

Tricia misconstrued my silence. "You really like him."

"No," I assured her. "He's hot, but as you said, he's an idiot. Moving on."

"I don't want you to get hurt. On any level."

"You're a doll. I'll talk to you soon."

In the elevator, I let the dread of having to go through Teddy's office give way to the excitement that I might find something that would help solve his murder. Helen wanted vengeance and I was beginning to get a little taste of that myself. Or maybe I was telling myself that to feel a little less vulture-ish about my Pulitzer Prize in the making.

The bullpen was painfully subdued as I made my way to Teddy's office. People were actually working, there was no superfluous chatter, and even the people on the phone spoke more quietly and politely than usual. The only loud voices in the whole place belonged to Yvonne and Gretchen, who were squaring off at Teddy's door. Gretchen was actually blocking the door, arms folded, jaw clenched, overplucked eyebrows drawn down into her approximation of a menacing look. Yvonne was trying to get past her, but Gretchen was immovable in attitude and size.

Yvonne turned as I walked up, brown paper crunching hideously underfoot. I only had time to smile helpfully before she launched into me. "What's going on between you and Helen?"

As I tried to flag down the express train Yvonne was driving, Gretchen explained, "Yvonne wants to go through Teddy's office, but Helen called and said you're the only one allowed in. The cops already did their sweep, took his PDA, that sort of thing, but you're supposed to handle everything else." Gretchen leaned against the doorjamb to emphasize her control of the space and I winced at the mental image Edwards had conjured up of Teddy leaning there as the murderer attacked.

Yvonne persisted. "There are files in there, work that has to be reassigned. I don't mean to be unfeeling. But we. Still. Have. A magazine to get out here. I am not above firing people to make my point." She stomped her foot and her heel punctured the brown paper. I actually expected blood to come bubbling up, Sam Raimi-style, but you couldn't even see a stain through the tear. Thank God.

Yvonne tried to mush the paper back in place with the toe of her shoe, then drew herself up in dramatic indignation. It was pretty futile. I'd never really noticed how short Yvonne was since she was always in the highest heels that structural engineering could manage. All Edwards had said was that the killer was shorter than Teddy, which meant less than five-ten. Even in her highest heels, Yvonne was still only in the five-six to five-seven range.

Yvonne?

I've thought some pretty nasty things about Yvonne in the time I've worked for her, especially when I was doing a feature article and she changed things in it that didn't make it any better, just different. Some editors are like that. They have to have it their way, not because your way is wrong but because it's, you guessed it, your way. But of the many colorful and clearly deserved things I have thought of her, I've never thought she might be capable of murder.

Time to think it now. Which meant it was also time to get her away from Teddy's office, because I was willing to bet she had personal rather than business reasons for wanting to get in there.

"Yvonne, we've had an awful night. And not a great morning. Let's not take it out on each other." I tried to guide her away from Teddy's office, but she plopped her bony rear end on Gretchen's desk, folded her arms across her chest, and made it quite clear she would not be moved.

"Why you?"

Who the hell knew. But I couldn't admit that or she'd be in there packing boxes with me, which struck me as a pretty bad idea about now. "I believe Helen was concerned it would be too painful for you. Or her. Or Gretchen." While I was lying, I might as well spare Gretchen's feelings, too.

"She said that?"

"Not in those exact words." Or words anywhere close to that, but there was no need to hurt Yvonne if she wasn't the killer. I made a mental note to pat myself on the back later for treating Yvonne as innocent until I could search Teddy's office and prove her guilty.

Yvonne struggled with some notion for a moment, perhaps that of Helen being concerned about her, then accepted it. She stood back up, her hand sweeping vaguely behind her to check for upended pencil cups, and walked back to her office without another word. As someone not particularly fond of silence, I was impressed.

Almost as impressed as I was by Gretchen's strength as she squeezed me in something closer to a chiropractic technique than a hug.

" 'Sokay, Gretch," I wheezed. Gretchen and I are about the same height, so my nose was mushed against her cheek. It made it hard to breathe on two counts—the whole mushing thing and the fact that Gretchen smelled like some strange, old lady perfume I couldn't quite identify. She usually favored the more exotic, dusky perfumes, but she mainly wore whatever free samples Teddy gave her, so maybe this was something new.

"Thank you for doing this," she moaned, then moved quickly to her desk to sob some more. I paused in the doorway, not sure whether she intended that I follow and comfort her, but Kendall Graham and Jason Jefferson, two of our bright-eyed editorial assistants, were beside her with tissues, water, and murmurs before I could decide. Kendall shot me a look like I'd made Gretchen cry. Since I've never been comfortable being the bad guy, I slunk into Teddy's office.

I wasn't sure where to start. There were framed issue covers on the wall, but those belonged to the magazine, not to Teddy. There were personal photographs on the credenza—the wedding picture, Teddy and Helen on Grand Cayman a couple of years ago, toasting the photographer as they laughed at some poolside bar. A beautiful walnut box held Teddy's collection of Montblanc pens. There were stacks of files everywhere, but those were Gretchen's problem. There didn't seem to be that many personal effects. That part might be easier than I'd thought. But what else was the office going to tell me?

I eased myself into the orthopedically correct desk chair and ran my hands over the polished wood of the desk. It was a big, lumbering old thing, the kind Spencer Tracy had whenever he played a lawyer. It had a certain grandness that I'm sure had pleased Teddy. It also looked quite capable of holding its share of secrets.

If I die and someone else has to clean out my desk, I will be mortified for eternity. Imagining someone piecing together my life based on the tampons, Advil, tea bags, Sudafed, toothpaste, and extra pantyhose in just my top drawer made me cringe. It also made me hesitate with my hand on Teddy's lap drawer. What if there was something in here I didn't want to know, couldn't handle? All my suspicions were abstract so far, but what if I was about to confirm them? I kept my head down so I wouldn't look up and look right at Yvonne's office, and slid open the drawer.

Men are ahead of the game right away because they are, on the toiletry level, lower-maintenance creatures and don't require intimate accessories on hand at all times.

Except for condoms. Not something you'd expect to find in a desk drawer, but there they were. Front and center, too, not even hidden back in the back behind a stack of Post-it Notes, which is where I squirrel away the tampons in my desk. Smack dab in the middle. Trojan Twisted Pleasures. I bet.

I slid the drawer shut so fast that I nearly pinched off both my thumbs. I was lightheaded and flustered, as though I had walked in on Teddy standing in the middle of the room naked. I tried to keep my brain from going to the next step, which was Teddy in the middle of the room naked and putting on a condom, but it was tough. I stood up, literally shaking my head to keep the image from lodging and becoming too clear. I forced myself to picture something else, anything else, like counting sheep. So I stood there for a few minutes, thinking of the claymation sheep in the Serta ads. But that morphed into Teddy naked with the sheep and that wasn't helpful at all.

Why would a married man keep condoms in his desk drawer? It wasn't like Helen came by the office a lot or they met for lunch a lot, even though she worked close by. These were not for Helen. But who? And where? I suddenly felt very voyeuristic just standing in the middle of the room and looking at the couch, the desk, the rug, trying hard to keep my mind a blank and failing miserably. Sometimes, an active imagination is a curse.

So, if Teddy was a bad dog, did that mean Edwards was right to be considering Helen as his prime suspect? No way. She was furious that this had happened. Probably blamed the mistress. And the mistress certainly made sense—someone who knew he kept late hours because she was one of the reasons he kept them, someone who knew her way around the building, someone who would feel the passion necessary to bury the knife in his throat and leave it there. So who was she?

I started going through his office like a junkie looking for a stash. It was easy enough to dismiss a lot of his desk—it had actual work in it. The top left-hand drawer had office hardware—staples, scissors, letter opener, buck slips. The top right-hand drawer was dominated by snacks—PowerBars, little boxes of raisins, a bag of trail mix. I started to close the drawer, then decided to dig deeper, pushing aside all the healthy snacks to uncover two Milky Ways and a package of strawberry Twizzlers. Somehow, that made me feel better.

Then there was the lap drawer. I slid it open again and pushed the condoms to one side, making a shiny green snake of foil squares coil itself in the front corner. Otherwise, the drawer also held the usual suspects of pens and pencils, a few subway tokens, Post-it Notes in varying sizes in yellow, blue, and pink, and a tin of Altoids.

I slid my hands all the way into the back and recoiled as I touched something soft and rubbery. I jerked my fingers away, only to hit more. A whole little colony. So many disgusting things ran through my mind at once that I surprised even myself. I took a deep breath and pulled the items forward into the light.

Soy sauce. Little take-out packets of soy sauce. And duck sauce. And ketchup, mustard, and even one sweet pickle relish. But no smoking gun. Other than the one I kept imagining in the condoms.

I was going to have to throw the condoms away—they surely weren't going home to Helen and I didn't want Gretchen to have to deal with them either—but everything else looked personal enough to pack. We seemed to be in one-carton territory here and I wondered if I'd find enough to comfort Helen. Or was she hoping I'd find something damning as much as I was?

I figured I'd start with the pictures on the credenza, then fill in with the random junk from the desk. I spun around in the chair, grabbed the picture of Helen and Teddy, and dropped it. I almost had a chance to grab it in midair, but my fingers just brushed it and turned its deadfall into a descending cartwheel. I winced as the glass shattered on impact.

The crash apparently wasn't as loud as it sounded to my guilty ears because Gretchen didn't come racing in. I stooped and picked up the shards of glass as quickly as possible. At least I hadn't damaged the picture. I'd offer to replace the glass for Helen. That would be a nice gesture.

I picked up the frame to shake the still clinging pieces of glass into the wastebasket. It was a simple silver frame, three by five, with little finials on the corners. My guess was, Helen had bought it for him. It seemed more her style. I shook the frame, the glass fell free, and the picture started to slide out. I pinched the picture against the frame with my thumb, but it had slipped enough to reveal another picture. I remembered my grandmother keeping our school pictures stacked in a frame like that so she could marvel at how much we'd grown from one year to the next. Was Teddy being sentimental or had he just been too lazy to remove the sample picture that had come with the frame?

I slid the top picture out to check the second. It was another cute couple picture and Teddy looked better in this one. Why did he prefer the other one? Oh. Because the woman in the picture wasn't Helen. It was Yvonne.

I had that creepy voyeur feeling again, but I couldn't put the picture down. They were at some black tie event,

Teddy in a classic black tux and Yvonne in an amazing Bagdley Mischka which, with the cooperation of strategic underwiring somewhere, flaunted all the cleavage she had. Judging by the cut of the dress and the color of Yvonne's hair, the picture had been taken last summer.

Now, Yvonne and Teddy had known each other for a long time. They were good friends. They went to a lot of swanky parties, both on behalf of the magazine and to support their own causes. So there was no surprise to see them together at such a function.

The surprise was *how* they were together. Teddy sat on a barstool. Yvonne stood between his legs, hip, breast, and shoulder nestled against his body, one hand holding a drink, the other comfortably, casually as high on his thigh as it could be without being directly on his crotch. Teddy's arm was around her, hand possessively on her hip. Yvonne was glancing at the camera, but Teddy's gaze was fixed on her face. More precisely, her mouth. He was leaning in, about to kiss her. They were relaxed, happy—this was not a mug-for-the-camera staged photo. This was a picture of a couple. Two people who were, at the least, sleeping with each other.

Honestly, my first thought was that I was impressed. How had they managed to be involved, right under our noses, and not have anyone suspect a thing? The consensus among the writing staff was that the bulk of Yvonne's most annoying character traits were a direct product of the lack of regular sex in her life. The staff was approaching a willingness to sacrifice small animals to pagan deities to get the woman laid so the world would be a happier place. But if my hunch about the picture was right, there was a different cause of Yvonne's lack of love for humanity.

Then, too, just because they had been a thing didn't

mean they were still a thing. Maybe their affair had ended badly and that had made Yvonne that much more of a joy to be around. I pulled the picture out of the frame to see if the date or anything was printed on the photograph. With the picture out of the way, a small key on a thin red ribbon fell out. It was tiny, less than padlock size. My sweep of the room hadn't revealed any locked drawers or any locked boxes inside locked drawers. What was the key to and why did Teddy keep it in the picture frame?

I turned my attention back to the picture. There was no date on the back, just an inscription: *You will be mine forever. Y.* Figures that Yvonne was as demanding a lover as she was a boss. Not "Will you be mine?" or "Hope you'll be mine," but "You will be mine." I wondered how Teddy felt about the issuance of that command.

Particularly because underneath the picture, MAARTEN was written in Teddy's big blocky handwriting. St. Maarten? I flipped the picture back over and looked at it hard, scrutinizing the details of the bar behind Teddy. Not that I spend a lot of time at bars staring at the back wall, but I'd be willing to put money on their being at the Ritz Carlton right here in Manhattan, not in St. Maarten. So what did "Maarten" mean?

I was sitting there with the picture in one hand and the key in the other when the door opened. With a move that was so smooth I couldn't believe I'd done it, I stood up and slid my hands into my pockets, concealing their contents, just as Gretchen stepped into the room. She looked at me, standing there with my hands in my pockets like I had all the time in the world, and smiled shakily.

"You want any help?"

I thought about asking her to help me sweep up the broken glass, just so she could feel useful, but decided it was far smarter to get her out of the room as soon as possible. "No, there isn't really that much," I assured her, now feeling that I could not take my hands back out of my pockets lest she discern the outline of either frame or key and want to know what I was stealing from the office of her dearly departed boss.

"Teddy wasn't much for clutter. He only kept the important stuff," Gretchen sniffed.

The picture in my hand seemed to give off heat as I nodded. "That'll make it so much easier on Helen."

Gretchen made an explosive sound that I mistook for a guffaw until I saw the tears streaming down her face. "Poor Helen!" was all she managed.

I nodded in what I hoped passed for sympathy, but I didn't want to encourage Gretchen's grief too much for fear that our boss, the murder suspect, would return to the scene of the crime to see what all the wailing was about.

So I assured Gretchen that I could handle packing, shooed her out with as much grace as I could muster, closed the door, and did what any sensible girl with a murder clue in her pocket would do. I called my best friends to see if they were free for lunch.

6

"*Murder is just an* extreme form of social interaction." I knew it was a bold statement, but since I was sitting on the floor of Cassady's office, barefoot, with lemon chicken dangling from my chopsticks, I felt I could get away with it.

Tricia reached over and felt my forehead, then shrugged to Cassady and returned to her beef and broccoli. "It doesn't seem to be a fever-induced delirium."

"What I'm trying to say is that you don't have to be psycho to kill someone."

"But it helps. Especially on the defense end of the process." Cassady was at her desk, multitasking mightily. Cassady's office looks more like a college professor's burrow than fancy lawyer digs. She has overflowing built-in bookcases on two walls, with windows I don't think she ever looks out, despite the view of Lincoln Center, on the third, and seascapes painted by her little sister framing the door. The Mission furniture is elegant but practical and there are books, files, and periodicals balancing on every available surface. I love it.

Cassady had agreed to meet for lunch, as long as "meet" consisted of all of us having Chinese in her office because she had a filing deadline. I had suggested that we wait until dinner in that case, but she'd snarked about the body count rising by then and a healthy lunch being a crucial step in the investigative process. Fortunately, all Tricia said was she had no plans she couldn't change and she'd be happy to meet.

Also fortunately, Tricia was her usual diplomatic self when I told her about Yvonne semi-volunteering her for Teddy's reception and my not exactly throwing myself in front of that train. "How interesting. A funeral reception," was her first reaction.

"I think Yvonne envisions it more as an industry party with a guest of honor who happens to be dead," I offered.

"Not exactly my stock in trade."

"I know. You can say no if you want to."

Tricia's hands seemed to be having a whispered conversation of their own, skittering back and forth across each other as she thought. I tried to anticipate the sticking point. Tricia loved a challenge, so that wasn't it. I'd already mentioned the money/no object thing, so that wasn't it. What was it?

Tricia's hands stopped, then softly wove themselves together. "It could help you with your investigation, right? Access to the guest list and all that sort of thing?"

She'd caught me by surprise. I hadn't thought of it that way and I never would have expected her to think of it that way. "Absolutely."

Cassady scoffed. "She'll have this thing cracked long before the funeral. Just plan the damn party."

Tricia agreed that she would, but I could see the gleam in her eye. She was starting to like the thought of helping me. I liked it, too. It was a vote of confidence, which led me to start expounding on what I knew so far and to offer up my theory of murder as bad manners.

The point I was trying to make was that just because Yvonne was acting normal—relatively—by the time I saw her didn't mean that she couldn't be a suspect. Particularly if Edwards was busy suspecting Helen and she had seemed far more normal than Yvonne. Though that was really an unfair comparison, given that she was far more normal than Yvonne, period.

"So do you think Yvonne suspects that you suspect her?" Tricia asked. She shot Cassady a worried look. Cassady sensed it coming, looked up to receive it, and nodded in agreement.

"What's that about?"

"You need to be careful, Molly." Tricia wanted to help, but she was still concerned. I could respect that. When I stopped and thought about what I was doing, I was a little concerned, too. So I was doing my best not to dwell on it.

"If Yvonne did kill Teddy, she did it because of romantic betrayal. Fit of passion and all that. Why would she want to hurt me?"

"Because you're going to prove she's guilty of murder?" Cassady frowned at me like I was a child who'd pressed both hands against a hot stove and then had the nerve to cry. I was definitely not going to dwell on this.

"It wouldn't cross her mind. I haven't said anything to her about the whole journalism deal."

"But she's bound to find out about your meeting with Garrett Wilson at *Manhattan* about your investigative article. Good news travels fast, but gossip travels faster."

"Please. Like that's going to happen."

"Like tomorrow at noon, sweetie." Cassady chuckled in delight, a rich, throaty sound that I find infectious and charming, except when I'm the laughee. I'm sure I looked confused, which just made her chuckle harder.

I looked to Tricia for help, but she was beaming almost maternally. She pointed back at Cassady with her chopsticks. "She did it, not me."

"Did . . . ?"

"Got you a meeting with Garrett."

Every morsel of Chinese food I'd just scarfed down, plus a few major organs, somersaulted into one big knot in the middle of my abdomen. Garrett Wilson. Features editor at *Manhattan.* A man known for launching—and crushing—great careers. At a magazine that mixed brainy with trendy so well that both sides benefited—less geek, more chic. It was the perfect place for an article about Teddy's murder but it never would have occurred to me to aspire to it. And now that Cassady had engineered a miracle that made such aspiration possible, I had no idea if I could pull it off.

"I sat next to him at a first amendment thingy a couple of weeks ago, I insisted that he keep his hand on his own thigh, and he insisted that I take his card. I figured someone should benefit from the whole experience, so I called him." Cassady got up from her desk and came at me, chopsticks raised. "And all it will cost you is one Szechuan dumpling." She speared said dumpling from its carton beside me and retreated to her desk.

"I don't know what to say." I was actually moved but I knew Cassady wouldn't tolerate high-flung emotion.

"My. Let's all linger and enjoy this historic moment." She winked at me and devoured the dumpling.

Panic started to sneak into the picture. "I can't tell him

I think Yvonne did it. I can't tell anyone that. Yet."

Cassady shook her head. "Sell him on the article being about the search, not about who actually did the killing. The fact that you're going to come up with the identity of the actual killer by press time is just a marvelous bonus."

"Who *are* you going to tell about Yvonne?" Tricia asked evenly. She has this way of withholding judgment that makes you so aware of the thin ice beneath your feet that you wish she'd just come right out and tell you you're being an idiot. In a polite and loving way. A helpful way.

Still, I knew what she was getting at. "No one. Until I know more. All I have is a hunch at this point."

"And a purloined key in your pocket." I'd shown them the picture and the key briefly before we ate. "Maarten" didn't ring any bells with them, other than vacation fantasies, and they agreed that it looked like the Ritz Carlton in the picture. But maybe the key was . . . key. Cassady drummed her fingers against her cheek in a caricature of deep thought. "What do you suppose it unlocks?"

"Yvonne's chastity belt?" Tricia ventured.

I shook my head. "It doesn't look antique." They chuckled and I dug the key out of my pocket, then pushed aside the law journals and periodicals swamping Cassady's coffee table to create a space where they could both see it clearly. "It doesn't have enough teeth for a safe deposit box or even a padlock."

Tricia started to pick it up and Cassady moved like she was going to smack her delicate hand. "Bad enough Agatha Christie has her prints all over it already, let's go easy."

I hadn't thought of that. Not only had I stolen evidence, I'd contaminated it. Assuming the key was evidence. Assuming that I was on the right track at all with my whole

Yvonne theory. Assuming that I wasn't in way over my head. But I didn't want to get into all of that right now, so I just said, "Damn."

"We can work with this. There's a reason you handled it, Helen asked you to pack his desk, so on and so forth, but you do need to go kinda easy from here on in," Cassady cautioned. I appreciated the use of the pronoun "we." Not that I wanted to drag either of them into harm's way. Assuming I could even see harm's way from where I was. Assuming—never mind, we've already been there.

Tricia leaned in close to the key, making a show of not touching it. "You know what this reminds me of?"

"Leaning over to put your nose on a glass coffee table reminds me of college, but I can't believe that's what you were going to say," Cassady admitted.

Tricia straightened up, but kept her eyes on the key. "You don't know everything, Cassady. Most things, but not everything."

Cassady and I exchanged a look of appreciation that Tricia sniffed at. "We're going to uncover all kinds of secrets here."

"My music box," Tricia persisted.

"That's where you kept your coke?" Cassady persisted in return. "I can't believe we never looked there."

Tricia deliberately turned so only I was in her field of vision, which just amused Cassady more. "I had a music box when I was little, really beautiful polished walnut. My father got it on a business trip to Vienna."

"And you wound it with a key like this?" I asked.

"No, it had a drawer in it for keepsakes and the key that locked the drawer looked like this one."

We all stared at the key for a moment and all I could think of was *Alice in Wonderland*, when Alice has to get the key off the table, but the cake makes her too small and the drink makes her too big. Or is it the other way around? And, as Grace Slick pointed out, the ones that Mother gives you don't do anything at all. "Eat me," indeed. Had I already fallen down the rabbit hole?

"So maybe Teddy gave Yvonne a keepsake box?" I ventured.

"Or just something special to keep in her box," Cassady said, enjoying the double entendre a little too much.

"Must be pretty special if she was willing to kill him over it," Tricia continued.

" 'If I can't have you . . .' " I suggested.

"Think he was breaking it off?" Cassady asked.

"Maybe Helen found out and told him to. That would explain why Yvonne thinks so highly of Helen these days." I got to my feet as gracefully as possible. "I think it's time to get back to the scene of the crime."

"Back to the office so soon?" Tricia stood like the perfect hostess, even though it was Cassady's office.

"Back to *Femme*. That's where Yvonne and Teddy met, as far as I know. My friend Stephanie Glenn's still there. Maybe she can tell me if that's where they hooked up, too."

"Think Woodward and Bernstein learned all about people's sex lives when they were chasing Watergate?" Tricia asked.

"Honey. That's why they call it Deep Throat," Cassady assured her.

"My brother insists Pat Nixon was Deep Throat." Tricia said it with the pained smile of someone admitting to a great family scandal. And given that her brother had recently registered Democrat, I guess it qualified.

"Okay, I have to leave before I start imagining the Nixons having sex in the Rose Garden. Thanks for lunch, I'll call you." I blew them both kisses and headed out, hoping that I was on my way to piecing together a story as opposed to making a fool of myself.

Fortunately, Stephanie and I talked pretty frequently and emailed even more often, so it wasn't a complete shock to her for me to call and ask if I could stop by. I hedged about giving her a reason on the phone and I think that intrigued her.

Femme is two buildings down from *Zeitgeist* and as the cab passed our building, I had this little palpitation of guilt, as though Yvonne could see me hunched in the back of the cab, looking up at her window to see if she was looking down at me. A fragment of song from childhood bounced through my head: "I looked back to see if you looked back at me at the same time that you looked back to see if I looked back at you . . ." Now that I suspected Yvonne, did Yvonne suspect that I did? It actually gave me goosebumps to consider it.

I met Stephanie Glenn five years ago when we were both writing for a mercifully short-lived magazine called *Sonic*. Brent Carruthers, this absolute freak who had been born into a maple syrup fortune, decided he was going to justify his existence by redefining New York culture. He had some theory about investing in cool businesses and then ensuring their success by pumping them in the magazine.

He threw a lot of money around and got people very excited, so excited that they didn't notice that he really had no idea what he was doing. The magazine was more an experiment in how many fonts could be crammed onto a single page before it imploded under the weight of its own pretension. Then Brent had to go into rehab and we found out how much of the maple syrup money had already been soaked up, and we all went and got other jobs having put out a whole four issues in nine months. But I met some cool people, so it wasn't a complete waste.

Stephanie landed at *Femme* shortly thereafter and had done a great job of ascending there. She was a contributing editor now, had a wonderful reputation, and had been on *Today* three times. As her assistant, an overly perky young man named Rico with two piercings in his left eyebrow, showed me to her office, I found myself honestly without envy about how well she was doing. I find that's a pretty genuine reading on how much I like a person.

Stephanie hopped up from her desk to greet me as Rico showed me in. Her office was lovely—not the corner but close to it, spacious, airy, Queen Anne desk, fresh flowers on the credenza, classic view of Lexington Ave. Good for her. She came right at me, arms open wide. Stephanie's short and bouncy and rarely still, but it's infectious, not grating. She'd gotten a perm since I'd last seen her and her dark blonde hair was a surprising mop of curls.

"I love your hair," I said as we hugged and she led me over to her couch.

She poked at it, wrinkling her nose. "I lost a bet."

"At least you didn't have to shave it."

She rolled her eyes. "We were about two shots short of that. So, this is such a nice surprise. Did Rico offer you something to drink?"

"I'm fine. And I don't want to stay too long, I know you're busy."

She shrugged. "Nothing breathing down my neck. What's up?"

I hesitated. I should have given my opening statement more thought on the way over, determined in advance how much information I could offer Stephanie. I was just going to have to feel my way along. "Did you hear about Teddy Reynolds?"

Stephanie sucked her top lip behind her bottom teeth and nodded. "I got an email from Francesca and I figured it was some ugly rumor, but then I talked to Mike Russell over at the *Post* and he checked it out for me. It happened right there in your offices?" I nodded and she shuddered. "Who found him?"

"I did."

"Ohmigod." Stephanie grabbed my hand and shuddered again. "Are you okay?"

I nodded again. "I'm just trying to make sense of it all."

"Of course."

I took a deep breath. "Yvonne's taking it pretty hard." I paused, trying to read Stephanie's reaction.

Her top lip disappeared again and she nodded. "I can imagine."

I proceeded cautiously. "I'm trying to figure out . . . the best way to deal with her and I thought you worked with both of them over here and maybe you'd have some insight . . ."

Stephanie nodded vigorously. "Did you know they were sleeping together?"

I couldn't help it. My eyebrows leapt up of their own accord and I squeaked out, "Really?"

"That's the whole reason he followed her when she moved to you. I mean, he's—he was—good at his job and all, but they wanted to be close to each other."

There's such an amazing difference between thinking something and hearing someone else say it out loud. When it's just a thought rattling around in your head, you can dismiss it. It has no weight, no form, you can convince yourself that you made the whole thing up like Jacob Marley born out of the chunk of undigested potato. But then someone else says it and it takes on a painful, undeniable solidity and you're staring your mortality right in the face.

"You look shocked," Stephanie said, patting my hand. "Sure you don't want Rico to get you something?"

"No, no, I'm fine. You know, I suspected, but I just wasn't sure . . ."

"They were very discreet, I'll give them that. And Yvonne gets the credit for that because everyone knows Teddy's such a dog."

I nodded, picturing the condoms in the drawer unrolling themselves and floating around like little ghosts. Don't the French call the orgasm *la petite mort*, the little death? Not that this was really the time for pondering that cultural puzzle. "Right."

"I had my suspicions when they were here, but I only know for sure because Yvonne and I were at this wretched charity thing to keep the rainforest from killing the baby whales or something and we both sneaked off to the bar during the after-dinner speech and got polluted. It was actually great fun. You know, trashing old bosses and complaining about writers—not you, of course—and all that good stuff. But then she takes this sudden weepy turn about love and the meaning of life and she winds up telling me way too much about Teddy and their sex life and how he keeps cheating on her but she always lets him come back. It was pretty amazing. Total buzz kill, though."

"Speaking of cheating, do you think Teddy's wife knew?"

Stephanie thought a moment, then chose her words carefully. "Yvonne seemed to think she knew in theory, but not in specifics, you know?" Stephanie tilted her head thoughtfully and her lip tucked back in behind her teeth. "But maybe that changed."

Another vote for Edwards' theory. I wasn't sure there was any point in defending Helen to Stephanie. "How long ago did you and Yvonne get soused?"

"Maybe three weeks." Wow. Current events, not history. So if Helen had just found out . . . Or if Teddy had decided to end it . . . Or both . . .

"How long had it been going on?"

Stephanie shook her head. "It started when they were working here, that's all I know. Oh. And that at first, they only did it when they were out of town. Fashion shoots, that kind of thing."

"St. Maarten?" I ventured.

Stephanie thought a moment, then nodded. "Yeah, we did a big travel-fashion combo issue and the main shoot was down there. Would've been about the right time. But after a while, they started justifying why they could do it in town."

In town, in the office, I was trying so hard not to visualize any of this. "No wonder she's taking it so hard."

"I wouldn't be surprised if she took to her bed with a load of pills and a crate of tissues."

Sounded pretty appealing to me, too. In fact, I needed to stand up before curling up on Stephanie's sofa and weeping for a while proved irresistible. Why did I feel like crying? Stephanie had given me the information I needed, but I felt like she'd taken something away from me. What had I lost? Hope? Deniability? I needed to go.

I squeezed Stephanie's hand. "This helps. A lot."

"You want me to call her? Obviously, I won't tell her we talked, but some extra sympathy at this point can't hurt, right?"

"You mean Yvonne, not Helen, right?"

Stephanie blanched. "God, I didn't even think about Helen. Isn't that awful. I should call her, too."

"I'm sure they'd both appreciate it." I stood and Stephanie stood with me. "Thanks."

"Sure. I mean, I can't imagine how you must feel, having found him and all. I think it's great that you're thinking of Yvonne at a time like this."

I forced a smile. If Stephanie only knew in what context I was thinking of Yvonne. "Like I said, I'm just trying to make sense of it."

Stephanie walked me to her office door. "You know, when you do make sense of it, it would make a great article."

My smile grew a little less forced. "Really?"

"Really. I wish we could publish it, but I'm not sure whether it would go under 'Beauty Tips' or 'New Spring Looks.' But you should think about it."

"Thanks," I said, actually grateful to her for easing my guilt for coming to her under a not-completely-honest pretense. "I will."

"But don't tell anybody you heard it from me," Stephanie added as I walked out. "I don't want to come off as a gossip-monger. At least until after the funeral." She gave me a crooked smile to make it clear she was uncomfortable with the joke she was making. At least she felt like she could make one right now.

I walked back to the office, Stuart Weitzmans and all. I needed the air—which was full of that ripe apple crispness that we get sometimes in October if the wind is just right and the rain hasn't started—and I needed the time. And I needed to decide what to do next.

What I didn't need was an absurdly large bouquet of

flowers on the middle of my desk when I walked back into my office. Since I work at home a lot, precious office space is otherwise allocated and I lay claim to a desk near Yvonne's office. I don't keep much on it and I quite often find other people's junk all over it when I do come in, so I had a moment of hope when I thought the bouquet might belong to someone else. That's how messed up my head was: I looked at a hugely expensive floral arrangement and hoped it wasn't for me. But seriously. Flowers at this point could only mean trouble.

Gretchen hurried over to meet me at my desk. "I'm so glad you came back. I was trying to figure out how I was going to get these to you if you didn't and I couldn't imagine carrying them on the subway."

"Cab. It's the only way," Kendall announced as she walked up. Kendall seems like a nice person, pretty smart, but she takes a strange pride in never smiling. Perhaps it's out of respect for the two inches of lipstick that she trowels on every morning, always in some deep earth tone that looks like something Starbucks scrapes out of their pots at closing. But since dark gray is the bright end of her wardrobe's color range, the lipstick works. Maybe it isn't a fashion thing. Maybe she just hates us all. But she was probably right about the cab.

"Yeah, the cab," I said, mainly because they were both looking at me expectantly so I felt I should say something.

But they didn't care about the cab. "Who are they from?" Gretchen asked.

Getting flowers at the office can be a very cool thing. It's an excuse to announce to everyone that it's your birthday or you have a new boyfriend or you're having great sex with an old boyfriend—all sorts of happy things. But there was no way this bouquet was good news. After all, whom could they be from? Even if Edwards could afford such a mongo display, he didn't seem the type to go this far to get an apology accepted. And as painful as it was to admit, I had to: There was only one other guy who could be sending me flowers right now.

"Peter," I told them after I opened the card and confirmed my suspicion.

"Is he your boyfriend?" Kendall asked. Without a smile, the question was as grim as I felt.

"We've been seeing each other." I smiled when I answered, thinking it might scare her back to her desk. She just nodded like I was passing on the great teachings of our beloved ancestors.

Gretchen buried her nose in the flowers and breathed deeply. "Must be going well," she said with heavy-handed wistfulness, in case there was any chance we'd forgotten things weren't so hot for her right now. She even sighed as she withdrew her face. She actually had pollen on one cheek from the day lilies.

I brushed her cheek off rather than responding. "Pollen," I explained.

Kendall leaned in to inspect Gretchen's cheek. "Your blush is all messed up now," she reported with a sidelong glance at me. The news seemed to distress Gretchen greatly, because she excused herself and hurried off to the ladies room. Mercifully, Kendall followed her.

I sat down and read the card again. R U OK? PETER. The only thing more distressing than Peter trying to be sincere was Peter trying to be cute. And Peter trying to be cute to cover up his lack of sincerity just took the cake.

I called him. What choice did I have? I had to acknowledge the flowers at the very least. And I couldn't exactly leave him dangling while I figured out the murder and

Edwards and everything else. I did have an emotional investment here, though the market seemed to have softened significantly in the time Peter had been out of town.

Not that the call was all about doing the right thing by Peter the boyfriend. This was also Peter the operator, and I had to figure out what exactly he was up to. Big flowers at the office were not his style. He wanted something.

"Dinner tonight. I don't suppose there's any chance you're free." I'd reached him on his cell, on his way to interview some baseball player whose name I was clearly supposed to both recognize and revere. Strike two.

"I might be able to make myself free." I had nothing on my calendar except solving Teddy's murder, but he didn't need to know that.

"I've missed you and I keep thinking about this horrible experience you're going through . . ."

And wondering how you can horn in on it? "That's very sweet of you, Peter."

"The Mermaid Inn. Eight. Okay?"

That was a lot to consider all at once, especially because having missed a whole night's sleep was beginning to wear on me a little, synapses hiccupping here and there. Let's take it one at a time. Mermaid Inn. Cozy but cool, not an overtly romantic place but not businesslike either. He was playing this one straight down the middle. That seemed doable. All right, then, eight. With proper applications of caffeine, could I make it to eight and still be good company? I don't mean to sound like a wimp on the sleep issue, but there was a certain emotional toll being taken here, too. I was beginning to feel a little battered and that usually leads to my being weepy and I had no interest in being anywhere near Peter if my body chemistry kidnapped my usual effervescent self and transformed me into Weepy Girl.

But with God and Starbucks on my side, I could probably make it until at least ten.

But then there was the big question: Was it okay? With my feelings as mixed as they were at the moment, should I be meeting this man for dinner? Was there any point? But how might he take it if I said no and what might he do—as aggrieved boyfriend or as journalistic rival? Well, if worse came to worst, we could go dutch and I could write it off as a business expense. Okay.

"Sounds good," I said with a tone I hoped was sweet but otherwise lacking in emotional indicators. "I'll meet you there."

It satisfied him. For the moment, anyway. "Great. Bye." I hung up and took a deep breath. Having something in the evening to look forward to always makes the afternoon go faster. And with one dead body already on my mind, why not add a dying relationship?

7

Dear Molly, Recently I was at dinner with a man in whom I am no longer as interested as I once was. In fact, I'm thinking about breaking up with him. During dinner, a man in whom I am increasingly interested walked up to us and engaged me in conversation. What is the etiquette in this situation? Should I have invited the man with potential to join us? Should I have asked him to call me later and let me get back to my date? Should I have run to the ladies room, snuck out the window, and met him out front? Did I mention the second man was a homicide detective who had, as recently as breakfast, suspected me of murder? Signed, Like Dating's Not Hard Enough

One of the fringe benefits of my job is that I can go to sleep every night knowing that there are women out there with far more serious problems than I have. Not *Schadenfreude*, exactly, more a lesson in perspective, a comfort in understanding my place in the universe. Said comfort began to slip away from me as I sat in the Mermaid Inn with Peter across the table from me and Detective Kyle Edwards coming across the room to me.

I'd actually managed to get some work done in the balance of the day, between agreeing to meet Peter for dinner and leaving to get ready. I'd literally kept my head down, reading letters and checking email, doing my best to avoid meeting Yvonne's eye as she bustled about the office, doing her best to pretend that nothing had changed. Of course, everyone was doing that to a certain extent, except perhaps Gretchen, who was being open and even a little showy in her grief. I wondered if she'd had a crush on Teddy. Maybe that's why she'd stayed with him longer than any other assistant.

I felt guilty, sitting there in the office and thinking about Yvonne as a murderer. It seemed like some bizarre violation of her hospitality or something. Plus there was no doubt she would can me in the blink of an eye if she knew how I felt. Would I stay at the magazine after she was arrested or would I need to move on?

My cousin Caroline dumped a guy after they'd been in this hideous car crash together, not because she blamed him or anything, but because every time she looked at him, she heard the squeal of brakes and the crunch of metal. There was probably something a little Freudian going on there as well, but you'd have to know Caroline to fully appreciate those possibilities. Still. Associating a person with something traumatic can wreak havoc.

On the other hand, my friend Danielle once stayed in a relationship about a year longer than she later realized she should have because she nursed the guy through some awful ulcer thing and started feeling responsible for him. She also worried that the stress of breaking up would bring back the ulcer, and it took her a long time to work up the resolve to accept that guilt. Of course, the ulcer didn't come back, but he started dating his dietitian and Danielle hasn't been with anyone serious since.

All of which was putting the cart before the horse. Why worry about what I was going to do after Yvonne was arrested when I wasn't sure she was going to be arrested? Because it kept me from having to worry about how I was going to get her arrested. I have a gift for worrying about things that might happen at some undetermined point in the future instead of taking care of things that need immediate attention in the present. If you're going to worry about something, which I do as a nervous habit, it's much less pressure to worry about what to name your children than worry about whether the man you're meeting for dinner has the potential to be their father.

That was not an issue here. At some point during the cab ride to the East Village, I realized I'd already decided to end my relationship with Peter. When we were first dating, I thought of him with excitement and anticipation. Now I thought of him with irritation. I told myself it had nothing to do with my territorial issues with the article. But even if it did, that had to say something, didn't it? If I really cared about the guy, I'd want to share with him, wouldn't I? Or I'd at least trust him enough to be willing to tell him what I was doing and ask him not to horn in.

A little wave of cold washed over me. That was it. I didn't trust Peter. How could I be involved with a guy I didn't trust? Had I withdrawn my trust at some point or had he never had it? Maybe this was one of those relationships that never got deep enough for it to be an issue. I'd apparently never given it sufficient thought. And that pretty much sealed the deal right there.

Now, it was all I could think of as I looked at him across the table, studying him as he studied the menu. It's a charming restaurant, walking that fine line between fun neighborhood place and destination of choice, with all sorts of seafaring and seafood art and memorabilia on the walls. The lighting in here suited Peter, the golden hues bouncing off the whitewashed walls and playing up the warm tones in his skin. He was a hunk, no question. He was rich, handsome, smart, good in bed, kind to animals—what a bummer that that wasn't enough.

I was also fairly sure that he would not be devastated when I broke up with him. But there was still that nagging thought that I would become "that bitch" in all his conversations for the next six weeks and that's a tough psychic hit to take, knowing you're sending someone out into the big, wide world who will speak your name as though he's spitting out rancid milk. If I was willing to be perfectly honest, I might say there were already people out there spewing my name, but I still had to psych myself up to add Peter to that list.

He put the menu down and smiled lazily. "Know what you want?" he asked with just the proper shade of innuendo.

"Order for me," I smiled. I wasn't going to be able to eat it, anyway, so what did it matter? Peter has this Old World streak in him that would get off on picking my dinner and I could keep my mind focused on more pressing issues—like the best way to break up with him. And when. After dinner but before dessert? As we walked out? Now, so he didn't feel like he was getting stuck with dinner?

He put down his menu and smiled. I smiled back. "Great. Now that that's taken care of, tell me how you are."

"Fine," I responded automatically. I needed to start getting myself in the break-up mindset. Hone in on his ex potential, make cons out of the pros. Like—he's good in bed. Okay, he's good in bed. Not great, just good. I deserve better. That's one.

"Must be weird in the office, with Teddy gone." He furrowed his brow. Man, the golden light in here really did suit him. Maybe it was the robber baron in his blood. Next thing you know, he's lighting up a cheroot and building a railroad. But he's rich. And the rich boyfriends can be hard work, because they aren't used to working hard. Things come to them—opportunity, power, other women—and they forget how to make an effort. That's two.

"It's . . . interesting. Tell me more about the wedding." I didn't want to talk about work. I wanted to make it as hard as possible for him to direct the conversation to writing an article. Especially now that I had a meeting at *Manhattan*.

"You should've come with me. It would've been more fun." He was deflecting my line of inquiry. It hadn't occurred to him until this very moment to take me to the wedding with him. We were barely dating at an in-town wedding level; we certainly weren't at the out-of-town-with-the-family-for-four-days level.

There's that whole weird thing about taking a date to a wedding—I'd rather take a friend and proclaim him to be such than take a boyfriend. And it's not the whole pressure-to-be-next deal that comes of being together at a wedding. It's really all the introductions. And the pictures. Not only are you constantly having to explain your relationship to the bridal couple, you have to characterize your relationship with the guy you brought with you. "And this is my boyfriend/special friend/lover/stopgap/occasional sexual partner/whatever, Peter."

Yeah, I know Miss Manners tells you to just say, "And this is Peter," and make it clear that it's nobody's business how close you are, but you gotta wonder—when's the last time she had to do it? Not as easy as she makes it sound. The only thing worse than having to characterize the relationship is not characterizing it at all, which leads to weird looks and/or smirks from the people around you and a pretty stony gaze from the non-characterized fellow himself. A glaring omission, I believe they call it.

And the pictures. Pressed between the sweet white leather covers of a dear friend's wedding album, you are forever paired with some guy you could come to loathe. Every time the pictures get dragged out, you have to put up with, "Good God, what did you ever see in him?" Of course, the same fate has been known to befall the bridal couple itself, so maybe that's not as big a deal.

"What's the craziest thing you did?" I persisted, driving the conversation back into shallow waters.

It worked. He got this goofy grin on his face, then leaned forward, looking around the restaurant as he did so as though checking to make sure his grandparents weren't somewhere within earshot. I leaned forward and scanned, too, figuring I should help him go for the joke, but instead I almost collapsed on the table.

As I scanned the indistinct faces of the other diners, one came sharply into focus. I couldn't believe it, but Detective Edwards was striding across the room, his eyes dead on me. I couldn't sit back up, I couldn't breathe, I couldn't do anything but stare.

"Molly?" Peter asked, probably concerned that I had had a sudden brain seizure of some sort, since I was staring, slightly open-mouthed, I will admit.

I straightened up and, in those three seconds, concocted a whole bunch of reasons Detective Edwards could be in the restaurant, none of them having anything to do with me. He had a date. He was meeting friends. He was a part-owner. He was in hot-foot pursuit of a nasty perp who had ducked into the kitchen from the alley and Edwards was heading him off here in the dining room. He wouldn't even see me.

"Ms. Forrester, good evening." So much for my great theories. He walked right up to our table, acknowledged Peter briefly—"Excuse me for interrupting"—then turned the big ol' blues right back on me.

"Detective Edwards." Out of the corner of my eye, I saw Peter react. Surprise doesn't suit him. Probably doesn't happen to him very often either.

"I'm sorry to intrude on your meal, but may I speak to you for a moment?"

Peter started to slide over like he was going to invite Edwards to sit down with us, so I got up as fast as I could. "Will you excuse us, Peter?" I walked past Edwards to the bar and hoped that only he would follow.

Peter stayed in his seat and Edwards followed me. Peter was displaying no possessive instinct, not even an appealing amount that he might be working to keep in check. That's three.

I put a hand on the bar to steady myself, but decided to stay on my feet. That whole subliminal thing about this conversation won't be long, so why bother sitting down. Edwards knew exactly what I was doing and leaned back onto a barstool. Okay, so who was going to be right?

"I have to ask. How did you find me?" No way he was having me followed. I didn't even want to have to decide if being followed was flattering or creepy, it was just way too expensive. Edwards seemed shrewder and more economical than that.

"I went to your office and the grim young woman I spoke to said she'd overheard you making dinner plans on the phone."

Had to be Kendall. Okay, we were having a talk in the morning. "Was she that helpful before or after you identified yourself as a homicide detective?"

"After. She stonewalled appropriately before." A smile flickered across his face, probably in response to the grimace stomping across mine.

"So now that you're here . . ." I prompted.

"What did you take out of Teddy Reynolds' office?"

I almost put my hand on my pocket. Tragically, the thing that stopped me was not good sense but remembering that I had changed clothes. The picture and the key were on my dresser at home. It still took a lot of concentration not to pat my hip guiltily. "Stuff," I told Edwards, a noncommittal shrug thrown in for good measure.

He sighed. "What kind of stuff?"

"Personal stuff. Why?"

"Because *stuff* is missing. I went back to his office to look for something and *stuff* is gone. Where did it go?"

I embraced what little righteous indignation I could justify. "Helen asked me if I'd pack up his personal *stuff*. She didn't feel up to it. I assumed she had cleared it with you."

He semi-nodded. "Where's the *stuff* you took?"

"In my apartment." I said it with as straight a face as possible, lest he read anything into it or worse, think I was hoping he would read anything into it.

"If you packed it up for Mrs. Reynolds, why doesn't Mrs. Reynolds have it?"

"Because Mrs. Reynolds has other things on her mind." It was infuriating to be standing in front of him, really angry about his insistence that Helen had something to do with Teddy's death and really captivated by those damn blue eyes. I hate talking to someone in sunglasses because I get self-conscious about seeing my own reflection, but right now I would've happily shelled out the cash to corral those blue orbs behind a pair of mirrored Armanis.

He squinted, which helped my concentration slightly.

"Which one are you protecting? The wife or the mistress?"

I gripped the bar as hard as I could and hoped the effort didn't show. He knew about Yvonne already? That was good, if it helped get him off Helen's case, but I was a little miffed somehow. I had wanted to present Yvonne to him in a pretty little package, slam-dunk, whaddya think of that? "I'm not protecting anyone. I'm trying to do—"

"The right thing by your friend, yeah, I remember." He shook his head. "I think you need a better class of friends."

"I beg your pardon."

"No disrespect, but even his mistress didn't have a lot of nice things to say about him."

"I find that hard to believe." Why wouldn't Yvonne have gushed for Edwards the way she did for the staff? She was smart enough to know that trashing him would make her look bad.

Edwards shrugged. "Of course, she strikes me as someone without a lot of nice things to say about anyone."

I had to nod at that one. Yvonne was abrasive on a good day, scathing on a bad one. Which made her affair with Teddy all the more fascinating, aside from the breaking-Helen's-heart part.

"I was actually kinda surprised. She looks so sweet in all those perfume ads."

I nodded again, but now it was to buy time. I had no idea what he was talking about. Yvonne in a perfume ad? Was he drunk? "Appearances can be deceiving," I said because it seemed to be a safe thing to say.

He looked me over, head to toe, then nodded. Okay, so maybe it wasn't a safe thing to say in the middle of a murder investigation. "Guess that's what being a model is all about."

Excuse me? A model? Teddy was having an affair with

a model? *And* with Yvonne? I clenched my teeth hard so my mouth wouldn't hang open. "How did you find out?" I asked.

"She was all over his PDA, which we did take out of his office last night. The first time I saw 'Camille,' I thought that must be one of the perks of the business. But she was in there often enough that Lipscomb and I decided to go have a chat with her. She's meaner in person, but she's prettier, too."

Model . . . Perfume ads . . . Camille . . . Oh, no way. No. Way. Camille Sondergard sleeping with Teddy? Our Teddy? No offense to Helen, but it's amazing he only bragged about it in his PDA and didn't rent a billboard somewhere. Suddenly, against my will, I could see the video clip playing on the Jumbotron in Times Square—with product placement by Trojan, of course. Camille was hot, in all meanings of the word. She'd gone from a couple of jeans ads to a huge deal with Chanel in what seemed overnight, even for her ridiculous business. Her ads were all over our magazine. Maybe now I knew the reason why. Wow.

"She said they just broke up." He looked at me for a reaction and I went back to nodding. "Why didn't you tell me?"

"I just found out recently myself." I smiled apologetically. How far can you bend the truth before you have to consider it broken? "So is she your suspect now?"

He shook his head. The lighting in the restaurant was even better for him than it was for Peter. Oh, yeah, Peter. I should probably be trying harder to get back to him than I was. In a minute.

"She was a celebrity auctioneer at some big animal rights deal uptown, alibi checks out solid."

I felt breathless, but did my best not to sound that way. "But if they just broke up, that helps Helen, doesn't it? Why kill your husband after he breaks up with his mistress?" *Because you realize he has more than one* would have been my guess, but I wanted to see what Edwards had to say.

"Because it's not enough."

I wanted to object, but I pictured Helen's face as she told me about regret and I couldn't summon the energy to convince Edwards he was wrong. Was I wrong? Had Helen found out about Camille, made Teddy break it off, and then found out about Yvonne and hit her breaking point?

"Let's get back to the stuff," Edwards said, having let me stew in my silence a moment.

"I'd rather get back to my dinner date."

Edwards shot a look across the room, then frowned. "Really?"

I didn't intend to laugh as loudly as I did. I didn't intend to laugh at all—it gave him the upper hand somehow. But still, there was something about his frown that cracked me up. I clamped my own hand across my mouth and glanced guiltily across the room. Peter was looking at us with his own frown and his was neither amused nor amusing.

Edwards looked at me, still smiling. "He'll keep."

I shook my head, more vigorously than before. "Nope, I'm thinking about throwing him back."

"Over your limit?"

"Not even close. I'm a choosy fisher."

"What do you use for bait?"

"It's not about the bait, it's about the lure."

"It certainly is."

"The trick is to get the fish on the deck before he even notices he's out of the water."

I've never been fishing once in my entire life, unless you count arcade games at the carnival and I'm pretty lousy at those, too. But when a metaphor turns itself into foreplay, you have to go with it, see where it leads you. Edwards' grin had softened, so had his gaze, and he was leaning toward me, his hand slipping along the edge of the bar toward mine. And I was loving it.

His fingers overlapped mine and his hand stopped, resting comfortably. "I don't want to be the enemy."

"Good."

"I've found out a lot about you in the last eighteen hours and I'd like to find out more."

"Good." If I could get away with the same answer for a while, it would free up some of my concentration for important things like breathing evenly and not drooling.

"So are we on the same side?"

"Good" wasn't going to work here and I took a moment to think. How sincere was this? I knew he didn't want to be my enemy because he didn't want me messing up his investigation. He didn't have a warrant or he would have played that card already. He probably thought he could use charm instead. But was the rest of it for real or just a sales pitch? His hand was warm and firm and I had a fleeting thought about how warm and firm the skin on his chest might be. But I forced myself to be careful. I wanted to be the one doing the reeling in here. "Sure. We both want the same thing, right?" I paused, giving him a chance to nod, before elaborating. "The murderer caught and justice served?"

The smile slid back into grin territory and his hand moved to cover mine completely. "Yeah. That, too. So when can I see the stuff?"

"Ask Helen."

"She doesn't have it."

"She will."

"Is it at all clear that I'm angling for an invitation to your apartment?"

"I'm just evaluating your pretenses."

"You're also obstructing a criminal investigation, but I didn't want to have to go there." His smile didn't change a bit as he said it, his eyes never left mine. It wasn't a threat, it was a simple statement of fact. And somehow I found that incredibly compelling. This guy was trouble. I really wanted to get into trouble. Not the "can I play with your handcuffs" kind of trouble, necessarily. But trouble on my own terms.

"I need to go home."

"I'll take you."

"That wouldn't sit well with my date."

This time, Edwards didn't so much as glance in Peter's direction. "Does that matter?"

"Yes."

"But only because your mother raised you right."

"Maybe."

"What if we tell him it's police business?"

"Is it?"

His fingertips moved lightly on my wrist. "Partly."

The word "swoon" has always fascinated me—it sounds just like it should, like Merle Oberon falling back against Laurence Olivier's arm. The actual mechanics of swooning, however, have always eluded me; how do you get your knees to give just enough so that they don't buckle and dump you on your rear end at the feet of a man who's trying to sweep you off your feet? I locked my knees because this didn't seem the best time or place to find out.

"I'm not the kind of guy to force an issue, but this has to happen tonight."

There actually was a moment when I wasn't sure if he was talking about the partly-police-business part or the partly-not-police-business part and I didn't want to overreact on either front. "Why?"

"Because I don't want to lay awake all night thinking about you . . ." He paused to measure how beautifully he was stringing me along before continuing. ". . . burning anything you don't want me to see."

I smiled because he deserved it. "You're not the enemy, remember?"

He leaned his head in Peter's direction. "He's not going to think so."

Now I paused, because I realized he really was going to make me give him Teddy's stuff tonight and because he was enjoying the idea of Peter sizing him up as a rival. This could be delicious or messy or both. It was certainly going to be interesting.

So much of the art of relationships is knowing when to stop—when to stop talking, when to stop kissing, when to stop seeing other people, when to stop seeing each other. Most of the time, it's difficult to make that decision in the heat of the moment. Occasionally, rarely, you can almost hear the music swell because it's so totally time to make a move.

I moved across the room, returning to my table and Peter, fighting the impulse to turn around and make sure that Edwards was following me. I was pinned between their gazes: I could see Peter glaring at me as I approached and I could feel Edwards' eyes on my back. Caught in the crossfire.

I couldn't blame Peter for being unhappy, but I was feeling pretty good, giddy even, and I knew better than to let that show. I dove in, taking the offensive before he could. "Peter, I'm so sorry, but I have to go." I stood beside the table to emphasize my point. I could feel where Edwards' hand had lain against mine and imagined for a moment that Peter could see it, like a sunburn or a tattoo. I covered it with my other hand. "Something's come up . . ."

"Obviously." Peter wasn't going to make this easy. Edwards was no help either, standing just slightly behind me, letting me take the brunt of Peter's displeasure.

I was considering how to pay him back for that when he stepped forward and gave Peter an official scowl. "I apologize, but—at the risk of sounding clichéd—this is police business."

I winced. I didn't want Peter to know any more about this than necessary and here was Edwards, enticing him with coming attractions. Peter cleared the napkin off his lap. "I absolutely understand." He flashed Edwards one of those annoying "let's all be sports about this, old chum" smiles that should come with its own navy blue blazer and deck shoes, and stood up. "Let's go."

"Excuse me?" Edwards was as surprised as I was, but I was the one who spoke.

Apparently, Peter was going to play the Gentleman card. Who coulda seen that coming? "I'm not going to abandon you, Molly. You've been through enough already. Whatever's going on, I want to help." I could smell the jealousy leaking out of his pores. The question was, personal or professional jealousy? I decided to be flattered on both counts, but that still didn't mean I wanted him around the rest of the night.

"Oh, Peter, that's very thoughtful, but it's really not necessary," I demurred, trying to send Edwards a telepathic message that this was the perfect time for him to flash his badge and tell Peter to sit back down and order the cioppino.

"I insist," Peter said, as much to Edwards as to me.

Edwards wouldn't look at him and apparently wasn't receiving my message. He sighed and shook his head, as though there were areas of civilian life in which he, gratefully, was forbidden to intrude. He wasn't going to help me out at all.

I had no card to play except to proclaim that I wanted Peter to stay behind, primarily in the hope that I could get Edwards alone and entice something more out of him than homicide theories. And announcing that seemed a little premature and a whole lot inelegant. It was like holding one of those original Polaroid photos in my hand, desperate to see the finished picture but knowing that if I peeled the paper back too soon, it wouldn't develop at all.

Which is how I came to leave the Mermaid Inn in the company of both Peter and Detective Edwards and driving back to my apartment in Edwards' car. I was braced for twenty minutes of stony silence or perhaps tense conversation with deeply charged undertones and a dollop of sexual tension.

But no. Peter and Edwards had the nerve to have a conversation. A friendly conversation. An animated one at that. About the Yankees, of course. If the Titanic went down today, half the men on board would be so engrossed in talking about the Yankees that they'd be in the water ten minutes before they knew they were wet.

I hate baseball.

8

Dear Readers, While Molly is in a cold, dank cell in Albion, serving the longest sentence for obstruction of justice ever handed down in the entire state of New York, your letters will be answered by Kendall and Gretchen, not because they're particularly insightful young women but because it will irritate Molly and make her time behind bars that much more miserable. Kisses, The Editor

Most of the time, you don't know you're going to truly hate yourself in the morning. Passion or mind-altering substances or emotions of some kind propel you headlong into a situation, you react first and think later, and then you hate yourself once sanity and sobriety have returned. But every once in a while, you do something knowing full well that you'll hate yourself in the morning and for many mornings to come. But you do it anyway. Is that bravery or cowardice? Daring or strength of conviction? Or is it just stupidity?

Leaving the Yankees fans in what passes for the living room of my apartment, I went into the bedroom, ostensibly to retrieve the box of stuff. What I really went to do was to hide the key and the picture of Teddy and Yvonne in my sweater drawer. I knew I wasn't going to give the picture to Edwards, not until I had an explanation for why it didn't draw a big red arrow to Helen and her guilt. I had the feeling that the key was equally treacherous. And on the off chance that either man wound up passing through my bedroom, for any reason at all, I wanted the photo and the key out of sight.

I picked the box up out of the chair where I'd dumped it when I'd come home from work. The thing to do was to march out into the living room, give the box to Edwards, and tell them both to go home. That was the prudent course of action. But, come on. If we always chose the prudent course of action, life wouldn't be nearly as interesting and I, for one, would be out of a job.

I lifted the lid off the box and looked again at what remained of Teddy's personal effects. I'd gotten rid of the condoms. More precisely, I'd stuffed them in an envelope and mailed them to Planned Parenthood's Manhattan office, hoping they might actually do some good there. Not that they hadn't done some good by preventing more Teddys, but I was thinking of a greater good here. I had even thought about mailing them to the Manhattan Archdiocese, but I figured I was racking up plenty of karmic problems without actively seeking them out.

I poked around one last time, but there didn't seem to be anything else in the box that could embarrass Helen or tarnish Teddy or trip me up. Plus, the longer I took, the more suspicious Edwards was going to get. Or worse, the more he might bond with Peter. So I took a deep breath and carried the box back out to the living room.

I half-expected them to be drinking beer and scratching themselves. It was possible, because I do keep beer in my fridge, two brands even: Tsingtao, because wine doesn't go with Chinese food, and Dos Equis, because Mexican carryout cools off too fast anyway and it just dies if you stop to make a margarita. To my relief, they were neither chugging nor scratching. They were having a far too earnest conversation about how you compare pitchers today, when no one ever pitches more than six innings, with pitchers from the "good ol' days" when guys would rupture their shoulders for love of the game. At least Peter wasn't grilling Edwards about the case.

Then again, maybe Peter was just waiting for me so I could observe his keen journalistic techniques in action. Because as I put the box down on my coffee table, Peter stopped and stared at the box with that slightly wide-eyed look little boys get when told they're about to catch a glimpse of a dead animal, particularly one that's begun to decompose. Repulsed, yet attracted. I don't know that they ever outgrow that phase; they might just learn to hide it better. "Teddy's effects, huh?"

"Desk junk," I assured him.

"The legacies we leave," Peter pursued, leaning forward to peek into the box.

I made myself laugh as I made big shoo-shoo gestures in his face and forced him to sit back into his slouch on the sofa, but I really wanted to smack his hand away. This time, I wasn't protecting my story or Edwards' investigation. I just had a sudden urge, maybe a flashback to a life as a temple guard in El Giza, to keep unworthy hands away from what was left of a man's life.

Edwards looked at me rather than at the box. I met his gaze with as neutral an expression as those blue eyes would permit and tried my darnedest not to think about the picture and the key. Besides, if he wasn't going to read my mind and help me out at the restaurant, he didn't get to leaf through my thoughts now. "This everything?" he asked.

"Other than some art on the wall," I answered. "Everything else was files and his assistant Gretchen will have to go through all that. And Brady, his second-in-command. But as far as what belongs to Helen now . . ." I shrugged.

"Thank you." Edwards didn't stand up. That was nice. He wasn't in any hurry to leave. Unfortunately, Peter looked like he was settling in for a long winter's nap himself. That was less nice. Fatigue was catching up with me and I didn't have the energy to play hostess to competing interests. I wanted Peter to go home.

"I'm sorry about all this, Peter," I ventured. "Guess I owe you a raincheck."

"Raincheck? It's early," he protested, checking his watch. It was only 9:30, plenty of time to still have dinner and really foul things up, but the momentum of the evening was shot for me. I didn't want to go out again. And I really wanted Peter to go home.

"The last twenty-four hours have been a bit much. I guess I'm more tired than I wanted to admit." I glanced at Edwards, but he was studying Peter and again, not receiving.

"You need dinner. We'll bring it in." Peter reached behind the couch to get the phone from the console table without looking. He was showing off for Edwards, demonstrating how familiar he was with my apartment. "What sounds good? Chinese? Italian? Thai?"

"No. I just . . ."

"Pizza?"

I can normally eat pizza at any hour of the day or night, hot or cold, thin, thick, or stuffed crust, may the spirit of

Dr. Atkins forgive me. But at this particular moment, all I could picture was how the grease coagulates in the pepperoni slices as the pizza cools, which led to the picture of the blood coagulating in the office carpet around Teddy's body, and I wanted to barf. I shook my head pretty emphatically.

Peter scratched his head with the antenna on the cordless. "Mexican?"

"She's not hungry." Edwards said it quietly, but with such authority that both Peter and I took notice. Peter looked from Edwards to me and back, trying to gauge the depth of the connection, if any. I watched his expression carefully, because a third-party reading would be very helpful about now. Edwards glanced up at me and Peter's eyes followed.

"No, I don't think I am." I should have quit there, but my deeply repressed inner Martha Stewart leapt up before I could squelch her. "But if you two want to eat—"

"No, thank you," Edwards said quietly. He nodded at the phone in Peter's hand and Peter reached back to set it in the base. But he missed and had to look back over his shoulder to fumble it back into place. I was fascinated by this turn of events. It wasn't that Peter was intimidated by Edwards, it was simply that Edwards had taken control of the room. He had to be amazing in the interrogation room. Among other rooms.

Peter sat forward on the couch, still watching Edwards. Edwards stood and Peter did, too. Edwards stuck his hand out and Peter shook it with formal restraint. Then he surprised Peter and me by smiling. "Maybe I'm the one who owes you dinner. Sorry to have busted up your date."

From where I stood, the smile was as effective on Peter as it would have been on me. Something about the wattage of the smile, after he'd been so serious so long, was disarming. Peter smiled back in spite of himself. "Official business, I get it. No harm, no foul."

"Can I drop you somewhere?" Edwards asked and I chewed the inside of my cheek in disappointment. Peter was going to leave, but so was Edwards.

"No, I'm cool. I'll get a cab." Peter blinked a moment as it registered that he had just agreed to leave. He looked at me and I forced a yawn, but it didn't take much effort. "You okay?"

"I'll be fine," I assured him. And then we all stood there, silent, everyone waiting for someone else to make the first move. I took a step toward the door, Edwards picked up the box, and Peter fell in beside him as we trekked all the way across the room. I felt like I should open the door and then offer my cheek to each of them for a chaste goodnight kiss as they went past. Doris Day would be so proud.

I kept my cheek in check as Edwards passed by. "Thanks again, Ms. Forrester. I'll be in touch." He stepped out into the hallway and then looked at his feet as though he wasn't allowed to watch if Peter was going to kiss me good night.

But Peter was still under the influence of Edwards' authoritative demeanor and he would've sooner kissed me in front of my father than kissed me in front of Edwards. I did my best not to let my amusement show and not to take advantage of his discomfort either. "Sorry again. Talk to you later."

"Yeah. Good night." He stepped out into the hallway, gestured to the elevator for Edwards, and started down the hall.

Edwards took three steps after him, then turned back to me. "Ms. Forrester, there was one other thing."

"Yes?" I said with what I hoped was a proper lack of

glee, though glee was trying its best to work its way in.

Peter paused, looking back curiously. Edwards threw him a quick look. "Thanks again. Pleasure talking to you."

Peter wavered a moment, then took the dignified option. He raised his hand in acceptance, said, "You, too," and punched the elevator button with focused vigor.

I stepped back, letting Edwards follow me. I closed the door behind him, then hovered near it. Not a time to appear overeager. "Yes, Detective? One more question?"

He didn't lead me back into the apartment, but he leaned in close. Deliciously close. "How serious are you?"

"About Helen being innocent?"

"About the college crew captain."

"He didn't make captain and it haunts him to this day."

"Answer my question."

"Why?"

"In my line of work, I'm used to people answering my questions."

"Aren't you also used to people lying to you, calling you names, and threatening you?"

"Let's save that for when we know each other better."

"Are we going to get to know each other better?"

"Depends how serious you are with Crew Boy."

"How'd we get back to him?"

"He doesn't seem like a bad guy and I wasn't raised by wolves, all rumors to the contrary." He straightened up, no longer deliciously close. That wouldn't do.

Now I leaned in, closing the gap back up. "Not that serious. Teetering on the brink of break-up, in fact."

He fought a smile. "Thank you for the clarification."

He started to put the box down, but I stopped him. "That was your one question."

"I'm sure I have others."

"I'm sure you do, too, but even though Crew Boy isn't the love of my life, I know him well enough to know that he's sitting down in the lobby, timing you. And while I might enjoy trying his patience, it wouldn't be very kind of me."

To his credit, his smile broadened. "My point exactly. Good night, Ms. Forrester."

"Good night, Detective Edwards." I opened the door for him, he shifted the box under his arm, took my face in his free hand and kissed me. Briefly, but firmly. Coming attractions, indeed.

9

"And you let him walk away?" Tricia reprimanded me the next morning. She'd been lying in wait for me in the lobby as I trudged into work and was not very happy with the fact that I had neglected to call her to brief her on "dinner" with Peter. She was even less happy when I told her about Edwards' appearance. But not so unhappy that she refused to hand over the extra vanilla cappuccino that she'd very thoughtfully brought along for me.

I led Tricia and our candied coffees through the limestone and glass canyon of the lobby and toward the elevator. We needed to get upstairs, not because I was in any hurry to get to work, but because Tricia had a meeting with Yvonne about Teddy's reception. Yvonne didn't like to be kept waiting and I didn't want to be part of anything that was going to upset her. Not that she was going to like being arrested, but that was different.

But first there was the matter of calming Tricia and finishing my story without divulging all my secrets to my fellow elevator riders. "It seemed like the right thing to do," I whispered, scanning the still-waking faces around me. No one I recognized, fortunately, but you never know who knows someone you know.

"Oh, you and the right thing. It's going to get you killed and make me crazy," Tricia hissed.

"In that order?"

"Could be neck-and-neck."

A few pairs of eyes moved our way, but didn't linger. They seemed more annoyed that we were talking than interested in what we were saying. So far, so good.

Tricia studied her coffee cup in tightly coiled silence, then said, far more loudly than necessary, "Must not have been much of a kiss."

Every pair of eyes moved our way. I didn't have to see them, I could feel them. I could also feel my face reddening in a good old-fashioned, junior-high blush.

Good manners prevented me from throttling my dear friend in the middle of the elevator with all those handy witnesses, so I gritted my teeth until I could march her off at the eleventh floor.

"It was amazing," I corrected as we proceeded to my desk.

"Then why let him go?"

"Because I was trying to be a lady."

"Because he's going to call your mother and report on your behavior after he crawls out of your bed?"

"Tricia, the moment wasn't right."

"Oh." The fight went out of her instantly and she smiled sweetly. Tricia harbors the heart of a true romantic and understands certain basic concepts, like the moment having to be right. "Why didn't you say so? That I get." She tapped her coffee cup against mine in a toast of acquiescence.

At this point, I had successfully propelled Tricia all the way to Yvonne's office and I gratefully leaned against her assistant's desk for a moment. I hadn't planned to start my day with an interrogation and I needed to catch my breath. "Fred, she's your problem now."

Tricia, ever the good girl, stuck her hand out to Fred, Yvonne's assistant. "Good morning, I'm Tricia Vincent, I have an appointment with Yvonne."

Fred Hagstrom is a sweet little guy in a thankless job and he knows it. He also makes sure everyone else knows it. Not that anyone stood much of a chance of ignoring him anyway. Fred has a Truman Capote fixation that hovers somewhere between endearing and annoying. The glasses actually work on him and I suppose it's his business if he wants to wear linen suits in New York City year round, but in October, you can get cold just looking at him.

"Yvonne's running a little late," Fred oozed, squeezing Tricia's fingertips in greeting. He looked at me, waiting for me to escort Tricia to the kitchen and out of his hair.

"We'll wait," I told him, and pulled Tricia behind me into Yvonne's office. Fred scrambled up out of his chair and tried to block us, but he wasn't quick enough. He stood in the doorway, hands on hips, and scowled at me as I pointed for Tricia to sit on Yvonne's torture rack of a couch. Wherever Yvonne and Teddy had their rendezvous, it wasn't there. One of them would have been limping noticeably a long time ago.

"This just isn't right," Fred protested.

"It's not like Tricia and I are going to strip down and make 900 calls, Fred. We're only gonna sit in here and gossip like good girls." I crinkled my nose at him because he seemed like the sort of guy who'd respond to that and eased him out the door. Normally, I wouldn't give Fred's orientation a second thought, but at this moment, I wished he would be deeply interested in going back to his desk and imagining Tricia and me naked, cooing into Yvonne's phone for $4.99 a minute. Instead, I had no doubt that he was going to stay on the other side of the door, his ear pressed against it, until the moment Yvonne arrived. I'd have to be quiet.

Yvonne last redecorated her office during her "roots crisis." Her grandmother died and left her estate to everyone but Yvonne, because Yvonne didn't seem to need it and didn't seem to care. Fact is, Yvonne *didn't* care, but she'd always thought she'd made a good show of caring, so it burned her that her grandmother had seen through her but never called her on it.

In retaliation, Yvonne dove into this demented flurry of antique acquisition, sort of assembling the roots she'd been denied. And then tweaking them along the way. As best one could tell from studying her office, Yvonne was descended from a long line of magnificent Mediterranean creatures who had bequeathed her heavy, dark woods and jewel-toned fabrics. Any rumors about their being Scotch-Irish and coming over in the '40s were just idle chatter.

Tricia perched on the edge of the sofa, which was designed for creating lower back problems. She looked around uncomfortably, but the décor had nothing to do with her unease. "I don't know if I can do this."

"It's an event, Tricia. You do great events."

"Oh, I'm not worried about the reception. I'm not sure I can sit here and talk to Yvonne like it's just another client meeting."

I threw open the door to check on our surveillance system, but to my surprise, Fred was back at his desk, ear far from the door. He glanced up, annoyed that I dared emerge and taunt him. I flashed him a smile he didn't buy. He went back to work and I closed the door again.

Tricia was lost in her own thoughts and didn't even notice as I pulled the little key on the red ribbon out of my pocket and started prowling through the office. "I've never been in a room with a murderer before," she said.

"That you know of?"

"Meaning?"

"That sculptor, two summers ago."

"Jean-Luc?"

"I was always convinced his next piece was going to feature his mummified mother, front and center."

"You never said anything."

"I didn't want to spoil the surprise."

"Are you looking for the music box?" Tricia let a whole boatload of opportunities to snipe at the dubious character of many of my past loves go sailing right by and jumped to her feet to assist me. I was sniffing around Yvonne's shelves, trying to find anything that looked receptive to the little key. If it was a music box, so be it. If it was a Barbary buccaneer bobblehead, that was fine, too. As long as it helped me nail Yvonne.

"How will we know when we've found the right piece of evidence?" Tricia asked, kindly hopping onto my wavelength.

"I'm figuring it's like the Supreme Court and porn. When we see it, we'll know."

"Try this." Tricia took a small porcelain box off the end table nearest the office door. It was rectangular, with little claw feet and a hinged lid that was locked with a tiny, heart-shaped padlock. It was way too cute for Yvonne to have bought for herself, especially in her Mediterranean phase, so it was perfectly plausible that it was a love token from Teddy. Love softens your definition of keepsake.

But the key didn't fit. It also didn't fit any of the drawers in any of the furniture in the room, desk and credenza included.

I was poised on the brink of thinking I'd actually been wrong when I saw it. It was on the lower shelf of the end table, the one where Tricia had found the cute box. At first glance, it looked like a wooden cigarette box, but it was deeper and more rounded than you'd expect a cigarette box to be. And a little golden keyhole glinted in the bottom panel.

I slid the box out and put it on Yvonne's desk.

"How lovely. It deserves better placement," Tricia said, eyes scanning the room for an open shelf.

"We're snooping, not redecorating, remember?" I slid the key in. It fit. It turned. The lid lifted slightly of its own accord as the catch released. I eased it open the rest of the way and tinkly calypso music began playing.

"Told you it was a music box," Tricia smiled.

Inside the box, a tiny ceramic woman dressed in a wild, multi-hued outfit of strategically placed feathers and a matching headdress pivoted before a series of mirrors attached to the inside of the lid. I've never been to St. Maarten—the men who want to take me away to some tropical paradise are rarely talking farther than Cape May—but I've heard they have a pretty cool Carnival, like the one in Rio de Janeiro. This little lady looked like she'd fit right in. But did she hold any secrets?

"There's no drawer," I hissed at my music box expert, suddenly feeling the need for absolute stealth.

"Poke around on the bottom."

I poked and was delighted when the poking at one end caused the other end to lift up. The box had a false bottom. Half of one, anyway. The floor of the box was cut into two pieces, probably to allow access to the mechanism that spun the little dancer. But it also created a very nice hiding place.

"For your real valuables." I fished the little plank out to be able to view the compartment fully and we were staring at a cardkey. One of those disposable cardkeys hotels use. And if I could just fish it out and turn it over, I could see that this one was from—

"What makes you think? I? Care?" Yvonne shrieked outside her door. Tricia and I nearly impaled each other with our heels, scrambling to our feet. I shoved the music box back together and onto its shelf, flipping the lid down as I straightened up and jammed the silver key into my pocket. The lid on the box didn't catch and it inched back open as I shoved Tricia across the room, but at least the music didn't start up again.

Yvonne walked in and looked at us without expression. Fred hovered behind her, peering unhappily. Tricia was using her reflection in the window to fix her hair and I was studying the blowup of the cover of Yvonne's first issue as editor. How guilty must we look?

"Good morning, Yvonne." I did my best to look right at her and not at the music box. Edgar Allan Poe's "The Tell-Tale Heart," a story that kept me awake three nights in a row in third grade, came back to me and I had a sudden image of me throwing myself on the music box, screaming, "There is the hideous syncopation of her silly souvenir!" Fortunately, the image amused me and I turned the smile into a greeting for Yvonne.

I was expecting a lecture for being in her office or for being in her life or something equally dour, but she smiled back. "So sorry to keep you waiting—Tricia." Yvonne closed the door in Fred's face and walked right by me to greet Tricia like some long-lost cousin. Tricia grimaced over Yvonne's shoulder as Yvonne hugged her, rolling her eyes at the open music box.

I nodded in understanding, but what could I do? Yvonne was already turning around to look at me. "You look like hell, Molly," was the greeting she offered me.

"Glad to hear it, Yvonne, because I actually feel like crap," I returned. Yvonne fluffed her hair as she put her bags down and it hit me: Her hair was a different color than it had been yesterday. She'd gone about three shades lighter, passing out of the blonde realm altogether and entering some bizarre peach sorbet area. She was late because she'd paid Sacha, her Croatian hairdresser, to get up at the crack of dawn and color her hair for her. Yvonne at nine o'clock was tough enough. I couldn't imagine Yvonne at 6 A.M. I hoped Sacha made her pay through the surgically altered nose.

"You, on the other hand, look terrific." I belatedly picked up my cue and eased myself back over toward the end table, hoping to position myself so she couldn't see the open music box at all.

"No, no. Weeping non-stop. Not sleeping. I look. Like Death itself."

Behind Yvonne's back, Tricia rolled her eyes again, which was not helpful at all. I swallowed hard. "Then Death should be on the cover next issue, because you look wonderful."

"Oh. I touched up my hair." She touched it with studied nonchalance. "I want to look good for Teddy's service. Out of respect." At the mention of Teddy, her eyes went to the music box. I hadn't gotten across the room fast enough. She saw the open lid and gasped like she'd seen a ghost. A little condom-shaped ghost came to my mind, but I hoped I was alone there.

Yvonne charged over to the music box and scooped it up like it was a wounded puppy. "Why is this open?" Before Tricia or I could endanger ourselves by attempting to lie, she continued. "Damn cleaning people. I should fire them all."

"Is something missing?" I tried to sound like Rebecca of Sunnybrook Farm, well aware that my Shirley Temple routine had never worked on my mother and had little chance of working on Yvonne.

Yvonne clicked the lid shut, locking the box and returning it to its place. "It just shouldn't be open. Ever again."

Tricia closed her eyes for a moment, bracing herself for a client meeting with a crazy woman. I would have felt more sympathetic, but I was puzzling over why the box should never be open again. Because the box was from Teddy and he was dead? Teddy had the key because only he was allowed to open it? Was the cardkey from Teddy? Which hotel?

If I could get Tricia to suggest to Yvonne that they talk in the conference room for some reason, I might be able to get back into the music box and figure out from whence came the cardkey. Short of dumping coffee all over Yvonne's desk, I couldn't think of why they'd need to move. I was actually hefting my coffee cup, trying to decide how much of a mess I could make, when the door banged open.

"I beg your damn pardon!" Yvonne barked.

"Y'all go right ahead, but this is vital and will not wait." Brady Cooper, assistant advertising director, who seemed to be grieving more over his shortened vacation than the death of his immediate superior, stood in Yvonne's doorway with an armload of files that looked precariously close to cascading onto the floor. Fred stood on tiptoe in an effort to be seen over Brady's shoulder, a tough task—not because Brady's all that tall, but because Fred is all that small.

Brady's a medium guy—medium height, medium build, medium color, medium intellect, medium personality. He does his best to get along, given the fact that he was born without the gene that allows you to laugh. Nothing in the world strikes Brady as funny. He's not one of these guys who's in a perpetual rage because of world injustice or anything that pathological and entertaining. He just has no sense of humor. Or sense of irony to appreciate that he can't even get the joke that he can't get the joke.

Which, of course, makes him a favorite target for the writing staff and any assistant with a half-decent joke to tell. Or, even better, to play. Something about Brady brings out the junior high school prankster in all of us and we should really be ashamed of how much we tease him, but if he didn't make it so easy, we'd probably move on.

"I tried—" Fred began behind Brady's back.

"Not hard enough," Yvonne growled.

"I understand y'all're in an important meeting and I do hate to intrude, but we have serious problems which do demand your attention pretty damn fast," Brady insisted.

"Serious problems?"

Brady hesitated before settling on, "Irregularities." Brady was uncomfortable that Tricia and I were in the room and didn't seem willing to say any more until we left.

"Maybe Tricia and I should come back later," I offered, not expecting the dirty look I got from Tricia.

"It would be very helpful to our timetable if I had a moment for a few decisions to be made," Tricia said in her most professional tone.

"What do you need decided this morning, Tricia dear?" Yvonne's eyes were still on Brady and they were worried.

"We need to at least choose a venue so I can arrange a tour for you and Mrs. Reynolds, ideally later today."

The mention of Helen brought Yvonne's eyes back around to Tricia. "You pick the venue. You tell Mrs. Reynolds and me when to be there. Thank you."

We were clearly dismissed even before she wagged her hand in the direction of the door. Tricia was about to protest, but we didn't have time for futility. Or to get dragged down in whatever was causing Brady's palpitations.

"Thank you, Yvonne," I said and ushered Tricia past Brady and Fred and out into the bullpen. Fred detached himself from Brady and attempted to follow us, but I turned and plopped a hand on his shoulder, stopping him. "Yes?"

"Did you upset her?" Fred asked with a straight face.

"No, I think you and Brady took care of that," I said, patting him on the shoulder.

"I thought I heard her shriek, through the door," Fred pressed.

"Her music box was open," Tricia explained.

Fred screwed his eyes shut and rubbed his temples. While fully appreciating his pain, Tricia and I exchanged a look of glee: The good and faithful servant was about to explain to us the significance of the music box and its being open.

"God help me, I need a different job," Fred sighed. Tricia and I exchanged a less gleeful look: Or not.

Fred slunk back to his desk and Tricia and I continued to mine. "Does he drink?" Tricia murmured as we went.

"Wouldn't you? Why?"

"We could ply him with sweet, girly cocktails and get

him to tell us what he knows. Assistants know everything."

She had a point. The finger that controls the hold button can flip off the whole world. I knew Fred was responsible for all facets of Yvonne's life—we could all hear her ranting to that effect on a regular basis. But would he be willing to dish about Yvonne and Teddy? I could ask my questions without coming right out and accusing Yvonne of murder. Though maybe Fred already harbored suspicions of his own.

Or maybe Fred wasn't the prime source. I scanned and actually was glad to find Gretchen standing across the bull-pen, even though tears were streaming down her face. Girl to girl, I could probably get more out of Gretchen than out of Fred. And as Teddy's assistant, she'd know more worth getting. I should've thought of her before.

Tricia looked over at Gretchen, her eyes widening in alarm at the tears. But emotionally overwrought probably worked to my advantage right now, so I motioned for Tricia to follow me and made my way over to Gretchen.

She wasn't trying to hide her tears, but no one sitting near her seemed to notice. Of course, she'd been crying off and on for over twenty-four hours now and there was work to be done. "Hey, Gretch. What's wrong?"

I held out an arm to her. Gretchen slid under it, forehead pressed to my shoulder, and muttered, "How mad is she?"

"Mad as ever."

"I mean, about Brady and the ads."

"She kicked us out before they got into details. Something about 'irregularities.' What's going on?"

Gretchen hesitated, casting an uncertain look at Tricia.

"It's okay, you remember my friend Tricia." Tricia gave Gretchen one of her best client smiles, the kind of smile that gets people to fork over big bucks without thinking twice. "What's going on?"

Gretchen glanced around the bullpen, then backed into Teddy's office, watching us as we followed her. I didn't relish the thought of stepping back into his office, but I did like the idea that Gretchen was about to tell us something that warranted some privacy.

"I know he's going to blame Teddy. And Teddy would never do anything to hurt the magazine." She took a ragged breath and her voice moved up the scale. "He would never do anything to hurt anyone. He would never do—"

"Gretchen." I couldn't imagine what the rest of the octave was going to be, but I knew it was going to shatter glass. I couldn't afford to let Gretchen get too operatic on me. "Are you talking about financial irregularities? Is there money missing?"

"That's what Brady says, but he's wrong. I know he is. Teddy would never—"

"Yes, he would never do anything to anybody. I'm sure Brady and Yvonne will get it all straightened out before we go to press."

Gretchen tried to pull herself together. "I just don't want them dumping on poor Teddy."

"We all want to protect Teddy's memory, Gretchen. That's why I need you to be completely honest with me. Can you do that?"

Gretchen seemed to shrink before my very eyes. "I'll try," she whispered.

I didn't want to play a lot of games and give Gretchen time to develop cold feet. If I wanted to draw another side to the triangle, I had to come right out and ask the question. "How do I get in touch with Camille Sondergard?"

The sob exploded from Gretchen with such force that I almost fell back a step. I looked at Tricia, perplexed. This was not the reaction I'd anticipated. Tricia looked at

Gretchen with detached wonder, like a child studying a hyena at the zoo.

"Gretchen . . ."

"How'd you know?" she wailed. Poor thing. Not only did she put up with all Teddy's crap in life, now she was left to try and defend his honor, questionable as it seemed, in death.

"His PDA. I talked to the detective. But I need to talk to Camille."

"Why?"

"I just need to. For Teddy's sake." Telling Gretchen I was trying to solve the crime was one step away from taking out an ad in the Sunday *Times*, so I had to be careful here.

"They broke up."

"Still . . ."

"I'm handling the guest list for the funeral reception," Tricia inserted smoothly. "In fact, I'll need to sit with you later and go over some names. But it would be inappropriate for Ms. Sondergard to attend unless she's willing to present herself solely as a business associate. That's a conversation Molly has volunteered to have with her."

News to me, but a brilliant idea. A little smile played at the corners of Tricia's eyes. She knew it was a great idea and she knew I'd owe her for it. But at the moment, she was focused on willing Gretchen into cooperation. Tricia's really good at this sort of thing, getting her ideas to look like other people's ideas. It can be a dangerous trait in a friend, but it's really nice when she's willing to throw her mojo your way when you need it.

Gretchen thought a moment, mashing her lips into all sorts of odd shapes. "I have a number," she finally admitted.

"Thank you." I hugged her lightly. "This will be so much help."

She nodded, not completely convinced. She took a notepad out of her pocket, wrote a number on it, and handed it to me. I decided to press my luck. "And there's no one else?" I asked as neutrally as possible. "Who might be a problem?"

The tears welled back up. She widened her eyes to keep them from spilling over, but it didn't work. Tricia quickly handed her a tissue. Gretchen took it and twisted it nervously, rather than using it.

"I really like working here, Molly," she protested.

"You're not getting fired. No one's going to even know we talked."

Gretchen sank into the armchair by the door. "Why did this have to happen? It's so wrong. It's not fair."

"It stinks," I agreed, sliding into columnist mode. "Especially because there's not much we can do now except remember him with love and help other people to do the same. But that means that any chance we have to minimize new pain for his family and friends, we have to grab."

Apparently, I scored on the sincerity scale, because Tricia's eyebrows lifted in approval and Gretchen's crying quieted slightly. Tricia handed Gretchen another tissue and Gretchen used this one, wiping her tears and blowing her nose. When she was finished, she took a deep breath. "There is someone else, but I don't think you need to talk to her. She knows all about keeping up appearances."

"Who, Gretch?"

"Yvonne."

My first instinct was to jump up and yell "Score!" but I pretended to be shocked. "Really?"

"She'll behave, though, because he just broke up with

her, so she wouldn't want anyone to know."

"Really?" Now I actually was surprised. I'd figured all signs pointed to the affair being current.

Gretchen nodded vigorously. "He broke it off."

"Why?"

"Why? Because Helen found out and she was furious. I overheard them fighting one night last week, here in the office. She was ready to—" Gretchen stopped herself, horrified by where that sentence was headed. She actually clamped her hand over her mouth.

"Don't go there," I advised. Not just because it was the opposite direction from where I was going, but also because it wasn't a pleasant place to go.

"I didn't mean that," she moaned from behind her hand. "Don't tell anyone I said that. Please."

"Of course not."

"You don't think Helen could—"

"Of course not." I said that with extra conviction and headed for the door before she could ask me anything that would be tougher to answer.

Tricia followed me, stopping to put her hand on Gretchen's arm. "I'll be in touch about the guest list. Thank you for everything you've done."

Gretchen erupted yet again and we left, pulling the door closed behind us.

"Damn."

Tricia led me back toward my own desk. "That doesn't mean you're wrong."

"Damn."

"And even if you are wrong, it's not like you've done anything as a result besides think evil thoughts about her, which you pretty much do anyway, so it's okay."

"Damn."

"Except that you hate to be wrong."

I stopped at my desk and retrieved our handbags from the bottom drawer, deciding in the process that I liked Tricia's much more than I liked mine. I had my black Fendi messenger bag. Now, I love it, I'll probably be buried with it because it will have grafted onto my shoulder by then. But she had her Kate Spade soho bag in porcelain leather and it didn't have a nick on it anywhere and taking a moment to covet it took my mind off other things for a moment.

"You're not going to respond to that, are you," Tricia chided as we headed for the elevators.

"That's the thing. I don't feel like I am wrong. But it's just a feeling."

"When you're investigating a homicide, I believe you're supposed to call it a hunch. Don't underestimate its importance. If you don't think you're wrong, you're probably not."

Her certainty made me smile in spite of myself. "You're a pretty amazing friend, you know that?"

"Is that a hunch?"

"More than."

"Then, thank you. What's next?"

"You go ahead and get the reception lined up. Call me when the walkthrough's set and I'll be sure to meet you there."

"Where are you going, so I can worry about you appropriately?"

"To paraphrase my grandfather, I'm going to see a woman about a dog."

10

I love the Metropolitan Museum of Art. Of course, I grew up with the Smithsonian Institution in Washington, DC, so it always strikes me as odd to have to pay to go to a museum, but I love the Met. I'm even a member. But still, it would never occur to me to shoot a perfume ad there.

I guess that's why I advise people about their personal lives and not about advertising. If anything, advertising makes my job harder. It's bad enough that we jack up our own expectations of what success should look like, what love should feel like, what happiness should sound like. When you add the tsunami of daily advertising with all its secrets for instant bliss, it's a little hard for real life to measure up. And the realization that life is not a Ralph Lauren ad can be difficult to embrace, especially when you don't have an appealing alternative in mind.

The travails of Western existence aside, I just needed a few minutes with Camille to get the break-up story from her and find out where she and Teddy got together to . . . get together. Not exactly something you can just drop into a conversation with a total stranger. But Teddy had always been a man of set habits, so maybe he took all his mistresses to the same hotel. Cuts down on the number of bellboys you have to bribe and that sort of economical thinking was Teddy's stock in trade. If I could figure out where he and Yvonne spent their time as a couple, I might be able to find someone who knew them as a couple, and that person might be able to shine the spotlight on Yvonne as a killer. And that's where it belonged.

It wasn't hard to find the gallery where they were shooting: There were tourists and security guards and policemen twelve deep in every available doorway. Camille, a breathtaking blonde whose perfection was a freak of biology, sat on a bench in front of Boucher's *The Toilet of Venus*, which features nude cherubim helping a similarly nude Venus primp. I could tell there were at least a dozen men among the onlookers who clung to the desperate hope that Camille was also going to strip down. Probably a couple of the women did, too.

The hairdresser was trying to get Camille's hair to fan perfectly across her shoulders and back as Camille looked up at the painting and wasn't having much luck. There were several suits sweating and watching their watches, but the photographer seemed cool with the delay. Or maybe he was stoned. Whichever, he was doing some yoga position on the floor in front of Camille that involved torqueing his hips in a way I can't imagine men are supposed to be able to bend, while his assistants scrambled to get all his equipment ready.

When I'd called the number Gretchen had given me, I'd spoken to Camille's assistant, Peggy, who didn't want to even confirm I had the right number until I said it was about Teddy Reynolds. She had then whispered their location to me and said she'd see what she could do, but stressed that she couldn't make any promises.

Now I could see why. Camille suddenly shrieked at the hairdresser, slapped her hands away, and got up. Suits descended like pigeons on spilled popcorn. Camille shook them all off and strode over to the far corner of the gallery where a cowering little brunette awaited the full brunt of Camille's wrath. Must be Peggy.

Peggy held up towels and water as soon as Camille got within reach; Camille grabbed a water, didn't acknowledge Peggy, and waited for the suits to start their portion of this afternoon's entertainment. One was already laying into the hairdresser, another was yelling into his cell phone. It was like choreography, watching them skittering around. I kept expecting them to burst into song: "When you're a suit, you're a suit all the way . . ."

I edged my way through the onlookers to try and catch Peggy's eye. It was going to be tough because Peggy seemed intensely interested in the floor while Camille and one of the suits ranted at each other. I waved, I bobbed and weaved, I cleared my throat, nothing. Finally, I dialed the number again.

Peggy jumped visibly and answered her phone quickly.

"I'm the friend of Teddy Reynolds who called you before. I'm in the north doorway," I explained, watching as she looked up and turned to face me. I gave her a friendly smile and a little wave. "This is probably not a good time—"

"No, no, it's perfect. It gives her an excuse to make them wait. She loves that," Peggy whispered into her phone. She hung up and skittered across the room to me. I thought of the captive mice enslaved in *The Nutcracker Suite*. This poor girl needed a new piece of cheese. She spoke to a security guard who ushered me under the ropes and over to her.

I shook her hand. "Thank you."

"I liked Teddy a lot," she said in explanation. I nodded in agreement and followed her over to Camille.

The suit pleading with Camille was running out of steam, so they were both open to my interruption. Camille told the suit she needed a few moments for a personal matter. He looked at me as though he were hoping I was there to have sex with her, anything to improve her mood, and withdrew, warning her that she had five minutes as he went. Peggy hurried after him. Or ran away briefly, I couldn't be sure which.

Camille looked me over as though I were modeling the outfit she was supposed to wear in her next ad. "Peggy said this was about Teddy's funeral," she said in an accent I couldn't quite place. Sweden meets Manhattan by way of London, maybe. Her vowels were tight and round, but so was the rest of her and that's why she's a millionaire and I'm an advice columnist. But I'd already coveted Tricia's handbag, I wasn't going to go down that path again so soon.

"I'm sorry to intrude," I began.

"They deserve to wait," she assured me.

"Is there somewhere else we can talk?" I asked, looking around. We were reasonably isolated in our corner, but the combination of lookie-loos and all the people in all the paintings staring down on us was creeping me out.

"No. Say what you have to say, it's fine."

Great. "I'm here as a friend of Helen's as well as a friend of Teddy's. I'm helping plan the funeral and I want to make sure there won't be any problems."

"You're afraid I will throw myself on his coffin and embarrass the widow?" She seemed vaguely amused by the picture she'd drawn.

"I don't mean to insult you—"

"No, it's sweet. Teddy was sweet, so of course he would have sweet friends. I wasn't exactly in a position to meet his friends." She smiled with a wistfulness that caught me unprepared. I hadn't stopped to think about how genuine her feelings for him might have been.

"I'm sorry for your loss."

It came out automatically, but it hit her hard. Her cool gray eyes were suddenly wet and her mouth tightened. She nodded, not trusting her voice for a moment, then proceeded carefully. "I really did care about him. The sex was amazing, but I cared about him, too."

My mouth tightened as I tried not to dwell on the amazing sex concept. Especially because I found myself wondering what brand of condoms he'd used with her. Still, in its own way, it was a segue to what I wanted to discuss next. I could only hope she'd follow along. "I'm also trying to help wrap up Teddy's business matters. Pardon me for asking, but are there recent hotel bills I should be looking for? I'd rather that his wife not have to deal with them, I hope you understand."

She shrugged rather grandly. "You don't need to protect her, she knows all about it. She caught us at the hotel together. It was a terrible scene."

I thought about passing out for at least two full seconds. How could Helen have known all this and not said anything to me? If she knew about Yvonne and Camille, why was she suspecting Teddy of sleeping with me? Or had she gotten to the point that she suspected him of sleeping with everyone? And had I gotten to the point of suspecting her?

"I'm sorry, I didn't realize. This was . . ."

Camille's perfect brow would have furrowed had it been able to move. Botox. Man, shatter all my illusions in one day. She thought for a moment, then said, "Early last week.

We are in our regular suite at the St. Regis and Paul, the concierge, calls up to the room that the real Mrs. Marquand was there and what did Teddy want him to do?"

"Mrs. Marquand?" I asked, confused.

"We always checked in as Mr. and Mrs. Marquand. It was a game Teddy liked to play." She shrugged tolerantly. "He loved games and I loved that in him."

The games I didn't want to know about. Was the name significant? J.P. Marquand, the novelist? Richard Marquand, the director? Was there a reference I wasn't getting? Or did Teddy just like the sound of the name? And how did Helen know the name? Did he use the same name with Yvonne? Ugh. That passed lazy on its way to sick.

"What happened?"

"What always happens," she said in a tone that implied every woman has been through it a hundred times. I declined to comment. "I hid in the bedroom while they had a screaming fight in the sitting room. But it was such a terrible fight, I was very moved. I thought, she must really love him. So after he sent her away, I ended it."

"You broke up with him?" Teddy had had a rough couple of weeks. Helen had found out about Camille and Yvonne, Camille had dumped him, and he'd dumped Yvonne. Not exactly going out on a high note.

"I don't like to be a part of messy things."

Then why sleep with married men, I wanted to ask, but that would make this conversation a messy thing. Instead, I said, "Thank you very much for your help and understanding. Someone will be in touch about the service and the reception."

"I'll be very discreet, I promise. Thank you for coming." She held out her hand. I thought she wanted me to shake it, but it was a gesture for Peggy to return. I took that as my exit cue and made a clean getaway. I was figuring out that investigating a murder is a lot like dating: Trust your instincts, pay attention to what the other person's really saying, and don't overstay your welcome.

Once I was out on the front steps of the museum, I took a moment to catch my breath and consider my next move. Should I go to the St. Regis and nose around or should I get back to the office and try for another look at Yvonne's music box, see if her cardkey was from the St. Regis, too? Or should I answer my cell phone?

It was Cassady. "I'm not the cute detective, so don't get all fluttery."

"Who says my heart doesn't beat just as fast when you call?"

"Take it up with your shrink, kiddo, and then explain to me why I have to hear about the big kiss secondhand."

"Cass, I'm a little crazed."

"And that's an excuse for a material breach of best friend etiquette?"

"No."

"Dish and I'll consider forgiving you."

"Meet me for lunch."

"I can't get away. Besides, you think you'll be free for lunch?"

"Yeah," I said, trying to figure out what she was getting at. Was this another dig about Detective Edwards?

"You don't think Garrett might invite you to stay for lunch?"

I didn't gasp into the phone, but I might as well have. I could feel the force of Cassady's sigh through my cell.

"Thank God I called. Go."

"Cass, I really am crazed—"

"And you can play that to your advantage. Make Garrett

think you're doing him a favor by stopping by, taking a moment out of your hectic crime-solving schedule to throw an idea at him. He'll eat it up with a spoon."

There was no point in telling her I couldn't do it. I already knew the lecture I'd get because I got it every time I confessed to self-doubt, and that's one of the reasons I love her so much. But I did have some misgivings about going to pitch an idea to Garrett Wilson when I had less than half an hour to pull my thoughts and myself together. "This may not be—"

"It's the perfect time, you're going to do well, just hang up the phone and get over there. My thigh only has so much allure for the man. We may not pass this way again."

"Cassady, I really—"

"I love you, too. Go. Then call me the moment you finish and tell me everything." She hung up and I hurried down the steps to hail a cab.

Fate gifted me with a cabbie who looked like he had as much on his mind as I had on mine and had no interest in striking up a conversation. I sat in the back and breathed deeply. I had to get organized. I was losing track of the rest of my life—important things that had to be taken care of, like this meeting and breaking up with Peter. Was the odd flutter in my stomach when I thought of that misgivings, anticipation, or too much coffee? That line of questioning was going to have to wait. One mountain at a time and Garrett Wilson came first. I took another deep breath, trying to find the perfect pitch and some calm spot in my soul from which to deliver it.

I hadn't found either thirty-five blocks later when I presented myself to the receptionist at *Manhattan*. You could tell they were a more serious magazine than we were just by the décor. Our offices were light and airy and always smelled like someone had just scorched popcorn in the microwave and had tried to cover it up with sandalwood incense. Their offices were full of deep, rich colors with thick carpeting and oiled wood paneling that muted sounds. Everything smelled of freshly cut flowers and perfectly brewed coffee.

The coward in me actually hoped the receptionist would sneer at me and announce to anyone passing by that I couldn't possibly have an appointment with Garrett Wilson because only real journalists got appointments with Mr. Wilson. Instead, she smiled with practiced charm, pointed to the burgundy leather armchairs in the waiting room, and told me Mr. Wilson's assistant would be out for me in just a moment.

I don't wait well. In the quirky physics of my world, a body at rest tends to become a body at worry. And I rarely worry about the right thing. For instance, I should have used the moments of waiting for Mr. Wilson's assistant to worry about whether I was going to make a complete fool of myself when I attempted to convince Mr. Wilson that I was worthy of pages in his magazine. Instead, I chose to worry about what hotel Teddy and Yvonne might have frequented if it wasn't the St. Regis. It was part of the story I wanted to sell, but not a part the editor was going to get very excited about.

Lucky for me, the assistant appeared before I could make the quantum jump to a new level of knotted worry. She was gorgeous—tall, sleek, perfect—and I concentrated on being intimidated by her rather than by her boss as I followed her down the hall and listened to her heels click on the polished tile hallway floors. Morse code, no doubt, for "Here comes a loser."

I'm not sure Mr. Wilson got the message. Once I was

in his office, I forgot what the assistant looked like and focused completely on being overwhelmed by him. He's the sort of guy Cary Grant played in the movies with the added benefits of a personal trainer and an eyelift. He's very well thought of in magazine circles, a darling of the charity circuit, and rumored to be a power broker in state politics. What was I thinking?

He sat down across from me, eschewing the mahogany desk large enough to support a production of *Phantom of the Opera* and choosing a sidechair I was sure had been hand-carried onto the Mayflower by his forefathers. The light pushing through the wall of windows behind him gave him an aura, or maybe just highlighted the one he already had.

"It's nice to meet you," he said as he flicked at a piece of dust that had dared land on his custom-tailored trousers. It was the only bit of dust in the entire highly polished room. "My daughter is a huge fan." Great. My reputation precedes me and gives me something to overcome. "I have to confess, I like your column, too."

I gulped back my shock and managed to say, "Thank you, sir."

"Strong point of view, crisp voice. Be interesting to see how it translates to narrative in feature reporting. So Cassady Lynch tells me you're working on a great story. Want to tell me about it?"

I couldn't catch my breath, much less tell him a story. Cassady had really greased the gears here. I might have to stop at Tiffany on the way home to find an appropriate reward. But as I scrambled to frame a response, I was momentarily afraid to share any of the story. I wanted to keep it in my head for fear that exposing it to light would make it shrivel up and float away. But how could I blow this opportunity? I took a deep breath and dove in. "It's a murder case."

"So Cassady said. I'm sorry about your friend, but I have to say—I love true crime. It sells well, too. Go on."

"I want to show the progress of the case from the point of view of a semi-detached observer. No emotional agenda, but someone who knows the players and may know the killer."

"May?" he teased.

I found myself smiling back. "I'm not going to give you all my secrets before I know how interested you really are," I responded, a little surprised by how flirtatious that sounded.

"I have to know more before I can tell you that," he volleyed back. "Tell me what the story is really about."

This is what I hate about trying to sell a story. Or about trying to discuss a relationship. It always makes me feel like I'm pinning a butterfly into an exhibit case while the poor thing is still alive. There are so many things you discover along the way and sometimes, they're the most important part of the journey. But that wasn't going to get me the sale. Or the validation that came with it.

Luckily, my subconscious slid into the driver's seat. "It's a story about appearances. Who we are when we get up in the morning versus who we become when we go to work or see someone we know or meet someone new. And how we alter that, tailor that, often without thinking about it." I gave him my best poker face so he wouldn't know I had no idea where that explanation had come from.

Garrett's smile disappeared and I didn't know if that was a good thing or a bad thing. He looked at me for a long moment and I did my best not to squirm, despite the nuclear forces at work trying to twist my body into a pretzel, as every microscopic bit of worry in me rushed to the pit of my stomach. The longer he looked at me silently, the harder I had to strain to stay untwisted. I was becoming a living experiment for The Anxiety Unification Theory.

He finally spoke. "That feels familiar. Most people realize we 'put a good face on' when we go out into the world."

The whirling mass in my stomach solidified painfully. Nothing pierces a writer—journalist, columnist, or scrawler on a bathroom wall—more than being told her idea isn't new. Every person who puts words on a page has to believe they have something new to express, or at least a new way in which to express it. Except for the bridal magazines, which get to run the same stuff issue after issue because you're either buying it once as you start planning your own wedding or you buy them compulsively, in which case the wedding industry has you addicted and you won't notice the repetition.

Garrett's reaction took the apprehension I had about the meeting and the guilt and worry I had about pursuing the article and fused them all into something completely unexpected. Something I was not, I'll admit, all that familiar with but that I'd felt when I first discovered Teddy's body: resolve.

I dug deep for a little confidence to dissolve the rock in my stomach and launched into what I hoped would pass for a blinding display of salesmanship and, even better, coherence.

"It's more than 'putting on a face' or playing a role. Yes, we all do that. To a certain extent, it's how we're taught to interact with people. Company manners and all that. I'm talking about something more basic, more innate, and less conscious. We all have facets. Like a jewel. Turn us slightly, put us in a new light, and a different facet emerges. It's still the same stone, but the new angle gives you a new appreciation for it, heightens its value. A lot of us go through life with most people only seeing one or two facets."

Garrett wasn't saying anything, not that I was giving him a chance, but he leaned forward in his chair. That was all the encouragement I needed. "Teddy was a vastly different person to everyone who knew him. A jewel of varied facets, some revealed to only a few. By assembling the facets into one jewel, by examining why he hid certain sides from certain people, we understand why we do it in our own lives. And what we gain or lose in the process."

Garrett opened his mouth, but I was caught up in my own chain reaction and powerless to stop. "And we frame it all in the fact that Teddy was a victim of violence. Did one facet facilitate that? And what about the facets of the killer? Which ones had Teddy seen, which ones have the rest of us seen? By learning who Teddy was to the person who killed him, what they saw of each other—"

"—we produce an article worth reading," Garrett finished for me.

I was afraid to move, to progress into the next moment. Had I grabbed him? He rubbed his forehead thoughtfully. "That's a pretty tall order."

I nodded. "That's what makes it compelling."

"Do you have the cooperation of the police department?"

I hoped I didn't blush as I thought of Edwards. "Occasionally."

That brought his smile back. "They can be tough."

"It won't be a problem," I assured us both.

"Who's the killer?"

"You'll find out when you read the article."

"Then I guess I better buy it." He kept talking, but I had a hard time hearing him over the rush of blood in my ears. Had he really said he wanted my article? I hadn't had to jump through flaming hoops or promise him my first-born or even agree to date him. He wanted my article. Had Cassady slept with him and left that out of the story?

"Give yourself a little more credit than that. And give me a hell of a lot more," Cassady said when I called her from the sidewalk. The fact that I was about to write a real article for a real magazine was still sinking in. My hand trembled and I almost dropped my cell phone. "Congrats, Molly."

"I don't believe this."

"A couple of hours, a couple of bottles of champagne, and you'll believe it. I'll help. Dinner?"

"Absolutely."

"Don't go into shock or anything."

"I won't."

"You can do this, Molly. You'll be great. All you have to do is solve a murder."

"Before or after I take care of world peace?"

It came out a little shrill and Cassady heard it. "Molly?"

"I'm fine."

"Yvonne did it."

"That's what I thought."

"Past tense. What happened?"

"A couple of people pointed me back towards Helen."

There was a longer pause on the other end of the phone than I would have liked. "And that's still Edwards' theory, too."

"Last I knew."

There was another pause and I braced myself for what

I was sure was coming next. "Then maybe you should leave it to Edwards."

"No."

"Why not?"

"Because it would be a lousy ending for my article. And because I'm right."

"Are you sure?"

Now it was my turn to pause. "I'll be sure by dinner." I always work best with a deadline.

11

"*My. God. Where have* you been?" Yvonne asked, not at all in the tone of someone who was happy or relieved to see me, but in the tone of someone who would have been just as pleased to see jackals drag in my corpse as to see me standing in the conference room doorway.

"I'm sorry, were you looking for me?" I didn't want to answer her question because truth was, I had been on my hands and knees in her office breaking back into her music box. Well, not so much breaking into it, since I did have the key, but entering it without permission, which was still unlawful on some level. But I'd gotten what I needed. By the skin of my teeth.

As I came back to the office from my meeting with Garrett Wilson, my concern over Camille's statements about Helen was giving way to the adrenaline that comes from getting a deal. Most of the writing I do outside the column is for our magazine, so it's a whole different thing to go out into the real world and pitch freelance ideas. And most of the outside freelance I do is light stuff, airy pieces for friends like Stephanie at other magazines. But this was a whole new ballgame and I was going to pop blood vessels keeping the news to myself. But whom at *Zeitgeist* could I possibly tell? "Hey, gang, I got a great gig writing about how our boss killed Teddy! Drinks on me!" I don't think so.

So I put aside the concern about Helen, contained the adrenaline, and took off an earring. I stowed the earring in the pocket of my skirt, which already held the music box key, and went to see Fred.

Fred saw me coming, his eyes wide in warning behind rimless glasses. "You don't want to see her," he hissed once I was at his desk.

"No, I don't, but why wouldn't I?"

"Not that this hasn't been a rough week for us all, but the woman is out of control. Hormones, emotions, medications—something is out of balance somewhere and I may not live until Friday at this rate."

"It's already Wednesday, Fred. Humpday. Hang in there. So is she in her office?" I asked, praying that the answer would be—

"No. She's in the conference room with Brady unless he's choked himself with his belt like a smart fellow."

"This still about the irregularities?"

"Oh, I'm sure she's moved on to defaming his mother by now."

"Poor guy. Well, I don't really need her, I need her office."

"Excuse me?"

I showed him the now empty lobe of my right ear. "I lost an earring and I think it might have been while Tricia and I were waiting for her this morning."

Fred twinkled. "Why? You two playing rough?"

I laughed, caught by surprise, and that pleased him greatly. "My secret's safe with you, isn't it, Fred?"

"Of course not." He tossed his head at Yvonne's office door. "Help yourself."

The door was closed so I felt it wasn't too conspicuous to close it again behind me. I went immediately to the music box, kneeling on the floor in front of it to support the missing earring scenario in case Yvonne came back in while I was . . . investigating.

I fished the cardkey out of the hidden compartment and paused a moment before I flipped it over. Did I want it to be from the St. Regis? Did I want Yvonne to be guilty or did I just want to be right? Before I could decide, I saw that there was something else in the little compartment. When I had opened the music box earlier, I had thought the compartment was lined with lighter material than the rest of the box. Now I saw that it actually was a layer of small, torn pieces of paper.

I flipped the cardkey over. The St. Regis. I let my breath out in a long, silent whistle and tried to decide how I felt. I couldn't. This seemed to indicate that I was headed in the right direction, but the road could fork. Helen could have tumbled to Camille because she knew about the St. Regis. Or Helen could have stumbled on to Camille because she knew about Yvonne and tracked her to the St. Regis. One way or the other, I was definitely taking a trip over there this afternoon.

Putting the cardkey aside, I fished the pieces of paper out of the bottom of the compartment. It was a sheet of lovely ecru vellum that had been torn up into tiny squares. I fumbled with the pieces, trying to reassemble the jigsaw puzzle in the palm of my hand. It was Yvonne's handwriting as best I could tell, but I wasn't getting a sense of what she had written until I saw "Dear Teddy—" on a piece. I had warring reactions: The investigator who had just sold a piece to Garrett Wilson thought, "Sweet." The heart of the colleague who knew them both actually sank a bit. A shredded love letter and a hotel cardkey. They made me unexpectedly sad.

I put the music box back together and replaced it on the shelf, smart enough to know that I couldn't sit there on the floor of Yvonne's office and play "Mend the Clue." I was trying to get to my feet, not a picture of grace given the narrow diameter of my skirt, when the office door opened. I changed my attempt at rising into a lunge between the end table and the sofa, my hand hidden under the sofa as I tried to ball up the fragments of the note into the smallest mass possible.

"Any luck?" Fred asked, doing a halfway decent impersonation of an interested party.

"Not yet," I replied, doing what I hoped was a more convincing impersonation of a woman desperate enough to retrieve a chunk of malachite and sterling silver that she would mash her body between and under pieces of furniture.

Fred eased the door closed behind him. "Mind if I ask you a—oh, sweet mother Mary."

I froze. I knew he couldn't see my hand from where he was standing, but I was nervous enough to imagine Fred whipping off his glasses and revealing his true identity as Superman, complete with x-ray vision. I decided the least incriminating thing I could say was, "What?"

"Was this open when you came in?" Fred strode over to the music box and picked it up. I could have kissed him for it, because it gave me a chance to stand up, step behind him as though I wanted to look at the music box over his shoulder, and stuff the wad of notepaper into my pocket out of his line of vision, x-ray or not.

"I guess I didn't notice."

Fred clicked the lid down firmly, making sure it latched, and replaced the music box. "The last thing we need around here is Yvonne seeing ghosts."

"Ghosts?"

Fred did a melodramatic take over his shoulder to make sure no one was lurking in the doorway, then leaned into me with a conspiratorial grimace. I'm tall enough that this entailed Fred essentially resting his nose between my breasts, but this was Fred and it seemed important, so I let it go. "It's a game she and Teddy used to play."

"A game?" I echoed in encouragement.

"He used to leave her messages in the music box, leave the lid open to let her know to look."

Atta boy! Now I really wanted to kiss him, but I couldn't risk distracting him. "No way." He nodded solemnly, but I pressed. "How do you know?"

"She called me once from some meeting across town, absolutely frantic. She said she'd run out that morning and forgotten to check and it was a catastrophe and Teddy mustn't know and all sorts of similar hysteria. Then she swore me to secrecy and made me check."

"Was it open?"

He nodded, a little less solemnly. "And there was a matchbook from Nobu there. She said she knew exactly what that meant and that I could take an extra fifteen minutes for lunch because life was good."

"So you think she met him there for dinner?"

"At least." Fred tilted his head to the side like a little dog waiting for instructions. He was waiting for a reaction, so I figured I'd better give him one.

I widened my eyes. "You mean Yvonne and Teddy . . . ?"

Fred put his finger to his lips, winked, and shushed me. As I continued pretending to be shocked, I ran the equations. If a matchbook from a restaurant meant "meet me for dinner," then a cardkey from a hotel meant "meet me for sex," and a hotel cardkey with a shredded love note meant . . . what? "We need to talk"? "I'm leaving you"? "You're not leaving me"? I needed to get out of there and piece things together on both the small and grand scale.

Fred, caught up in his drama, continued. "After that, I started watching the music box. I figured the days it was open, she'd be happy and my vile existence of servitude would be a little less bleak."

"Did it track?"

"Right up until Monday. The box was open and she didn't seem that happy about it." Fred frowned as though considering this fact for the first time, but then shrugged, apparently not interested in considering it all that deeply. "And then it was open this morning when you and Tricia were in here and after you left, she got all feverish about it being a message from beyond or some such hysteria." Great. Not only am I trying to finger Yvonne for murder, no matter what Camille said about Helen, but I have her seeing ghosts in the meantime. I'm Employee of the Month material.

Fred gestured dismissively at the music box. "It's just a cheap little thing, the latch is probably breaking down." Now if we could just get Yvonne to embrace that theory. And if I could just make a clean getaway. "Any luck?" Fred continued.

I pulled on my earlobe and headed for the door. "No, I must have dropped it somewhere else. Thanks for letting me look, though."

"I exist to serve," Fred drawled and I hurried away, wanting to be well clear of Yvonne's office before she returned, especially if she was in a foul mood.

What I needed to do now was find a private spot where I could reassemble the note—not exactly an operation that could take place in the bullpen. Or anywhere else, for that matter. Our offices weren't designed with privacy in mind. Except for the conference room and Yvonne was in there, which made it forbidden territory. The only real shot I had at uninterrupted, unobserved activity was the ladies restroom. Unfortunately, to get there, I had to walk past the conference room.

I walked briskly, head down, most thoughtful face on, praying the door would be closed. But as I drew closer, I could hear Yvonne quite clearly, as well as Brady and Gretchen, who were trying desperately to get a word in edgewise. The door was open.

Yvonne stood at the far end of the conference table with Brady and Gretchen flanking her. Files, artwork, and billing statements were splayed across the table. Yvonne was the picture of wrath, a Herrera harpy. Brady looked like he would volunteer for the Bataan Death March if it meant he could leave the room. Gretchen wept, quietly but deeply.

I kept walking. I passed the door. I shifted my eyes back to the floor. And still it came, loud and shrill and jarring, like I had tripped an alarm at the Guggenheim: "Molly! My. God. Where have you been?"

"I'm sorry, were you looking for me?"

"This doesn't concern Molly—" Brady began.

"And it's not the only thing that concerns me!" Yvonne roared at him. "Surprise! Other worries!" Her eyes still on

Brady, she pointed her sharply manicured talon at me with such force and precision, I froze as though it were a poison-tipped spear. Or, more likely, a fully armed ICBM. "Do not move!" I stayed in the doorway.

Brady sank down in a chair, defeated. Gretchen tried to stand her ground. "It's been paid for. Teddy wouldn't have told me to log it in if it hadn't been paid for. It's Accounting's mistake."

Yvonne turned the full heat of her wrath on Gretchen. "Other worries. Hear me?"

"Yes, ma'am," Gretchen demurred.

"Anything I can do?" I said, more to distract Yvonne than to actually get involved.

Yvonne held up the talon again, this time commanding me to wait while her eyes bored into Gretchen. "Even if this were all I cared about. What are you?"

Gretchen didn't seem to understand the question. Her eyes flicked to me in the briefest show of panic, then went right back to Yvonne. Yvonne leaned in closer. Spittle-spewing range. "An assistant." Yvonne said it as though it were a curse in some ancient tongue and Gretchen flinched like she understood it in her bones.

In sixth grade, I punched Justin Dietrich in the nose because he called Amanda Mapleton "fat." She was, but it was stupid and petty of Justin to make an issue of it. Those instincts don't go away, even when someone like Yvonne is loaded for bear. Now I had to get involved. I walked up to the table and tried to make sense of what they were looking at. "What's this, Brady?"

Brady didn't protest this time. He must've figured he'd live longer if someone else caught flak for a while. "We've got a bad ad and we're up against the deadline. Can't find the agency's check, keep trading calls with them." He slid a file marked NACHTMUSIK AGENCY across the table to me, but I was happy to take his word for it. "Sophie's still out on medical and her assistant isn't any help. She couldn't track a payment if it were all in pennies stuffed in her pantyhose." My protective instincts have limits. I knew Wendy, the assistant in question, and Brady was actually being gracious.

"So you're going to pull it?"

"No!" Gretchen all but stamped her foot. "I remember when Teddy met with their agency, I remember him show- ing me the check. It's a good ad. If Teddy were here . . ."

Gretchen dissolved into tears again, melting into a chair. Yvonne sneered at me like it was my fault. "More ques- tions?"

Why not. "Is it a good ad?"

Gretchen nodded rapidly through her tears and pushed a piece of paper across the table to me. It was just the match print, but it was still dramatic. It showed a woman's leg from just below the knee, the foot in a gorgeously simple black high heel. Around the heel was wrapped a lovely piece of jewelry, for lack of a better term. It was a climbing vine made of gold wire, studded with delicate golden flow- ers with jeweled centers. Other vines in other designs and color combinations lay next to the woman's foot. Appar- ently, you slipped these up the heel of your shoe. The ad read, "Walk in ever-changing beauty. Shoe Jewels by Noc- turne," and listed a web address. "Nice ad, cool idea," I had to admit.

Gretchen nodded again, struggling to get her tears under control. "Teddy said they were a brand-new company with lots of promise. He talked to them a lot, even told the agency they could have the page facing you, Molly."

Teddy had often teased me that he could get a premium for the page across from my column because a survey had indicated I'm one of the first things people read. Me, their horoscope, and the diet tips. Everybody who offers quick answers gets an early look.

"That's great," Brady interjected. "I hope they all get rich and famous. But what did Teddy do with their check?"

I slid the artwork back to Gretchen. I knew what really upset her was the implication that Teddy hadn't been doing his job properly, not the fate of this new company. Though it would be a shame for them to take a hit because Teddy was gone. It would also be a shame for Gretchen's heart to be broken and Brady's life to be miserable because Yvonne couldn't handle her guilt over Teddy.

"We still have a day or two, don't we? Maybe Gretchen can help Wendy track down the check?" I asked, giving both Yvonne and Brady my best *Zeitgeist* cheerleader smile.

Gretchen brightened immediately, looking to Brady for a reaction because she was smart enough not to look at Yvonne. Brady was smart enough not to answer until Yvonne did. I was smart enough to know I had done what I could and any further pressing on my part would backfire on us all.

Yvonne wrestled with a couple of inner demons, then turned to Brady, snubbing Gretchen and me. "Friday. Close of business. Deal with it." She swept away from the table and I didn't get a chance to register Brady's or Gretchen's reaction because she swept me up with her and we were suddenly out in the hallway. "What does Tricia say?"

"I haven't spoken to her yet," I said, pretending I didn't have whiplash from the sudden change of subjects. But maybe we hadn't really changed subjects at all. In a way, this was all about Teddy. And as soon as I could get somewhere and read the note, I'd understand why even better.

"I want answers!"

I had to bite the inside of my lip to keep from shouting, "Me too! And so do the police!" But I opted for an understanding nod and said, "Let me give her a call, see where she is in the process. Tricia is meticulous, she's not going to make a hurried or ill-informed decision."

"I would hope not."

For an awkward moment, I didn't know if I'd been dismissed or not. For an even more awkward moment, Yvonne glared at my hand in my pocket. The hand clutching the pieces of note in my pocket. She even snapped her fingers, expecting me to hold out my hand and divulge its contents. "So call her."

With great relief, I slid my hand out of my pocket, leaving the note concealed, and showed her my empty hand. "I don't have my cell. Let me go back to my desk."

Yvonne gave the practiced sigh of a boss who employs only morons—and bosses who believe that never seem to notice that were that true, it wouldn't say much for their skills in hiring and management—and stalked back to her office. I hung where I was, happy to create a little distance.

What I also created, though, was the impression I was waiting for Brady and Gretchen, which pleased them both as they came out of the conference room. Brady actually thanked me before he trudged back to his office and Gretchen threw her arms around me in another one of her boa constrictor hugs. "Thank you, Molly."

"All I did was persuade her to wait a little, Gretchen. You think you can get this straightened out in time?"

"Absolutely."

"Teddy wasn't skimming, was he, Gretchen?"

Her eyes teared up before her hand could get to her mouth. Seemed like a genuine reaction. "See, this is what I was afraid of."

"I know and I'm sorry for asking. But I have to."

"Why?"

An excellent question and me without an excellent answer. "For my own peace of mind. Because I liked Teddy," was the best I could do, but Gretchen bought it. I was starting to understand the appeal of lying and getting away with it and that worried me. But I was grateful it worked in the moment.

Back at my desk, I checked in with Tricia. She'd talked to Helen and the funeral was set for Saturday morning at St. Aidan's Church with the reception site still undetermined. She'd already talked to three restaurants and four hotels near the church, but wasn't done yet. "Please, not the St. Regis," I implored.

"Why not? That's one of the places Helen requested," Tricia replied. "I'm headed over there shortly."

"You're kidding."

"I know it's pricey, but I think she's deriving some comfort from spending Yvonne's money."

"It's not that, it's just . . . twisted."

"How so?"

"Meet me there and I'll explain."

"Can you do three o'clock?"

"I'll have trouble waiting until then."

Tricia girl-squealed into the phone and my ear throbbed. "How could I not ask first thing? How did the meeting with Garrett Wilson go?"

"Great. I got it. I'll tell you all about it at three."

"How lovely that some good will come out of this. Congratulations! Love you."

"Love you, too." I hung up, grinning because Tricia and Cassady were more excited about the article than I was. Actually, that's not true. They were just able to sit in their offices and scream in delight and I couldn't do that.

Especially because Gretchen was hovering over my desk. "Hey, Gretchen."

"I'm sorry to bug you, Molly, but I heard you and Yvonne talking about Teddy's service and I wondered when it was going to be."

"Saturday at eleven with a reception to follow. We'll make an announcement to the staff."

"That's not much time."

"It's what Helen wants and Tricia's great at pulling things together on short notice."

"No, no, I meant that's not much time for us to get ready."

"Us?" I asked gingerly, fighting off the image of Gretchen and me doing a soft shoe number on the main altar as our parting tribute to Teddy.

Thankfully, Gretchen gestured to the magazine staff bustling around us, but I still wasn't sure I got her point. My perplexed silence urged Gretchen on. "I don't know what to wear," she confessed in a stage whisper.

I actually found her concern touching. It seemed to come from a real desire to be appropriate, not anything narcissistic. "There's a reason the little black dress is the cornerstone of the female wardrobe," I assured her.

"I don't have a little black dress," her confession continued. "You know how it is, black hasn't been black in such a long time—gray was last season's black and taupe was black the season before—and somehow, I don't have a black dress anymore."

"It's Wednesday. You've got time. Talk to Caitlin, get

some advice from her." Not that Caitlin, our fashion editor, had dressed anyone over a size two in twenty years, but she still might have some good suggestions for Gretchen.

Gretchen nodded but didn't move. I had a pretty good idea of what was coming next, but I thought I might be wrong, might be flattering myself. So I stood in the middle of the street and let the truck hit me. "I was wondering . . . if you'd go shopping with me."

Asking a woman to go shopping can be like asking a man to go to dinner. It can even be worse. There are the same opportunities for rejection, for misunderstanding what level of intimacy is being assumed, for feelings being stomped on. But with two women going shopping, even if the asking part goes well, there is a whole pantheon of pitfalls awaiting as you discover how disparate your senses of style and your budgets really are, how leisurely a process you think it should be, how differently you treat salespeople. And where a man and a woman have to confront the issue of whether to sleep together after dinner, two women out shopping have to confront the issue of whether they know each other and like each other enough to share a dressing room. Guess which one is usually the easier call to make.

"Gee, Gretchen, I don't know," I stammered, looking at my watch and hoping it would be much closer to three o'clock than it was.

"You have an appointment. It's okay. I'll figure it out." Gretchen drifted away from my desk backwards, hands wafting apologies like a hula dancer.

"No, wait," I vamped, trying to figure out how to help Gretchen without encouraging any hint of dependence. "I do have an appointment, but if you can go now, I could hit a place or two with you first."

"I don't want you to go out of your way," Gretchen said, thrilled by the notion that that was exactly what I was going to do.

"Where were you thinking of going?"

"Panoply, over on Fifth."

The St. Regis is on Fifth. And she was looking at me with the earnest eyes of a kid who never got to be captain in kickball and choose the teams. This was important to her for some reason. "That's actually on my way," I vamped again.

I was still vamping when we got to Panoply. I would have liked to walk because it's easier to vamp when you're walking—traffic noise requires that you repeat yourself a lot, other pedestrians distract you and allow you to go off on tangents, window displays demand that you stop talking about yourself and start talking about them. But time and distance forced us into a cab and into focused conversation.

"Do you think they'll ever figure out who killed Teddy?" Gretchen asked me before we'd gone half a block.

"Yes," I answered because I felt I had to.

"Do the detectives have a suspect?"

I dove for the first subject change that came to mind. "Every time I think of the detectives, I think of that Elvis Costello song. 'Watching the Detectives.' It's been going through my head a lot lately. Have you ever seen him live? He's amazing."

Gretchen smiled politely. "I prefer jazz."

"Well, now that Elvis and Diana Krall are together, maybe he'll start doing jazz."

"What kind of music will there be at Teddy's reception?"

Nice feint as Gretchen drives for the basket. This was going to be harder than I'd thought.

I tried several more times to change the subject, yanking

us over to weather, movies, even politics, but Gretchen kept homing back in on Teddy and the funeral. I suppose she had a right to be obsessed, but it was frustrating me to the point that I nearly vaulted from the cab when it stopped in front of Panoply, thankful for the task of paying the driver and sending him on his way.

I checked my watch again. I had enough time to go in with her and didn't have a good enough reason not to. As I steeled myself to go in, I realized I'd made a mistake in the cab. I should be taking advantage of the situation. Instead of steering conversation away from Teddy, I needed to guide it toward specific information about Teddy, but subtly enough that Gretchen wouldn't recognize the interrogation for what it was. With a new plan in mind, I happily followed her in.

I have a love/hate relationship with shopping. I love looking through clothes, feeling the fabrics, listening to their rustling and the whisper of hangers and security locks across the bar. It's great fun trying to discern the possibilities within each piece, imagining the magnificent fun I will discover if I can just get the right shoes with the right skirt and blouse.

But I hate the salesgirls. That's cruel of me, I know, but how cruel is it of them to stand there with their perfect little outfits on their perfect little bodies and ask if they can show me anything? Yeah, they can show me what they do with the two hours of their day that they're not at work or in Pilates class.

And now that they all wear headsets, they come off like some super-secret branch of Homeland Security, ready to call in the National Guard if I take the wrong pair of slacks off the rack: "You can't wear those! Your butt will look huge! Put the hanger down and back away. Strike Team, I have a Taste Violation in Sector Four."

It's enough to make you want to shop in the suburbs and deal with the bored teenagers. Of course, I used to be one of those bored teenagers, hence my bias.

A chirpy little headset-wearer was upon us moments after we walked into the store. The store was spacious and airy with clothes hanging in isolated yet strategic locations. It was the mating of a walk-in closet with an airplane hangar. "Good afternoon, I'm Deirdre, can I help you find something special today?"

Gretchen blinked at her and I went for the preemptive strike. "She needs a dress for a funeral."

"I'm so sorry for your loss," Deirdre said, her chirpy inflection not changing one iota. "You'll find what you're looking for over here." Deirdre led us to a delicate rack draped with black fabric in various configurations.

"Thanks. We'll take a look and let you know," I said with a really nice smile, but Deirdre still took offense, frowning at me as she huffed off, her DKNY slides making little *tsks* of disapproval on the hardwood floor.

I moved hangers around like a picky eater pushing food around on her plate. "Gretchen, you don't need to worry so much about protecting Teddy's reputation. We all know he was a good guy."

Gretchen didn't even look up from the dress she was examining. "I'm not so sure Yvonne thinks so."

"Well, the whole thing with Yvonne is so complicated. And I'm not talking about his personal life, I'm talking about the ad and all. You'll get that straightened out. Teddy wouldn't have screwed the magazine."

"No," she echoed in emphatic agreement.

"I mean, everybody pushes the envelope here and there—the occasional lunch on an expense account that shouldn't be, that sort of thing. No one's going to cause an uproar over those." She nodded, watching me now, trying to guess where I was going. "Unless it was something big, like a house account somewhere." Like the St. Regis, for instance, but I wanted to see if she'd say it first.

She shook her head. "Teddy was a good man who did the right thing. He had such a big heart. You know that ad Brady's all freaked about? A brand-new company that probably has its whole future riding on that ad and Teddy saw that and was impressed by it and wanted to give them great placement. Because Teddy believed that people deserve a chance, that there are talented people out there in the world besides Tommy Hilfiger and Kate Spade and those people might have something to contribute. And he knew how awful it could be trying to get your foot in the door, so he opened the door for them. Isn't that wonderful?"

I hadn't expected Gretchen to clamber up onto a soapbox, but I was fascinated, so I just nodded and she kept going.

"But of course, there are always spoilers like Yvonne who get all their joy out of stomping on people's dreams and playing with the affections of good men like Teddy just because it makes them feel special. Even if she wasn't the one who stabbed him, she killed him, Molly. She broke his heart and a man like Teddy couldn't live with a broken heart."

Her passion knocked the air out of me. As I groped for a response, Ms. Headset returned, wearing her plastic smile. "Have you found anything?"

"Yes," Gretchen barked at her. "I found your clothes

trite and derivative, overpriced and badly produced, and I wouldn't wear them if you paid me."

Gretchen charged for the door and I hurried to catch up with her, waving to Ms. Headset over my shoulder. "I think we're leaving."

I grabbed Gretchen's arm once we were outside and made her slow down. "Where are you going?"

"I don't know."

"Slow down a minute."

She stopped and burst into tears. "I didn't see a thing I liked in there."

We both knew that had nothing to do with her tears, so I stood quietly by while she wailed. I smiled uneasily at the random passersby who looked askance at Gretchen's wailing, but most people just kept walking. When the tears began to slow, I put one hand on her shoulder and hailed a cab with the other. "Maybe you should go home for a while. Everyone will understand."

"No," she sniffed, "I need to get the ad straightened out. That'll make me feel better."

She'd pulled herself together for the most part by the time I got a cab to stop and I bundled her into it. "Hang in there. Everything will get sorted out and we'll make it as right as we can."

As the cab pulled away, I started to hail another one for myself, then decided against it. The hotel was only a half dozen blocks down Fifth Avenue and I could use the walk. I needed to clear my head and my heart.

One of the things I love most about walking in Manhattan is that it's a way to be by yourself without being alone. The sidewalks are always full and you can enjoy the circus parade of people as they rush by, intent on the dramas of their own lives. You can smell anxiety in the air, but there's hope and promise, too. You make your own way, unbothered or maybe unnoticed by your neighbors, but they're right there, right next to you. Contact is a breath away. It's a patchwork quilt that might not match anything in your home, but having it on hand is comforting. The thought alone keeps you warm.

That had to be the hardest part of getting involved in a crime like this—fighting against that instinct for connection and keeping yourself from drowning in other people's sorrow. Do this sort of thing too long and it had to harden your heart a bit, as a protective mechanism if nothing else.

But how to reconcile that with Detective Edwards and his amazing kiss, which I had been trying very hard not to think about all day? Had the kiss been the mechanical, instinctive move of a hardened heart looking for action? Certainly hadn't felt that way. Or had it been the kiss of a heart so aware of the frailty of life that it sought connection that much more forcefully? There was only one way to answer that question before I got too caught up in my own poetry. I had to kiss him again.

12

Tricia was waiting for me in the lobby of the St. Regis, a delicate splash of coral amidst all the gold and white opulence. "I don't know what Helen was thinking," she said before I'd even made contact with the brocade chair next to her. "You can't have a funeral reception in a place that looks like a twelve-year-old's wedding fantasy."

The St. Regis is one of those stunning places with high ceilings and glistening floors that make me feel like my face is dirty and my hair isn't combed, no matter how swanked up I am. "I dunno. Heaven could look like this. The streets are paved with gold, aren't they?"

"I'm not going to engage you in theological debate."

"Not without a cocktail, anyway."

"And it's only three o'clock, so that's not an option."

"It's always five o'clock somewhere in the world."

"Aren't we both here because we have work to do?"

"You're done. You've already scratched this off your location list. But I'll tell you the real reason we can't have Teddy's reception here. This is where he brought his mistresses and where Helen busted him on it."

Tricia's face spun into a spiral of disgust, then righted

itself. "So she has some revenge scenario in mind that she wants to enact at the reception?"

"Thing is, she doesn't actually seem the type. It might be more of a case of quiet satisfaction that she's honoring him at the scene of his crimes and only she and the mistresses know."

"That's cold."

"So's cheating on your wife. Wanna have a little fun?"

"Are those related thoughts?" Tricia looked a little alarmed.

"Maybe you do need a cocktail." I stood and she followed, but I didn't take her to the bar, I took her to the concierge desk. "Yvonne is very anxious to talk to you about the plans for Saturday," I warned her on the way.

"I told Helen I'd have something to go over with her at the end of the day, I'll call Yvonne as soon as Helen signs off. What are we doing?"

"You're being sweet, innocent, and insightful and I'm digging around in the mud. Only it won't seem so dirty because you'll be so sweet, innocent, and insightful as a diversion."

Tricia rolled her eyes. "It won't be the first time I've been a beard. Not even the first time at this hotel." I made a mental note to revisit that statement, but we'd reached the concierge and it was time to focus.

"Good afternoon, ladies. How are you today?" The concierge spoke in the mashed and clipped tones of someone who would rather die than admit he'd grown up in Brooklyn. The nametag on his custom suit read "Paul," but it was a safe bet he'd been called Paulie until he was at least fifteen. But that was far behind him now that he was attending to the needs and wants of people with obscene amounts of money. I thought he pulled it off nicely, but I'm a big fan of sleek Mediterranean types, on an aesthetic level anyway. Tricia, whose tastes run WASP-y by definition, was less impressed.

"Paul, I need your assistance with a difficult, delicate matter."

"Of course."

"Our brother was often a guest in your hotel. He just . . ." I paused for effect and Tricia sniffed, right on cue. I tilted my head slightly so she wasn't in my field of vision before continuing, ". . . passed away."

"I'm so sorry," Paul said evenly.

"We're trying to tidy up his affairs, and I use that word deliberately, Paul. We want to spare my sister-in-law any hurt possible."

"I understand," Paul said. This didn't seem at all unusual to him. I guess there were plenty of people in the city with enough loose change to spend hundreds of dollars for a tryst. My thought was, if you're going to shell out half a grand for an afternoon of pleasure, go shoe shopping. At least you take something tangible home with you.

"I'm not sure if he had an account with you or how he was handling the billing, but it's a bill our sister-in-law doesn't need to see."

"A delicate situation, to be sure." Paul's polite smile never wavered, but nothing else moved either. He wasn't exactly leaping at the opportunity to be of service.

Tricia opened her purse, slid her hand in, back out, and onto the counter of Paul's station in one fluid movement. It took me a moment to realize that she had her hand over a bill, but Paul knew what she was doing right away. He put his hand next to hers and they executed the transfer like Houdini and his wife passing a key. Before I knew it, Paul had pocketed the money, Tricia had closed her purse, and we were in business.

Paul placed his hands on the keyboard of the computer that nestled discreetly in the corner of his station. "Let me see what I can do. His name?"

"I believe he used the name Marquand when he was here."

Paul thought a moment. "I don't recognize that name." He typed, waited, then shook his head. "We haven't had a guest by that name since the first of the year, anyway. A more extensive search would require my speaking with my associates in Accounting."

Tricia stepped in delicately, probably tallying how many associates in Accounting would need bribes, too. "Perhaps we got the name wrong," she said more to me than to Paul.

"If he came here often and was a gentleman of distinctive demeanor, or had a particularly memorable lady friend . . ." Paul offered.

Given the choice, I bet on the fact that Paul would remember Camille over Teddy. "His most recent lady friend is very tall, very lovely, very Scandinavian."

"She looks like a model," Tricia said with as close to a wink and a nudge as Tricia is capable of giving.

Paul worked to keep a straight face, no doubt dictated by the employee handbook. "Could you mean Mr. and Mrs. Maarten?"

"Yes," I said quickly, thinking of Camille's mangled pronunciation and of the MAARTEN printed on the back of the picture of Teddy and Yvonne. The picture. I'd forgotten about the picture. I started rooting around in my purse. "Absolutely. I must have misunderstood."

"Camille—that is, Mrs. Maarten—has a bit of difficulty pronouncing it." We both looked at him in surprise, but he kept that impassive expression in place. "I find it charming."

"You know who she is," I confirmed.

"And we are the soul of discretion. Though the staff here at the St. Regis uniformly salutes your late brother on his . . . success."

I found the picture in my purse and laid it on the counter for Paul's inspection. I wanted to be sure Camille wasn't in here with multiple partners and confusing things. "This is my brother—"

"With your sister-in-law. Yes. I've met her as well."

I felt like I was holding a compass that had suddenly swung south. I tapped the picture. "You've met her?" It wasn't Helen that Camille had encountered, it was Yvonne?

"The real Mrs. Maarten, as she referred to herself, yes. It was an unfortunate incident and I would rather not divulge—"

"You were here the day she caught Camille and Teddy together."

"Yes. Your sister-in-law is a memorable woman. I also remember because she mentioned to him, quite forcefully, that he had never brought her here and she was very upset about that. Which I took as a compliment to our hotel."

Tricia smiled at him. "And I'm sure that's exactly what she had in mind."

"Did you see my brother Monday night?"

"No, ma'am. And I would have, had he come in. He always checked in with me."

Always looking for that something extra, I'll bet. "Is there an account we need to attend to?" I asked.

Paul stepped out from behind his station. "If you'll just give me a moment."

We nodded and he hurried over to the front desk. There was bound to be a lot of whispering and snickering, but it didn't look like it was going to cost us extra. "How much do I owe you?" I muttered to Tricia.

"Nothing."

"Tricia—"

"I'll put it on Yvonne's bill."

"There's a certain poetic justice in that."

"So let me get this straight. Teddy brings Camille here, Yvonne finds out and busts him, but as far as we know, Helen stays out of the loop."

"And then Teddy invites Yvonne here, probably thinking he can make it up to her, but he winds up dead."

I looked around at the thousands of dollars worth of fresh flowers in the lobby alone, the exquisite furnishings glittering regally under all the chandeliers, the intensely rich people coming and going, all to the accompaniment of Gershwin tunes being played on a grand piano back in the bar. Exceptional, but to die for? Or kill for?

"Why'd she wait a week to kill him?" Tricia asked.

"I don't know. Maybe he pleaded for a second chance."

"Do you think he got it and blew that, too?"

"Could be. I think I have her 'Dear John' letter in my pocket."

Tricia growled in vexation. "Why do you keep mentioning the good stuff as an afterthought?"

"I'm not sure what the note says. I need to reassemble it."

"They have very nice tables in the bar here. Let's go." Tricia grabbed my wrist and made to march me off to the lobby bar, but Paul returned at that moment.

"Thank you for waiting, ladies. Your brother's account is handled by a third party."

"That wouldn't be *Zeitgeist* magazine by any chance, would it?" I asked.

"You didn't hear it from me," Paul cautioned.

So Teddy was cheating on the boss and billing it to the company. Talk about living dangerously—and paying for it. We thanked Paul profusely and moved off to the bar. This counted as an acceptable reason to start drinking early.

We picked a table near the piano, figuring that the music would cover our conversation, hushed though it was. Tricia felt that the landmark status of the hotel demanded a classic drink and ordered a vodka gimlet. I suspected we had a rough evening ahead of us and ordered Glenfiddich neat.

I'd been twisting so many mental puzzles around in my head that it was actually soothing to have a physical one to spread out across the table. Whoever had torn up the note had done it very precisely so all the pieces were about the same size. Tricia called Cassady and told her to come meet us, listened to a lot of guff about the bar at the St. Regis not being Cassady's kind of bar, then buckled down to help me move the tiny pieces around until we started to get a sense of what Yvonne had written.

We were just finishing the reconstruction when Cassady arrived. We could tell she was approaching from the way all the businessmen lifted their heads from their drinks for a moment, like lions around the watering hole catching a new scent in the air. And she wasn't even dressed up. It's one of the reasons she doesn't like this kind of bar—you can't exactly slip in unnoticed, you have to walk right through the middle of everybody. Not that Cassady doesn't like being noticed sometimes, but most of the time she can't be bothered.

She gave us each a quick kiss on the cheek, sat down, and sniffed our drink glasses. "What's going on here?"

"The ambiance demanded it," Tricia explained.

Cassady beckoned to our waitress, ordered Grey Goose on the rocks, and held her arms out to the sides. "Am I supposed to roll up my sleeves next?"

"We actually have it almost put together," I told her. Tricia brought her up to date as I carefully laid in the last few pieces of the note.

"I knew you were on the right track with Yvonne," Cassady said when Tricia was done.

"But the reasons might be more complicated than I thought," I warned, scanning the completed note.

"They can be downright medieval as long as you get the right person. Court-ordered psychiatrists will take care of the rest," Cassady assured me.

"So what does it say?" Tricia asked.

We all hunched over the note, pressed as closely together as possible, lab partners all trying to peer into the microscope at the same time. The note read:

Dear Teddy,

> *This has to stop. I can't allow it to continue. I have given you ample fair warning but you have persisted and left me no choice. I'm not happy about this decision, but I can't see any other answer. Forgive me. In my heart, I will always be—*

Yours, Yvonne

I walked us through it. "So she gives him this note and his answer is to tear it up and put it back in the music box with the cardkey. He wanted her to meet him here and give him one more chance."

Cassady shook her head in disagreement. "Seems like an awkward way to fire someone."

"Fire?" Tricia and I looked at each other, making sure we both found that a ridiculous interpretation.

"She's not going to fire him, she's going to break up with him," Tricia explained.

"She's going to kill him," I corrected them both.

"You think this is a death threat?" Cassady asked. "You're jumping to that conclusion because you know what happened."

"Read the note," I responded. Problem was, while Cassady read the note again and tried to imagine it coming from the killer's point of view, I read it again from the point of view of a boss forced to fire a friend and lover for embezzlement and, possibly, other infractions. It worked both ways. Then I read it a third time with Tricia's more romantic interpretation. That worked, too. Damn.

"So who's right?" Tricia asked.

"Maybe we're all right," I suggested. "They aren't mutually exclusive feelings. Maybe the combination pushed her to homicide."

Cassady hummed thoughtfully. Tricia clapped her hands quietly. "Good work, Molly."

But was it? Something about this wasn't right. There was still a piece missing. I couldn't put my finger on it.

Since I didn't respond, Tricia turned to Cassady. "Didn't she do a good job, Cassady?"

Cassady jingled the ice in her drink for applause. "A little free in her handling of evidence, but a good lawyer will be able to work around that. As long as the cops are scrupulous once she hands it over."

"Cops?" I echoed automatically, still searching to identify what was nagging me.

"You've already gone above and beyond, you don't have to arrest and try her by yourself, Molly. We have people who are paid to do that. I hear some of them are even intensely cute."

Edwards. Was I ready to talk to Edwards? It all added up in my head, but when I thought about telling him, I felt more nervous than I'd been with Garrett. It was even more important that Edwards buy my story than Garrett. So I had to nail down this extra piece first. As my mother always said, "For want of a nail, the shoe was lost."

Shoe. The ad. That was it. That was the missing part. If Yvonne suspected Teddy of financial impropriety, why wasn't she telling Brady that? Why was she giving Gretchen time to try and straighten things out? Did she really not know that he had been skimming or kicking back or whatever was going on with that ad? Was she hoping to protect Teddy out of guilt after his death? Or was Yvonne involved too and hoping that, if third parties "discovered" the problem, she could blame it all on Teddy and walk away unsullied?

"Have either of you heard of a company called Nocturne?" Tricia and Cassady shook their heads and I described the product in the ad Brady had shown me.

"What a terrific idea," Tricia sighed enviously. "Don't you hate that, when someone comes up with a cool idea that makes so much sense that you should have thought of it quite some time ago?"

"Who's behind it?" Cassady, ever the commerce maven, was already flipping through her mental Rolodex.

"I don't know."

Cassady took her little Coach leather notepad and Tiffany silver memo pen out of her purse and scribbled down the name. She asked me for the name of the ad company, too, and wrote that down. "Let me make some inquiries."

" 'Inquiries' is so much more ominous than 'phone calls,' " Tricia observed.

"Same thing, I just bill 'inquiries' at a higher rate," Cassady explained. She closed her notepad with the little flip of the wrist that she'd learned from Officer Hendryx Monday night and smiled. "This is pro bono, don't worry."

"It's about money," I said with increasing certainty. "The love affairs might be part of it, added fuel to the fire, but this is about money."

Tricia nodded. "That would explain why she didn't kill him when she caught him here with Camille."

Cassady was watching me with cool appraisal. "You need to call Edwards. You need to make him aware of what you know."

"For Helen's sake," Tricia added.

"And for her own," Cassady told her. "If she sits on this too much longer, we're getting into obstruction and all sorts of other unpleasant areas." She turned back to me. "You need to call him. Unless you really don't think you're right."

That last little bit was Cassady issuing a challenge more than giving advice. She said it because she knew it would cut through everything else and make me pick up the phone. Which I did.

Tricia nudged Cassady. "Look. She has him on speed dial."

Cassady nodded in approval. "Every single woman in Manhattan should have her shrink, her colorist, her favorite restaurant, and a police detective on speed dial."

My mouth was suddenly dry. I took a sip of my drink

and, of course, he answered the phone as I was swallowing. But as I choked, I realized it wasn't him. "Homicide, Lipscomb."

I tried to find my voice and my cool, but both were pretty shaky. "Detective Lipscomb, this is Molly Forrester. I spoke with you—"

"Yes, Ms. Forrester. What can I do for you?"

"Is Detective Edwards available?"

"I'll see." Detective Lipscomb put me on hold and I couldn't help imagining Edwards standing right next to him, the two of them counting off some male-endorsed amount of time before Lipscomb picked the phone back up and told me Edwards couldn't talk to me because he'd had time to think about how stupid he'd been to kiss me and he didn't have time for these complications and would I stop—

"Detective Edwards."

Oh. I really had thought he wasn't going to take the call. "Hi, it's Molly Forrester."

"Hello." It was neutral, but it wasn't cold. So far, so good.

"I'd like to talk to you."

"Go ahead."

"I'd prefer to do it in person."

"That may not be possible."

"You don't want to see me in person?"

"It's a matter of logistics," he said and I realized Lipscomb was probably standing right next to him, filling in my half of the conversation for himself.

"If it helps, it's about the case. Nothing else."

"What about the case?"

"I have information I think you need."

"You took something out of Reynolds' office."

"No. Well, I mean, there's more to it than that."

"Molly . . ."

"It's not Helen. I know it's not."

There was a pause and I held my breath. Cassady and Tricia leaned forward, willing their support into me. Cassady also pushed my drink back into my hand in case I needed a more concrete form of support. I pushed the drink away and held my hand out for their hands instead. Cassady and Tricia each grabbed two fingers and clung.

"Nine o'clock."

My stomach flipped for the fourteenth time that day. "Fine. Do you want me to come to the precinct?"

"No."

There was another pause and I decided to time this one. "Would you like to come to my apartment?"

"That would be good."

"Great. Do you need the address?" I asked, solely for the benefit of eavesdroppers. Tricia squirmed in her chair with delight and Cassady's grip on my fingers increased by about 100 PSI.

"That won't be necessary. Nine o'clock."

"See you then." I hung up and put the phone down on top of Yvonne's note as a paperweight. "He's coming to my place at nine."

"That is so wonderful," Tricia enthused.

"He's coming so I can tell him about Yvonne," I reminded her.

"For starters," Cassady pointed out. "Who knows where things might lead?"

13

"*Stay with me. Please*," I pleaded. I don't like pleading, but it's the only thing that works in certain situations. Not that it was working at all at the moment.

Cassady and Tricia were pushing me out of the cab, depositing me on the sidewalk in front of my building, and giggling with delight. We'd never made the transition to dinner, just started adding hors d'oeuvres to our cocktails, so here I was at 8:40, a little buzzed, a little hungry, and a little unsure of how to handle Detective Edwards when he showed up. So I was pleading with my two best friends in the entire world to please, please stay with me, and they were delighting in my apprehension.

"We'd only be in the way," Cassady insisted. "You have work to do."

"Important work," Tricia emphasized.

"You have all your evidence?"

"All I have so far."

"It's enough to get him thinking. Remember, this is what he's trained to do. Though I have no doubt he has other talents."

That struck Tricia as very funny. They were clearly not getting out of the cab. They were beaching me and sailing off. So be it. "Remember that I invited you to stay when you call me tomorrow morning begging for details."

"The kind of detail I want isn't going to happen if we stay, sweetness." Cassady closed the door, they both blew me kisses and drove off into the night.

Twenty minutes later, I was showered, changed into my most presentable Levis and lawn blouse, and fortified by a vanilla Coke and a dose of peanut butter—Jif, reduced fat but extra crunchy—eaten right off the spoon.

Ten minutes after that, I was pacing, twirling the empty spoon in my fingers, and chomping an Altoid. Edwards had my phone number and could call me if something had come up to prevent his arrival. And ten minutes late wasn't all that late. Especially for a cop, I had to imagine. Still, it was making me nervous.

But not as nervous as the sight of Edwards in my doorway at 9:18 made me. I was braced for the big blue eyes, but his cheekbones seemed to have gotten higher and sharper since the night before. For a moment, I wasn't sure I was going to be able to pull this off.

Then Detective Lipscomb stepped up. "Sorry to keep you waiting, Ms. Forrester."

"Not a problem, detectives. Please come in." I thought about kneeing Edwards in the groin as he walked by since he'd called from the lobby and just said, "It's Edwards," not "It's Edwards, and my partner and I are here."

I offered beverages, but they declined. Edwards wouldn't look me in the eye, which put me on edge. They sat in the two chairs in the living room, leaving me with the couch. I don't know if it was deliberate, but in one smooth move, they made me feel that I had not summoned them, they had come to interrogate me.

I wasn't going to let them take the upper hand. I was

going to speak first. "My boss Yvonne Hamilton killed Teddy Reynolds."

Edwards still wouldn't look at me. He picked at the corner of his notepad instead. Lipscomb looked at me with a professionally bland mini-smile. "Do you have evidence to support your statement?"

"I know Camille Sondergard told you she was having an affair with Teddy and broke it off because his wife found out." Edwards glanced up at me now, but his eyes quickly returned to his notepad. Did Lipscomb not know about our meeting at Mermaid Inn? "I spoke to Camille myself," I continued, to clarify the situation for both of us, "but I learned subsequently that the woman Camille thought was Helen Reynolds was actually Yvonne Hamilton."

Edwards' eyes came up and stayed up. Lipscomb flipped open his notebook. They were listening. I told them about all the people who could vouch for the affair, including the concierge at the St. Regis. They looked at each other. They hadn't been to the St. Regis yet, but they'd be going in the morning, I could tell.

"Is there anything else you'd like to tell us?" Lipscomb asked, pen poised.

"I think it's more than an affair gone wrong. I think both Yvonne and Teddy are tied to financial irregularities at the magazine." I gave them the highlights of the ad problem. "That's probably just the beginning. Sophie in Accounting may be in on it, too, because this only came to light when she went out on medical leave." I was thinking out loud and I needed to stop doing that because I could hear a conspiracy theory trying to work its way into things and that wouldn't help anyone.

"And in your theory," Lipscomb proceeded carefully, "what does that have to do with Ms. Hamilton killing Mr.

Reynolds?" I could feel Edwards' eyes on me, so I kept mine on Lipscomb. I couldn't get distracted and start sounding like an idiot now.

"I think the fact that he was betraying her in both business and in love was too much for her."

"Pretty potent combination," Lipscomb acknowledged.

"I know she was at her breaking point." I handed them the scraps of the note in a Ziploc baggie. "This is a note she wrote Teddy, telling him it had to end."

" 'It'?" Edwards asked quietly.

"Their relationship. I think it can be read as both their emotional and professional relationship."

Lipscomb took the bag by the very edge and held it up, looking at the pieces inside. "It can be read at all?"

"It fits back together like a jigsaw puzzle."

"Where did you get it?" Edwards asked as Lipscomb slid my bag into an evidence bag and put the whole thing in his jacket pocket.

"I found it in Yvonne's office."

"Did you take it out of the trash?"

"No, I took it out of her music box."

"Why were you looking in her music box?"

"Because you think Helen killed Teddy and I know she didn't and I was trying to find a way to prove it to you."

Lipscomb closed his notepad. That wasn't good. Edwards sighed. That wasn't good either. "I wish you had talked to us before you gathered and potentially compromised evidence by yourself," Edwards said. He looked me right in the eye for the first time since he'd come in and it still rocked me, even though I was getting irritated with him. I was also getting irritated with myself. Why was I letting this man make me crazy?

"I thought I should have something to back up my statement instead of just mouthing off like a crazy person," I said, trying to keep my voice smooth and even.

"But this is all—" Edwards began, but Lipscomb gave him a small shake of the head.

"—very interesting and we appreciate it very much. We'll be in touch." Lipscomb stood, shook my hand, and started for the door, trusting Edwards to follow him.

I followed more closely than Edwards.

"Detective Lipscomb, I know a kiss-off when I see one," I protested.

"Ms. Forrester, we truly appreciate everything you've done and said, but it's important for the integrity of the investigation that you let us take it from here. You wouldn't want to see Mr. Reynolds' killer go free because of tainted evidence, would you?"

"Of course not—"

"Thank you, Ms. Forrester. We will be in touch," he repeated carefully for the obedience impaired, and walked out.

I spun around, expecting Edwards to be right behind me. He wasn't. He was standing ten feet back, watching me with that unreadable expression of his. I glanced over my shoulder, but Lipscomb was not in sight. Was this some variation of good cop/bad cop? Lipscomb is polite but brusque and Edwards stays behind to read me the riot act?

"I'm sorry," Edwards said after a moment, catching me completely off-guard.

"About?"

"Last night."

I forced myself not to touch my lips. "I didn't object. And I certainly didn't tell anyone." Cassady and Tricia don't count.

"It was inappropriate."

Was he covering his butt or backing away? "I'm sorry you feel that way."

He walked toward me slowly and I actually felt apprehension instead of excitement. There was something in his manner, something dark I hadn't seen before. I held my ground and he walked right up to me until we were practically touching. "I just don't want you to get hurt."

Then don't hurt me, I thought, but I knew enough not to push it. He seemed to be talking about a much bigger picture, so I just said, "Thank you." We were so close I had to tilt my head back to look him in the eye. If I rose up on my toes, I could press my mouth against his. It seemed like a great idea and a horrible idea, all wrapped up together.

"When this is over, we'll do this right," he murmured, brushing the back of his hand against the back of mine. I forced myself not to quiver as his whole body brushed against mine as he passed me and walked out the door. I'd read about tantric sex and wondered if I'd just experienced tantric foreplay.

I was still trying not to quiver three hours later. I had debriefed Cassady and Tricia and I had worked my way into a bottle of Chatter Creek Syrah. I don't pretend to be a wine connoisseur because I think that's just setting yourself up, taunting your friends into giving you some obscure Virginia wine and telling you it's the latest thing from the central California coast and then sitting back and watching you make a fool of yourself talking about rose petal finishes and complex acidity and migrant labor.

And then there are all those rules about what to drink with what—red with beef, white with fish, rosé with whatever your grandmother serves because it's the only wine she buys, that sort of thing. I have yet to find a satisfactory explanation of the more important set of rules—Cabernet with a bad break-up, Pinot Grigio with nostalgia, Merlot with revenge, something like that.

In the absence of any set dictates, I decided Syrah went well with anxiety attacks and extracted the bottle of Chatter Creek from my kitchen cupboard. The name seemed appropriate, too, since I was hovering at the edge of that level of anxiety where my teeth begin to clack together.

I had channel surfed endlessly, finally watching the last twenty-five minutes of *The King and I* because I thought a good cry would help me relax, and I still couldn't unwind. That's what cable really needs. A Weeping Channel. A channel that shows nothing but the tearjerker scenes from movies so you can tune in at any time of the day or night and be bawling your head off within five minutes. It would be very therapeutic.

But even after the closing credits, I couldn't decide. Had I done the right thing? Cassady and Tricia assured me I had. Did Lipscomb and Edwards think I was a lunatic? Probably. Was I? I hoped not. And what to make of Detective Edwards? But that just made the quivering worse.

I poured the last glass of wine, wrapped up in my comforter, and tried to think of nothing but *The Lion in Winter*, which was starting next on Turner Classic. I should've been watching *Gaslight* but no one was showing it. Right about the point where Anthony Hopkins hides behind the curtains in Timothy Dalton's bedroom, I finally drifted off.

The next morning, I felt like I had gone to war with France and Spain myself. I wasn't hungover, I was wrung out. Falling asleep on the couch rarely leads to a peaceful night's sleep, but I felt like I'd slept with every muscle tensed as hard as possible. And I bet I wouldn't get a bit of toning or firming out of the whole ordeal. Where was that feeling of freedom and renewal that's supposed to come with doing the right thing?

Two bottles of water, a banana, and a Frappuccino later, I was still wrestling with that question. And arriving at the office in time to see Yvonne ushering Edwards and Lipscomb out of her office didn't help as much as one might expect.

Everyone in the bullpen was pretending not to notice the presence of homicide detectives in our midst. But there was a notable absence of tapping on keyboards or talking on telephones. Yvonne stood in the doorway of her office, shaking hands with Edwards and Lipscomb like they'd dropped by for cocktails and had to leave now because they had theater tickets. Fred spotted me across the bullpen and tried to warn me off, but Yvonne spotted me a split second later.

"And of course, if you have more questions," Yvonne announced to the entire bullpen, if not the entire floor, "Molly's the one to talk to. This has been Molly's party all along. Hasn't it, Molly?"

She wasn't in handcuffs, so who knew what they'd talked to her about and what they'd said about me. This kept getting messier instead of getting straightened out. It occurred to me to turn and walk back out, maybe walk all the way to Cape Cod and find work in a nice bookstore there, but I thought there was a chance that would be misinterpreted by the authorities. At least Edwards and Lipscomb weren't telling Yvonne they'd already talked to me plenty. "I don't think it's been anyone's idea of a party," I said, mainly because everyone seemed to be waiting for me to say something.

"Of course. The columnist makes better choices than the editor."

"That wasn't my intention, Yvonne."

The only thing worse than the whole bullpen listening to this exchange was Edwards and Lipscomb listening to it and probably committing it to memory. I didn't want them to think that I had some personal agenda fueling my suspicions of Yvonne. It was difficult for me to believe her capable of murder, not convenient.

Yvonne didn't return my last volley, so I walked over to my desk, trying to project the aura of a woman with no animosity, no guilt, no emotional traumas of any kind. Edwards and Lipscomb left, walking out through the center of the bullpen and avoiding me rather neatly. I sank into my chair in relief.

"Molly!" Yvonne screeched before my chair cushion had even finished settling. I popped back up to my feet because of a physical reaction to the pitch of her voice, not out of any instinct to please.

I walked toward her, wondering if she was going to lecture me about my bad manners in accusing her of murder. Instead, she marched back into her office, her demeanor demanding that I follow. Great. She was going to chew me out behind closed doors. I hoped there would be something left to send home to my parents.

She gestured for me to close the door behind me. I did so reluctantly, leaning against it to stay as far away from her as possible. Was I going to want witnesses?

Yvonne clearly didn't, since she sat down behind her desk and burst into tears. "This is the most awful thing I've ever been a part of."

I nodded because I didn't want to derail her and because

I didn't want to have to offer fake sympathy. What did she expect when she knifed Teddy? Maybe she hadn't thought it through sufficiently. A common fault in crimes of passion, I would imagine. Of course, this was looking like a crime of passion plus commerce now, but that didn't mean it was any better thought out. Still, I was having a hard time feeling anything but uneasy and maybe a little queasy about this emotional display.

"I hate him being gone," Yvonne continued to sob. "I miss him so. Don't you?"

"Yes." I wanted her to get to the point so I could leave.

"The police had a lot of questions . . ." she said, struggling to compose herself. I was glad to hear that they'd grilled her. Maybe that was part of all the tears. Then she continued, "About you."

"Excuse me?"

I almost fell over from shock and from the fact that I was still leaning against the door and Fred opened it from the other side without knocking.

"Tricia Vincent is here," Fred announced, oblivious to the multiple calamities occurring on our side of the door. He didn't bat an eye at Yvonne's tear-streaked face or at my gasping one. He just ushered Tricia in, deposited her, and withdrew quickly. He could probably smell the female hormones crackling in the air and was wisely taking cover.

"Good morning," Tricia said with professional calm.

"Tricia. Thank God." Yvonne snapped a tissue out of the box on her credenza, wiped her face, and hurried to embrace Tricia. I should have saved Tricia by hugging her myself, but I was still trying to recover from the revelation that Edwards and Lipscomb had asked Yvonne questions about me. Who was playing whom here?

"We're wrecks. All of us. It's good you're here," Yvonne

told Tricia. I had to refrain from pointing out that we were wrecks thanks to Yvonne and offered to take Tricia to the conference room to wait for Helen. It was a ploy on my part to get a moment alone to vent to Tricia, but the moment we stepped out of Yvonne's office, there was Helen, so that blew that.

Helen was dressed in a conservative black suit and clutching a black handbag like it was a life preserver. Her face was so completely drained of color, no doubt from weeping two days straight, that even makeup wasn't helping. I wondered if the expression "widow's weeds" came from the notion that there would be no more flowers for the woman who wore them. Helen certainly looked as though she believed that.

I didn't know if we were supposed to hug Helen, shake her hand, or say hello. Tricia hugged her, but Tricia hugs everyone, so that wasn't a good barometer. Yvonne hugged her, too, but that was a guilty conscience at work. But I went ahead and hugged her myself so I wouldn't look conspicuous in my difference. Apparently, I hadn't been giving enough thought to my own conduct in this process if Edwards and Lipscomb were asking Yvonne questions about me. Damn Edwards.

Or wait. Could this be like Yvonne's note to Teddy— its meaning depended on how you wanted to read it? Could Edwards and Lipscomb be asking questions about how people were reacting to the death, people who were friendly with Teddy, and Yvonne kept pushing them toward me, mainly to push them away from her? I clutched that theory harder than Helen clutched her handbag and vowed to take comfort in it, at least for a little while.

We trooped into the conference room—me, Tricia, Helen, Yvonne, and Gretchen. Fred half-heartedly offered to come take notes, but Gretchen said she could do that. Fred was happy to be spared.

No surprise at all, Tricia did a great job of laying out the plans for Saturday so everyone was on the same page. She had fabric swatches, photographs of flowers, sketches of how things would be set up at the church and at the reception. Tricia remarked that we had been very fortunate in that a wedding had been canceled at the Essex House and we'd been able to grab their ballroom. Tricia and Helen had decided that the reception should be at the Essex House because, Helen told us, "It was a special place for Teddy and me." She said it without irony or bitterness, which earned her major points in my book. She also said it without looking at any of us, which might have helped. How much did Helen know? Did she really want to know? Unfortunately, she was going to have to find out, but maybe the timing would work and she wouldn't have to face it until after the reception.

Helen produced a list from her handbag. "Tricia asked me to draw up a guest list for the reception."

"We drew one up, too. Friends of the magazine. Who adored Teddy. That you might not have had the pleasure to meet," Yvonne said, waving her hand at Gretchen. Gretchen pulled a list out of a file. Just eyeballing the two lists, we were looking at three hundred people easy, and two-thirds of them were coming from Yvonne and Gretchen's list.

Tricia already knew the total number, since she'd needed it to select a room, but Helen seemed to be doing the math for the first time. She made a quiet, baby-bird sound of discomfort. Tricia reacted to it immediately, placing her hand on Helen's arm. "Helen, are you all right?"

"This is larger than I had imagined," she said quietly.

"We're taking care of everything, Helen," Yvonne assured her.

It was like someone had flipped on a circuit breaker. Helen went livid before our eyes. "This isn't about money, you bitch," she spat, pinning Yvonne back in her chair with the force of her rage. "That might be a difficult concept for you to understand and that might make me feel sorry for you if I weren't so damn busy feeling sorry for myself right now. I know what matters to a woman like you, Yvonne, and it's not what matters to a woman like me. What matters to me you took away."

I was afraid to move, to breathe. Had Helen just accused Yvonne of killing Teddy? Edwards and Lipscomb shouldn't have left so soon.

"What do you mean?" Yvonne seethed.

"You took away time I could have spent with my Teddy. Time I'll never get back. Time that would have meant even more . . ." She tried to finish, but she couldn't. She was crying too hard.

Yvonne saw a moment she could play to her advantage and moved toward Helen to soothe her. But Gretchen was sitting right next to Helen and scooted up even closer, putting an arm around her shoulders before Yvonne could make her move. Helen didn't even seem to notice. But Yvonne did. She made an angry gesture for Gretchen to get away from Helen. Gretchen looked her right in the eye and ignored it.

The transference of emotion is a fascinating thing. When you can't, for whatever reason, confront the true object of your rage, you take it out on the most convenient target. The target spends a lot of time trying to figure out what he or she did wrong to set you off like a Claymore mine and then, probably, turns around and does the same thing to someone else. It starts a chain reaction and that's why they created the United Nations.

Yvonne came out of her chair like one of those spring-loaded skeletons that jumps out of the coffin as you come up someone's walk on Halloween. "Do what I tell you."

"You didn't tell me anything," Gretchen said in a voice I didn't quite recognize. There was a little frost in it.

"You know exactly what I wanted you to do. Now. Do. It."

"No."

My first instinct was to applaud. My second was to jump up and yell, "Don't push her, she's a killer." I dropped down the list to my third instinct and said, "This is a very emotional time for everyone—"

"That's no excuse for insubordination!"

The vitriol was flooding the room rapidly enough that even Helen noticed. "I don't understand—"

"How many times must I remind you? You are an assistant! You will always be an assistant!"

Gretchen looked like she'd been gut-punched, but she didn't let go of Helen. She spoke quietly but forcefully. "And you'll always be a bitch."

"Get! Out!" Yvonne shrieked.

I tried again to intervene. "Yvonne, please—"

"You!" The talon was in my face for the second day in a row. I should have bitten it. "Can go, too!"

"And you can get a grip!" I wish I could say I was emboldened by the new career path which Garrett Wilson had opened for me, but truth be told, I was just flat-out furious. "Gretchen's out of line, but the emotions are flying pretty high right now, so I think that can be excused. It's abundantly clear that this is hard for you, but I'm willing to bet it's just a little bit harder for Helen and you should lift your gaze out of your own navel and recognize that other people have the right to grieve and they certainly have the right to comfort each other."

I had the big cat cornered and I braced myself for the teeth to be bared. Yvonne was ashen: I doubt any staffer had ever talked to her this way. Except maybe Teddy and we all knew what happened to him. She sneered at me. I half-expected a growl to come out when she opened her mouth. "Being an advice columnist does not make you the perfect judge of human nature."

"But I know more than you think I know."

Alarm swept across Tricia's face before it went back to its professional calm again. She knew, or she was at least praying, that I knew better than to confront Yvonne right now, especially in front of Helen.

Yvonne took a moment to read my face. I did my best not to give anything away. She was trying to figure out what I knew. The affair? The murder? The financial mess? Wasn't she going to be surprised.

Fred leaned into the doorway, a Christian inching his way toward the lions. "Excuse me?"

"What?" Yvonne and I snapped in unison.

"I'm very sorry to interrupt but there's someone here to see you, Molly. She says it's urgent."

It actually seemed like an ideal moment to leave and regroup. I turned to Helen. "Will you excuse me?" She nodded. "Tricia, I'll be right outside." She nodded, too, a little windblown by the proceedings. I gave Gretchen a look to let her know I was sure she could handle herself and followed Fred out.

Cassady was waiting by my desk, surprisingly agitated for her. I quickened my pace, took her hand. "What's wrong?"

"That's what we're going to find out," she said with a sly grin. "I'm getting why you enjoy this whole seek-the-truth thing, even without the hot detective."

"What are you talking about?"

"Your ad agency. It's bogus."

14

Dear Molly, How do people manage to have affairs and not give themselves away? How do people learn to turn off the blush switch, cancel the stammer button, and put their conscience out to pasture? I think I could really enjoy the heightened passion, the regular sex, and the serious jewelry that come with messing around if I could just get past the notion that I would blurt out a confession the minute someone looked at me wrong. Is there somewhere I can take lessons? Signed, Lusty but Leery

"She knows, doesn't she." I was in a cab with Tricia and Cassady, my heart pounding with guilt. "Yvonne knows that we know."

"Not to diminish her pain at losing her lover—" Tricia began.

"Pain she fully deserves since she knifed him," Cassady interjected.

"But I think Yvonne is a little too self-centered to be picking up on your tension and extrapolating it to that extent," Tricia finished calmly. She then stuck her tongue out at Cassady, but in a relatively polite fashion. Tricia does just about everything in a relatively polite fashion. Which is really cool, because she gets away with a lot more than those of us with more naked emotions. Tricia can rip off someone's head, hand it back to them, and leave the room before they can say thank you.

"I don't get how she can walk around, having killed Teddy, and act like everything's going to be fine. Especially when I lie to her about why I'm leaving the office and I figure God will punish me for doing that much."

"You have a moral compass and she does not," was Cassady's assessment. "A moral compass with some deeply twisted roots, but you have one and we love you for it." I considered sticking my tongue out at her, but I knew it wouldn't come close to the delicate gesture of contempt Tricia had made it. I rolled my eyes instead.

It had nearly made me implode to wait for Tricia to finish her meeting with Helen and Yvonne after Cassady made her pronouncement, but Cassady insisted. Gretchen came out of the meeting not long after I did, went straight into Teddy's office, and closed the door. I figured if Yvonne had fired her, she'd be wailing to get everyone's attention and standing on a desk to announce her imminent departure. It was more likely she was just having a good cry; she deserved it, and I wasn't inclined to share it.

When Helen, Yvonne, and Tricia emerged some time later, they all looked somewhat depleted. Helen went right past us, headed for the sanctuary of the elevator. Yvonne slammed into her office, and Tricia practically draped herself over my desk. "Can I go home now?" she moaned.

"No, you have a funeral to plan, but first—a mission," I said, patting her hand briskly.

She sat up and every hair on her head fell into place without her having to as much as flick a lock. It's not fair. "Mission?" she said with more dread than I was expecting.

"Come on. It'll be fun," Cassady encouraged.

"More fun than mediating between Helen and Yvonne anyway," I promised.

"Ingrown pubic hairs are more fun than those two," Tricia sighed. "But we settled everything except who's going to cry more at the funeral. So I have a lot to accomplish today. How important is this mission?"

"Crucial," Cassady insisted. "Molly, go lie to your boss about where we're going and let's go."

Our cab was headed north. Cassady's little bombshell about the bogus ad agency had grown out of some research she'd done on her own and some serious flirting she'd done with Officer Hendryx. She had started off looking for documents related to Nachtmusik, pursuing the theory that Yvonne or Teddy might be involved in the agency and doing kickbacks or money laundering or some other variation on white-collar crime that could have led to murder. She was hoping to find Yvonne or Teddy on the board of directors or as an officer of the company, some tangible link.

What she found was nothing. Not just nothing connecting Yvonne or Teddy. Flat-out nothing. No business license, tax records, or articles of incorporation, no paper trail that proved such a company even existed. Just the phone number that had been in the file Brady had shown me.

That's where Officer Hendryx came in. Cassady, wearing a particularly alluring Caroline Herrera fitted jacket and skirt in pewter, no blouse, and a superb pair of scarlet Stella McCartney pumps with a heel that qualified as a deadly weapon, "dropped by" to say hello to Officer Hendryx and thank him again for being so understanding the night of Teddy's death. The poor guy never knew what hit him, and Cassady walked out with a last name and an address matching the phone number plus a dinner date for a week from Thursday.

I'd humbled myself sufficiently to ask if my name had come up in the conversation, especially in conjunction with the name of Detective Edwards. Cassady took a little more glee than necessary in telling me that neither one of us had come up at all.

The address was uptown, in Morningside Heights. Not exactly the neighborhood of choice for advertising agencies in my experience, but I was prepared to be surprised.

Tricia was prepared for the worst. At the very least. "What if this is all an elaborate cover for drug dealing or gun running or something worse? We should have brought the lovely detective with us."

Our cabbie, a bug-eyed rotundity who swore his name was really Jim Bond and refused to pinpoint his Midwestern accent for us because he was "trying to erase his past," stopped the cab suddenly. "I can't afford to be mixed up in no sort of illegal nonsense."

"Neither can we," I assured him. "We're just kidding." That didn't seem to mollify him much, but he didn't put us out on the sidewalk, either. He drove us to the address we'd given him and deposited us in front of a brow-beaten apartment building still trying to maintain some dignity despite the ravages of time.

We wanted Cervantes, Apartment 14. I pressed the buzzer for 14, debating how truthful to be when someone answered. But no one did. Wonderful.

"Are they not home or simply ignoring us?" Tricia asked.

"It's gonna be a little tough to figure that out from here," I admitted.

Cassady scooted me away from the buzzers. "You don't go to the movies often enough." Using both index fingers, she pressed Apartment 9 and Apartment 26 simultaneously. Nothing. She added her middle fingers, now buzzing four apartments at a time. Still no response. Six. Eight. No answer.

Tricia dared ask, "And this works in the movies?"

Cassady growled and drove all ten fingers against buzzers like the Phantom of the Opera attacking the organ. She leaned into it, the buzzers shrilling together. "Somebody's got to fall for it!"

The buzzers made such a racket we almost didn't hear the front door open. By the time that sound registered, the resident who was exiting had almost let the door close again behind her. She sneered at Cassady and reached as though to push the door closed, but Tricia darted past her and grabbed it.

"Thank you," Tricia smiled, manners perfect in any situation.

The resident, a woman a few years younger than the three of us, was dressed in baggy khakis, a Tori Amos T-shirt, and a heavily pilled brown cardigan. She carried an armload of books and her hair was caught up in a bun fixed with pencils. A denizen of Columbia University, no doubt. She barely acknowledged Tricia, preferring to glare at Cassady. Cassady took her hands off the buzzers and put them on her hips. "What?"

Ms. Columbia assessed our midtown dress and demeanor, then dismissed us with a shake of her head, which infuriated Cassady. "So I forgot his apartment number," Cassady hissed.

"Did you get his name?"

Ms. Columbia had no way of knowing how rare Cassady's look of surprise was, so she didn't linger to enjoy it. As she walked away, Tricia and I made supreme efforts not to laugh and gave Cassady a moment to compose herself. "Women's Studies. Graduate level. Bet you fifty bucks," Cassady huffed as she marched into the building.

We walked through the squeaky front door, down a hallway with threadbare carpet and once-green walls that smelled of fabric softener and browning onions. Apartment 14 was at the end of the corridor with a cheerful little decal of a smiling angel stuck next to the peephole. We could hear a woman's voice, speaking in rhythmic tones too low to understand through the door.

I knocked and the woman's voice didn't stop, it just moved closer to the door. The closer it got, the more we could hear it. It was difficult to reconcile the image of a woman walking to answer the door with a sultry voice saying, "Yeah, right there, baby. Oh, that's so good. Oh, yeah, yeah, yeah!" As she screamed in climax, the door opened a little.

The safety chain permitted us a glimpse of a gangly but attractive redhead in her early 20s, dressed in a Rhode Island School of Design T-shirt and low-rise jeans. Holding a paintbrush and wearing a hands-free telephone headset, she held up a finger for us to wait as she finished her phone conversation: "Oh, baby, that was fantastic. You're amazing. You call me again soon, you promise? I'll be right here waiting for you." She purred and disconnected the call, then looked us over and frowned. "You're not Jehovah's Witnesses."

"Likewise, I'm sure," I answered.

"Sorry, through the peephole you looked like you had to be selling something and that was my first guess. I figured I'd give you a little taste of what I was selling and scare you off."

"Didn't work," Cassady noted.

"Worth a shot," the painter shrugged. "What can I do for you?"

"I think there's been a mistake," Tricia began, but Cassady shushed her.

I was inclined to agree with Tricia, but I pressed on, just in case. "Ms. Cervantes? We need to talk to you about Nachtmusik."

Her lip curled like she'd just taken a swig of coffee with rancid cream. "Oh, crap," she said, leaning her forehead against the edge of the door. "You guys Charlie's Angels or what?"

"We're not law enforcement, but we can bring them into play if necessary," Cassady promised calmly.

"We're just trying to find someone, that's all," I told her.

"Yeah, I bet," she said and closed the door. I started to get frustrated, but then I heard the safety chain drop off and the door opened again before I could get too worked up. Ms. Cervantes gestured for us to come in.

It was more studio than apartment. There were canvases on easels, leaning against what little thrift shop furniture there was, and stacked against the dull lemon walls. The piece she was working on was on an easel in the middle of the room and appeared to be a naked woman wringing the neck of a swan. It was powerful and unsettling and we all stared at it in appreciation for a moment.

"I call it 'Leda's Revenge,' " the painter shrugged. "I just got out of school, I got a ways to go."

"And the phone sex?" Tricia asked politely.

"Helps pay the rent. Occasionally inspires me. Different

strokes, pardon the pun." She put her paintbrush behind her ear and I could see from the multi-hued streaks on her temple that she did it often.

If we were about to uncover a major conspiracy as Tricia suspected, we were being lulled into a false sense of comfort and being lulled well. On the other hand, there was a chance she was as nervous about us as we were about her. She took the plunge first. "So tell me why I'm going to regret ever getting involved with Nachtmusik."

"Well, Ms. Cervantes—"

"Alicia."

"Alicia, we need to contact the corporate officers of Nachtmusik and that's proving to be a little difficult," I explained.

She snorted. "Yeah, I bet. Corporate officers. They wish."

"What's your connection to Nachtmusik?" Cassady asked.

Alicia fidgeted with her paintbrush, readjusting its position behind her ear. "You aren't IRS either?"

Trying to mask her offense, Tricia smoothed her Dolce & Gabbana skirt. "Do we look like civil servants?"

"I wanna be careful," Alicia explained.

"And we appreciate we may be putting you in a difficult position. But a friend of ours who was doing business with Nachtmusik has run into some pretty serious problems," I tiptoed, "and we're just trying figure out what might have happened."

"These aren't heavy hitters, trust me," Alicia said. She seemed sincerely distressed by the notion that the company was involved in anything shady or sinister. Then a thought occurred to her. "Wait. Did they borrow money from your friend and not pay it back? That I'd believe. But they'll pay the minute they can. I swear to you."

In championing the underdog, which Gretchen had so proudly proclaimed Teddy was wont to do, had Teddy gotten in over his head—borrowing money from the wrong people or kiting or skimming? And had he been about to take Yvonne down with him, which is what homicidally provoked her?

"What exactly is your connection to Nachtmusik?" Cassady asked again.

"A phone line." Alicia pointed to a telephone and answering machine unit on a small formica table jammed into the far corner of the room. "I'm more or less their receptionist."

"Why do you take their phone calls?" I asked.

"Because even if they were a real company, they don't have enough money to rent an office. They call it 'start-up mode,' but it's more 'ain't-got-squat mode,' far as I can tell."

"Who's 'they'?"

"My cousin Will and some friends of his. They've got Big Plans, don't we all." She did a spare-me eye roll.

Cassady said, "So you answer their phone for them and then what?"

Alicia shrugged. "Not much. It hardly ever rings. Except this one magazine's been calling, all frantic about an ad they supposedly placed." The three of us refrained from looking at each other, but we all looked at the floor at the same time instead, which probably looked even more suspicious in the long run.

"What've you been telling the magazine?" I asked when I looked back up.

"That Mr. Cervantes—that would be my cousin, the dreamer—will get back to them as soon as possible. And then I call Will and tell him to take care of it, because these people are driving me nuts."

Well, at least Gretchen was doing her job and hounding them. If Mr. Cervantes wanted to hide from her, there was only so much she could do.

I took a chance. "Do you know a Teddy Reynolds by any chance?"

She shook her head. "I don't deal with anyone but Will."

"What do you get out of this?" Tricia asked.

"Dinner," Alicia admitted. "Will buys me dinner once in a while. Besides, he may be a nut, but he's my cousin. I'd want him to help me out if I had a lunatic scheme."

"What's his lunatic scheme?" I asked. "Is he trying to break into advertising?"

Alicia shook her head. "He worked for an agency when he first came to town, but said it didn't feed his soul. He says this is an interim step to something big, but he also enjoys being mysterious. And in case it turns out to be less than legal, I'd rather not know a lot of details."

"You have any reason to believe it's less than legal?" Cassady's lawyer antennae sprang up.

"Secrecy's a lot of hard work, so why put yourself through it if you don't have to," Alicia posited.

Tricia pointed to Alicia's headset. "Some people just find it more exciting."

"As I said, different strokes," Alicia shrugged.

"How can we get in touch with Will?" I asked.

"I'll call him for you," she offered a little too quickly.

"Like I don't have enough men dodging my phone calls.

You can't warn him off, I really need to talk to him, Alicia. It's very important."

Alicia looked us over carefully, weighing our sincerity as we had been weighing hers. After careful consideration, she shook her head. "I can't. I gotta have his back, you know?"

I wasn't sure what to do next, but Tricia was. "Would you like Jasmine Yamada to see your work?"

"Don't jerk me around, girl," Alicia breathed. Alicia obviously knew that Jasmine Yamada ran Galleria Mundial on West 57th and could make her career with a couple of phone calls.

"If you tell us how to reach Will, I'll get you a meeting with Jasmine next week."

"Who are you guys?" Alicia wanted to believe us, but she didn't dare.

"We look out for our friends, that's all. Want to be our friend?" I asked.

She was weakening, but she wasn't quite there. "I can't put you on his doorstep."

Tricia whipped out her cell phone, hit the speaker button and the speed dial, and held up the phone so we could all hear the conversation. The phone only rang once before a crisp voice answered, "Galleria Mundial."

"Tiffany? It's Tricia Vincent."

"Hey, Tricia! How are you?" the voice on the phone enthused. Alicia looked impressed.

"I'm great, how are you?"

"Wonderful. You looking for Jasmine?" Now Alicia looked really impressed.

"As a matter of fact, I am."

"She's in Milan until next Wednesday, but she'll be calling in."

"I can talk to her when she gets back. I think I may have a new artist she needs to meet," Tricia explained, looking into Alicia's eyes.

"Oh, she'll be so excited. She says one of these days she's going to convince you to come work with us."

"We'd have too much fun and wouldn't get anything done."

"True! I'll have her call you next week."

"Thanks, Tiffany." Tricia snapped the phone closed. Even Cassady and I were starting to look impressed at this point.

Alicia was stunned. She pulled her eyes away from Tricia and started writing a phone number down for us.

"Of course," I felt compelled to clarify, "if we don't hook up with Will, you don't hook up with Jasmine. So calling him and telling him we're on our way would be a bad idea."

I could tell it had crossed her mind and I could also tell that in a quick weighing of options, a showing at Galleria Mundial won out over a long and happy friendship with Cousin Will. Altruism is rarer than humility in this town.

Alicia gave me Will's phone number and Tricia took down her non-900 number and promised to call her as soon as we had talked to Will. We thanked Alicia and beat a hasty retreat, lest she have second thoughts.

In a cab driven by a large Jamaican woman who must have spilled a gallon of patchouli in the front seat and mopped it up with pizza slices, we headed south again. I watched Tricia slide Alicia's number into her wallet. "I gotta tell you—you're a little too good at this."

"You also gotta say thank you," Cassady prompted.

"Absolutely. Thank you."

"You're welcome."

I leaned back over to Cassady. "But this whole operator side of her—you're not surprised?"

"It's a big part of what I do all day, Molly. Just like you get people to tell you their problems, I get people to tell me what kind of deal will make them happy."

"I guess I'm not used to having a front-row seat."

Cassady nodded. "I love friends who maintain the capacity to surprise me."

"They make Molly nervous," Tricia smiled.

"I'm dealing rather well with the number of surprising things I've learned about friends this week. Aren't I?"

"Actually, you are," Cassady admitted. "I'd be drinking much more heavily than you are at this point."

"Are you suggesting we start drinking? Three-martini lunch, anyone?"

"Maybe that's what you should do. Call Will and ask him to lunch."

That was the question of the moment, how to approach Will. I didn't want to mention the magazine, not knowing where he stood on the whole non-payment question or on any other business with the magazine, Teddy, or Yvonne.

"If he's seat-of-the-pants, maybe the way to get him is to offer him a new pair of pants."

"You're going to take him shopping?" Tricia asked.

"No, just fuel his ability to shop himself," I said. I dialed Will's number on my cell and got an answering machine that simply said, "This is Will. Sorry I missed you."

"Hi, Will, my name's—" In a split-second, I realized that if I was tracking a conspiracy at my own magazine, I shouldn't give him my real name, since that could tip anyone left on the inside of the magazine that I was closing in. I looked at Cassady and said, "Cassie." She grimaced, but it was done. I continued spinning my tale to Will's answering maching. "I'm a friend of your cousin Alicia and I'm hugely jammed up and hoped you might be able to help me. I've got this ad that has to be done and fast, but good, and I will pay you *beaucoup* bucks if you can save me. Call me ASAP." I left my cell phone number and hung up.

Cassady shot Tricia another look. "Talk about front-row seats."

"It's not lying, it's creativity," I insisted.

"Careful, next thing you know, you'll be a lawyer," Cassady warned.

"So what do we do now, while we're waiting for Will to call back?" Tricia asked.

"We could go thank Officer Hendryx again so Molly could run into Detective Edwards."

"No, thank you. I don't think daily doses of Detective Edwards are all that healthy."

"I feel sorry for the poor guy," Tricia offered.

"The poor guy? How does he get to suspect me of murder and come off as 'the poor guy'?"

"You're not thinking it through. He's torn between desire and duty, trying to do his job but completely distracted by you. It muddies his thinking."

"Tricia, this is me and Edwards, not *The Four Feathers*."

"Why do they keep remaking that movie? It gets worse every time," Cassady opined. "There should be a law controlling what movies can be remade and how many remakes will be allowed per century. I mean, really. *Psycho*. What was Gus Van Sant thinking?"

"You're the intellectual properties lawyer. Write one," I suggested.

Tricia squinted at us both. "Are we done discussing Detective Edwards already?"

"I am," I said.

"Cassady?"

"Tricia, I can hear her grinding her teeth from here. I think she needs some time away from him. Absence makes the heart all hot and bothered, right?"

"Then let's go shopping."

Cassady nodded. "I cleared my calendar."

I hesitated, feeling a traitor to my gender, but also wondering if I should be back in the office, picking up what intelligence I could there.

Cassady repeated. "I cleared my calendar."

"Thank you," I acknowledged, "I just think—"

"You don't want to go back to the office. You can't talk to Will there. You'll only draw Yvonne's ire and Gretchen will want to sit next to your desk and weep all afternoon and Peter will call to see how you're doing and you'll have to talk to him as well."

"Peter," I groaned guiltily. I still hadn't dealt with him.

"Later," Tricia assured me.

Cassady didn't acknowledge either interruption. "That's why you're going to come with us and help me with a few loose ends for the reception and also make sure Cassady has something to wear that won't cause cardiac arrests at the church." Tricia looked me in the eye and dared me to argue.

It is hard to argue with a well-thought-out plan. Especially because she was right. I didn't want to go back to the office unless it was absolutely necessary. I could check on Gretchen's progress on Nachtmusik at the end of the day, but I was pretty sure she wasn't going to get anywhere. Higher-priced heads than hers were behind this mess. And the more distance between Yvonne and me, the better. No question there.

So I signed on. "Sounds great."

And it was great. Spending time with Cassady and Tricia is like going to a spa for the soul. I feel better, happier, smarter after I've been with them. We alternated between items on Tricia's to-do list and looking for an outfit for Cassady—and whenever possible, looking at shoes for all three of us.

We were down at Balenciaga which is like shopping on the holo-deck of the Enterprise with its shifting light and surreal mix of store and art gallery. I'm always a little intimidated there, but Cassady insisted. She was trying on this amazing pair of ankle boots with great tucks in the leather and stunning heels. I actually found myself trying to imagine those shoe jewels from the ad on Cassady's shoes. They'd work. It was a cool idea. I hoped the company making them wasn't involved in this whole Teddy mess.

My cell rang. I answered it quickly, automatically, not stopping to think who it might be. "Hello?"

"Cassie?"

I almost told him he had the wrong number, then I realized who it had to be. "Yes?"

"This is Will Cervantes at Nachtmusik. You called?"

Yes! "Will, thanks for getting back to me so quickly."

Cassady stood up so fast that she almost impaled the salesman's hand with her heel. Tricia hurried back from where she'd been eyeing a pair of slingbacks. Cassady mouthed, "I'll take them" to the salesman, just to make him go away, and she and Tricia crowded next to me to hear the conversation.

"I'm not really sure I can help you," he began.

"Money's not an object."

There was a significant pause. "What's your timetable?"

"Sooner than later. Maybe we could meet, go over the particulars face to face. I know it's so last century, but I hate doing business on the phone."

"I'm a little jammed up myself," he parried. If he was involved in Teddy's death somehow, of course he was jammed up. But I had to convince him that it was worth taking the time to meet me.

"Help me out here and I can promise you a pretty steady stream of work," I lied. I don't like toying with people's dreams, but I was kind of in a hurry.

"I have some commitments this afternoon," he said. "It would have to be tomorrow."

I didn't want to wait, but I didn't want to press too hard and scare him away either. "No way you can do it today?"

"No. I've got other deadlines."

He had no idea how intriguing I found his choice of words. I paused so he could think I was agonizing before I answered. "Then I guess it'll have to be tomorrow. Where and when?"

"Two thirty? We're right off West 14th, down in the meatpacking district. Above Vinnie's Grill."

Somebody lucky enough to snag a miserable walkup in a rundown neighborhood that then exploded into the "new SoHo." There might be more to this guy than Alicia had let on. "Thanks. See you then."

I hung up quickly so he wouldn't have time to reconsider.

"I'm going with you," Cassady announced as she paid for the ankle boots.

"I'll arrange to be there, too," Tricia added.

"You can't both keep skipping work for me. I'll be fine."

"Don't argue. It gives you crow's feet," Tricia warned.

So I gave in and we continued with our errands, with

me concentrating on not thinking about anything but shopping. It worked in five- to ten-minute stretches and I thought that was pretty good.

We had blown through the afternoon and Tricia's to-do list and were contemplating cocktails when my cell rang again. It hadn't rung at all since Will's call, mainly because Tricia and Cassady were with me and didn't need to call me, and the magazine was apparently able to limp along in my absence. I wondered if it might be Will again and I didn't want to answer it in case he had reconsidered, but then I remembered I do have other friends and a life outside of all this weirdness and it might actually be a call about something else.

I said hello and heard nothing but static. What I thought was static, anyway. I said hello again and realized it wasn't static, it was hoarse, ragged sobbing. "Who is this?" I glanced at the display pad on my phone, but I didn't recognize the number. "Who is this?" I repeated, not sure if I should be worried about someone I knew or annoyed by a crank call.

"Molly . . ." the weeper finally said. "Oh God, Molly . . ."

"Who is this?" I repeated, willing the person on the other end of the phone to pull it together and answer me.

"Gretchen . . ."

I should have known. I should have recognized the sobbing, given all I had heard in the last couple of days, but this had a raw quality to it that was new. "Gretchen, I need you to take a deep breath and tell me what's wrong."

"You better . . . come . . ."

"Gretchen, did Yvonne fire you?" A fresh wail keened out of the phone and I jerked the phone away from my ear for a moment. "Gretchen, what the hell is going on?"

"Yvonne's dead."

15

I don't like déjà vu. Probably because in my line of work, you go to all sorts of extremes not to repeat yourself, so that little glitch feeling of having done or said all this before isn't a pleasant one.

Yet here I was Friday morning, standing before the assembled staff of the magazine and talking about untimely passings and service times to be announced and how awful it all was. Somehow it had fallen to me to find the words to explain something that made no sense, even to me. Why was Yvonne dead? How far did this mess go?

Tricia, Cassady, and I had rushed to the hospital as soon as I hung up with Gretchen. I didn't want to get into the whole story on the phone, I wanted to talk to Gretchen face-to-face.

It was a pretty banged-up face. Gretchen was sitting on a gurney in the St. Vincent's ER, holding an ice bag to the back of her head, a bruise blossoming on her right cheek, her lip split, her eyes swollen from crying. She started hyperventilating when she spotted the three of us doing a strength-in-numbers approach on a nurse who asked us to please wait outside. Finally, Cassady identified herself as a lawyer and us as her associates and the nurse gave up and let us pass.

"What the hell happened?" I asked. The whole cab ride over I'd been trying to line everything up. If Yvonne had killed Teddy, then who had killed Yvonne? How deep did this go, how big was it that it warranted two murders? As if anything warranted two murders.

"She needed a new outfit for Teddy's funeral," Gretchen sobbed.

"You went shopping?" My voice almost squeaked with disbelief. Sure, I had recently succumbed to Gretchen's tears and gone out with her, but Yvonne, rest her soul, was made of stronger stuff than I. No way waterworks and wheedling had moved her.

Gretchen's lip curled, either in scorn or from the sheer power of her sniffing. "I didn't say that. She needed to go out and that meant someone had to come along and carry her bags and juggle her cell phone and wineglass and zip her up in the back."

"Fred bailed?"

"He said he couldn't participate in anything that might involve Yvonne being naked."

"Understandable," Tricia murmured.

"So she picked you?" I asked, trying to make it sound inquisitive and not mean.

"I'm an assistant, remember? Never, ever more than an assistant. What better way to rub my face in it?" Gretchen's nostrils flared in indignation, but that made her nose start running again, so she went back to sniffing. Tricia mercifully produced tissues from her handbag and gave them to Gretchen.

"So you felt you had to go," Cassady prompted.

Gretchen nodded. "She wanted to take the Jag and come to Chelsea."

"Her Jag? Why not a cab?" I asked. Driving didn't seem practical, but that's coming from someone who believes parking prices in Manhattan are a conspiracy to bankrupt the American people. The only thing worse than being extorted for a daily parking space is being extorted for a daily parking space and then leaving it during the day to be extorted for a short-term space somewhere else.

Gretchen shrugged. Her mouth jerked like she was try-ing to force a smile, but it didn't come off. "At least I got a chance to ride in it." It was a classic XKE, an automotive work of art. Yvonne drove it to attract men, but it was still a beautiful car. "So she pulls onto this little side street, says she knows a great lot, and these guys come out of nowhere . . ." Gretchen gestured, indicating that the guys had walked in front of them, as her sobs increased in speed and volume.

"I know this is hard, honey," I coaxed, selfishly wanting her to finish.

"Yvonne slammed on the brakes to keep from hitting them. They started yelling, she started yelling, one of them banged on the hood which really freaked her out. Then all of a sudden, the other one—really big guy—rips open Yvonne's door. I tried to help her, but the other guy opened my door."

"He waited until you were distracted," I offered, hoping it sounded comforting rather than patronizing.

"Of course," Cassady prodded, leading me to believe it hadn't sounded comforting at all.

I opened my mouth to offer a defense of myself this time, but Tricia gave us both a silencing look. "I'm listening," Tricia said, taking Gretchen's hand. "What happened then?" To me, Tricia was employing the same even tone she'd use to coax a client torn between gazpacho and consommé. But such was her charm that Gretchen squeezed her hands and continued without acknowledging our interruption.

"I smacked my head on the pavement. I pretended they knocked me out 'cause I thought they might think I was hurt worse and freak and run. But Yvonne wouldn't get out of the car."

"She fought them?" I interrupted again, absurdly thinking of an article we'd run only two issues before about safety basics for women in the city. "Give them the car" was pretty high on the list, but I guess "Don't think you're invincible" should have been even higher.

"She called them all kinds of names and she wouldn't get out of the car. I was just sitting up to tell her not to argue . . ." She clamped her free hand over her eyes, willing the memory away, but it didn't work. "The big guy shot her," she finished in a whisper.

Tricia gently hugged her. "I'm so sorry."

I felt numb. My brain didn't want to move forward. Was this connected to Teddy's death? It had to be. It was just too weird to think that this might have happened independently, some cosmic justice stepping in because we weren't going to figure it out for ourselves.

Gretchen had already talked to the police at the scene, so we just had to wait for the doctors to release her. The main concern was a concussion, but Gretchen swore she'd go home and take it easy and her roommate would keep an eye on her, so the ER doctor let her sign herself out.

Tricia wanted to escort Gretchen home, but Gretchen insisted that she just wanted to be alone for a while. So we put her in a cab, then hailed one for ourselves and went out for a morose round of cocktails. None of us was very enthusiastic about dinner, so we split up early and went home. I soaked in the bathtub so long that I had to add new hot water twice, but I still couldn't figure it out. Loan sharks? Drug dealers? Nothing made any sense. But violent death doesn't make any sense, so maybe that was the whole problem right there.

The next morning, I went in early. I had to tell Fred and then I had to send him home, he was so freaked out. Gretchen came in with a little makeup on her bruises and an air of crushed optimism that was palpable. She'd told people bits and pieces of what had happened by the time I called everyone together, but there were still gasps throughout my little talk as the staff tried to grapple with this double-whammy.

A double-whammy that explained the appearance of my dear Detective Edwards and Detective Lipscomb as I wrapped up my rambling comments. Gretchen glanced at the approaching detectives in alarm, but I told her not to worry about it.

"Ms. Forrester," Detective Edwards said, in greeting or in warning, I couldn't be sure.

"Detectives," I responded. "I'm sorry to be seeing you again so soon."

"We know this is a difficult time for all of you here at the magazine, but we have some questions," Detective Lipscomb said in precise understatement.

"I can imagine. Let me make sure the conference room's open."

"That's okay," Detective Edwards said. "We'd rather do this at our office."

"I don't know that Gretchen's up to that at the moment."

"We don't need to talk to Gretchen. She gave a statement yesterday."

Gretchen took her exit cue and walked quickly back to her desk. Even though I'd been immersed in it for the last three and a half days, I was still new to this whole homicide deal and it took me a minute to understand what he was saying. When I did understand, I didn't want to believe it. "You've got to be kidding," I said, trying to keep my voice quiet and light.

"That's usually a waste of time," Edwards replied.

"You don't want to talk to the whole staff?" I offered, giving them an elegant out.

"Not at this point."

Not only was he serious, he was going to make me say it. I glared at him with every ounce of strength I could muster. Oh, to be that Cyclops guy from *X-Men* right about now. "You want to talk to me at the precinct."

"If you could make yourself available, we'd really appreciate it," Detective Lipscomb said, trying to keep things polite.

"And if I can't?" I asked, a little shrill but not without cause.

"We'll have to insist," Detective Edwards said. At least he was having difficulty looking me in the eye for any length of time. I'd take that small satisfaction for the moment.

"This is so bogus," I said, grabbing my purse and jacket.

Driving to the precinct with them was definitely a different experience from driving to Helen's with them on Monday night. I sat in the back seat alone, not wanting anyone to see me. The detectives were content to let me stew in silence, so I hunkered down and tried to lay in the new pieces of the puzzle.

Teddy was dead and my interest in that was perceived as too keen. Now Yvonne was dead and the only link between the two anyone could come up with was me? What is it they say about no good deed going unpunished? But this wasn't about me. It was about Teddy and Yvonne and missing money and affairs and God knows what else. How was I going to get them to see that?

The detectives walked me through their dreary, government-issue bullpen, strangely devoid of all those saucy prostitutes who are always leaning against the desks in TV shows. We threaded our way between battered metal desks and backbreaking chairs until we reached an interrogation room. We entered and Detective Edwards closed the door behind him. I could have sworn I heard the hiss of the room being hermetically sealed.

In this brave new world of ours, preemptive seems to be the way to go. I sat down at their ugly metal table. "I can't tell you anything," I said to open.

"Can't or won't?" Detective Lipscomb clarified.

"Can't. I don't know anything you don't already know. This is an exercise on someone's behalf."

"Tell me about your relationship with Yvonne Hamilton," Detective Edwards said quietly, sitting down across the table from me. He scooted the chair in a bit closer and it grated horribly, nails on a blackboard. I bet they practice that one.

"I'm sorry, but you must be joking. It's bad enough that you had your doubts about me with Teddy. I can almost forgive that since I found the body and was a little too eager to help. I understand all that now. Believe me, this has not been an easy week for anyone at the magazine and since I'm inclined to take things to heart, it's been pretty miserable for me."

"Take things to heart? That mean you hold grudges?" Detective Lipscomb followed up.

"Wow, that was nice. I didn't see that coming. Point to Detective Lipscomb," I said with a fake smile, then dropped it. "No, it doesn't mean I hold grudges. It means I don't feel emotionally capable of handling the death of two colleagues in the space of one week."

"How do you suppose that happened?" Detective Edwards asked. Here, he was more willing to look me in the eye. Home court advantage.

Something about being unjustly accused turns me back into a mouthy fifteen-year-old. "I'm sure if I'd paid more attention in math class, I could give you a formula for why two random events occurred in circumstances that make them look less than random. But I'm sure I was drawing on my blue jeans when that was discussed."

"You think these two deaths are unrelated?"

No, I didn't think that but I didn't want to offer a theory that was only going to get me into more trouble until I had something to back it up with. Better than what I had provided so far, apparently. My silence provoked a glance exchange between the detectives and that provoked a response from me. "No, they could be related since both Teddy and Yvonne worked for the magazine and they were having an affair. But then we're talking about hit men, aren't we?" Were they making me say all that for someone on the other side of the mirror? Otherwise, I felt stupid telling them what they already knew. I also felt sad it made it look bad for Helen again. But then, was Helen sitting in the interrogation room? No, thank you very much.

"Are we?" was all Detective Edwards offered.

That was what I'd sat up most of the night trying to figure out. If Yvonne had killed Teddy, who had killed Yvonne? Had Helen hired someone out of rage and revenge? Or was this whole phantom ad agency thing the tip of some huge financial iceberg where Powers That Be had told Yvonne to kill Teddy and then had killed her to clean up? I'd know a lot more if I got to keep my appointment with Will at two thirty. They wouldn't keep me that long, would they?

"How did you feel about the affair?" Detective Edwards asked.

"I didn't know about it until after Teddy died. They didn't let it affect anything at work," unless their financial shenanigans were undermining the fiscal health of the magazine. Man, I hoped not.

"Yvonne told us you didn't like her very much," Detective Edwards continued. Detective Lipscomb had dropped back, leaning against the wall, letting Edwards drive.

"She wasn't very likable. Not to speak ill of the dead."

"Were you jealous of her?"

I surprised myself by laughing. "Is that what she told you?" I suspected he was pushing my buttons and I was going to do everything in my power to stay unpushable.

"Was the way you spoke to each other yesterday morning typical of your relationship?"

"Do you know anything about women?" I asked, not caring who was listening. "If you think that little spat was significant, the women in your life are on Prozac. Maybe with good cause."

"No need to get personal," he said with a hint of warning.

Maybe I was the one pushing buttons now. "Why not?

This has been personal since the get-go. I have a dead co-worker, I try to help, I have another dead co-worker, I don't even get a chance to help, and you insist on reading all sorts of dark, ulterior motives into that. Do I look like I know hit men? This job's gotta be a breeding ground for cynics, but I'd think it also forces you to develop a sixth sense about people and yours has to be completely out of whack if you think for one damn minute that I'm capable of killing anyone."

Detective Edwards was at a loss and I savored the moment. I was so angry at him, I knew it wasn't just what he was saying, it was that I wanted to believe that he felt something for me that would make him dismiss any doubts that were raised by Yvonne's sniping or anything else. Sure, he had to do his job, but he had to respect me, too. Or I was the biggest fool on Manhattan since the Indians sold it.

I opened my mouth, prepared to dig myself in deeper, but the door banged open and Cassady strode in, wearing her brand-new Balenciagas and prepared for battle. I was tempted to push up her sleeves and look for the Wonder Woman bracelets. "You're not talking to them? Haven't I taught you anything?" she growled at me.

"You remember Cassady Lynch? She wasn't my lawyer then, but she is now."

The detectives nodded in acknowledgment.

"Are you charging her with something?" Cassady asked.

"We're just talking," Detective Edwards attempted.

Cassady gave him a withering look that made it clear to all that she knew everything that had occurred between Detective Edwards and me since the moment we met. "How nice you have time to just talk. Ms. Forrester and

I, on the other hand, both have jobs to do. If you'll excuse us, we'll go do them."

Tight-lipped, Detectives Edwards and Lipscomb dismissed us and Cassady marched me through the bullpen and hallways on a single-minded path to the front door. "Nothing. They have nothing. You have an alibi, for God's sake."

"Yeah, but it's you and Tricia."

"Don't you dare start sympathizing with them. They're grabbing at straws and you're an idiot if you allow yourself to be treated that way."

"Thanks so much."

" 'Idiot' is a legal term for a client who doesn't stick up for him- or herself."

"Look at all the fun things you lawyers know. How did you know I was here?"

"I called to see if you wanted to have lunch, thank God. You should've called me."

"I didn't want them to think that I thought I needed a lawyer."

Cassady stopped in a relatively quiet corner by the front door and dropped her voice to an earnest whisper. "I don't like this anymore, Molly. I don't like that you're nosing around in something that's gotten two people killed and has the police looking at you—"

"Excuse me?"

"I know you didn't do anything, idiot, but getting dragged into this and sullied by association could be a major pain in the ass and really screw your life up for a while."

I thought of Garrett Wilson and his impeccable office, his stunning assistant, all that perfection, and nodded. "So what do I do now?"

"Drop it."

"I can't."

Cassady started to protest, but she's known me too long. "I know," she sighed and guided me out the front door.

There's an acrid quality to the air of a police station; probably all those years of flopsweat and anguish get into the wallboard and don't come clean. It was a relief to be out in the noise and dirt and stink. I give Gershwin a lot of credit for listening to the city and coming up with *Rhapsody in Blue*. Maybe New York was quieter in those days, but it's still a pretty magical transformation. I tried to hum it to calm myself as Cassady and I hurried down the steps, but then a cab stopped in front of us, its rider got out, and I choked.

Peter came rushing over as though I needed mouth-to-mouth. Yeah, that was going to happen. I only coughed for a moment, long enough to embarrass myself, not endanger myself. "Molly. I came as soon as I heard."

I wanted to ask "Why?" but what came out was "Heard?"

"A friend was down here, saw you come in with detectives, thought I'd want to know."

I wanted to ask why again, but on second thought, I didn't want to get into that discussion. I was exhausting myself trying to look at most of the people I knew on at least two different levels—that facets concept that had seemed so intriguing and entertaining when I was pitching it to Garrett Wilson—and at the moment, I had neither the strength nor the patience to add Peter to that list.

"Anything I can do?"

"It was just an interview, Peter. They're not carting her away," Cassady interceded.

"You here as a friend or a lawyer?"

"You here as a friend or a writer?" she zinged back. God, I love my friends. I could've hugged her, but that really would have confused Peter.

Peter played the hurt card, ignoring Cassady. "I came because I was worried about you, Molly. The last time I saw you, a police detective needed to talk to you. And now—"

"Same detective, different body," I explained. "You heard about Yvonne?"

"I'm very sorry," he nodded. I was sure it was the talk of every other magazine staff in the city. What the hell are they into over there?, stuff like that. And more than a few people shaking their heads mournfully, then making sure their resumes were up to date and ready to mail. "What can I do?"

"Nothing."

"How about I take you home?"

"How about you take no for an answer?" Cassady snapped. Wouldn't that be a sight—Cassady taking Peter apart on the precinct steps. She'd win, no question.

"No one has to take me home or do anything for me," I mediated. "I'm going back to work. I have things to do, promises to keep, all that nonsense." I avoided looking at Cassady because she knew I was talking about keeping my meeting with Will and she still didn't approve. I looked at Peter instead and tried to make it a look of sincerity.

"How about dinner?"

"I don't know, Peter." Meaning I didn't know when I'd have the energy to give him an appropriate kiss-off, but it wasn't going to be tonight.

"I really am worried about you." He chose not to look at Cassady either, probably as leery of her reaction as I was.

"Thanks. I'll call you."

His pride kept him from pushing any further. He put his hands up in a gesture of surrender and backed away. "Okay. Talk to you later." He hurried up the precinct steps. So had he come to check on me and was going in to check on my story or was the whole thing a song-and-dance? I felt dizzy.

"I've just about had it with men today," I told Cassady as we hailed a cab.

"Learn to live with them. I tried to give them up once and the withdrawal symptoms are pretty ugly. Cats, vibrators, sensible shoes . . ." She mock-shuddered and a cab stopped. Small wonder. A twitch from Cassady can stop traffic.

She dropped me at my office and pledged to be back for me at two o'clock since there was no way I was going to Will's alone, especially now. With Yvonne gone.

I couldn't believe Yvonne was dead. I was glad that I didn't have to see her body, since the image of Teddy's body was going to be with me for the rest of my life, but it did make her death a little more abstract. All along, it had been weird enough to contemplate that something had gone down that was worth one person being killed. Now there were two. This was unreal. Surreal. Screwed up.

My feet got me back up to the office without my brain having to participate in the process, thankfully. I half-expected to find a sign in the elevator that the eleventh floor had been quarantined due to contagious murder and the elevator would no longer stop there.

But it did stop and my feet took me to my desk where yet another delight awaited me. Conversation stopped as I entered the bullpen. Cassady stops traffic, but I stop talk. Only because when last seen, I'd been carted away by homicide detectives, but it was nice to have an impact. For about ten seconds. Then it creeped me out. Kendall and Gretchen were watching me like they had to hold each other back from rushing to me and inundating me with compassion. Wouldn't that be fun.

"Thank you all for your concern," I said to the bullpen at large. "It's nice to be back."

I plopped down at my desk. I should immerse myself in my job, right? Isn't that what the Puritan work ethic demanded? Work hard and everything else will be all right. How many stress-related heart attacks does that explain?

I'd immersed myself all the way up to the first knuckle on my big toe by powering up my computer when Gretchen and Kendall descended. "Do you need anything?" Kendall asked, sounding more like a hospice nurse than an assistant.

"A husband, children, big house in Connecticut, and a job on the *Times*," I suggested. "I can take care of the rest."

Apparently, it came out more snarky than I'd intended because Kendall burst into tears. I would've felt bad if Gretchen had cried, but I was also pretty used to that by now. But Kendall in tears was alarming. I had never seen her express emotion of any kind and to see her blubbering because I'd mouthed off was just the extra helping of guilt that I needed right now.

"Kendall, I'm sorry. This is no time to joke, is it," I said, getting up and easing her into my chair. Kendall put her head down on the desk and I awkwardly patted her heaving shoulders. Gretchen stood next to me, staring into space just past Kendall.

"How you holding up?" I asked, hoping I wouldn't send her over the edge, too.

Gretchen shrugged but it took an effort to raise her shoulders that high. "Pretty unbelievable."

"Yeah. You really should go home."

"I can't. I'm afraid to be alone." My heart broke for her. I was haunted enough by the image of Teddy's dead body, but I found him dead. She'd seen Yvonne die. I couldn't imagine.

All the department heads had met with The Publisher to figure out what to do and emerged with the edict that we should go ahead with Teddy's service on Saturday and a separate one would be planned for Yvonne after The Publisher had a chance to talk to her family. I hadn't even thought about her service. No one asked me to get involved with Yvonne's and I was happy to lie low and escape notice.

Once Kendall got her crying under control, I apologized again and persuaded her to take Gretchen downstairs and have a cappuccino on me. I also whispered to Kendall that she needed to convince Gretchen to go home. I sat back down at my desk and tried to focus on the latest letters to arrive, but it was hard to concentrate. I doodled diagrams on a legal pad with lots of arrows pointing back and forth between Teddy and Yvonne and money launderers or cocaine kings or evil geniuses bent on world domination. It wound up looking like bad art, but not like a solution. With any luck, that would come from meeting Will.

16

"I don't like the fact that we're going to a neighborhood where so much blood has been spilled," Tricia said in the cab. She was working her thumbs back and forth on the handle of her Miu Miu crocodile handbag like she was praying a rosary.

"First of all, it's bovine blood. Secondly, find me a blood-free neighborhood on this island," Cassady challenged.

"It's just so . . . fresh in MePa," Tricia replied, gazing out the window. She had called me twice the night before to ask me not to go see Will. Since I was soaking in the tub, I let the machine pick up. By the time I got out, there was a third message from her, saying that she understood why we still had to go and she hoped her understanding wasn't her undoing.

I have to agree with her to a certain extent. The fact that the slaughterhouse district is the new cool place in town is a little unnerving, on an aesthetic and symbolic level if nothing else. I've had friends explain it in terms of the dynamic forces of a limited real estate market, but it's still odd.

The cab let us off in front of a scruffy neighborhood

bar and grill with an exhausted awning that read VINNIE'S GRILL. Next to the grill's entrance, a deeply battered door—with no buzzer installed yet, much to Cassady's relief—led us to a narrow staircase that took us up to Will's place.

There was a doorbell barely discernible under three or four generations of paint. I leaned into it, unsure it had worked until I heard footsteps approaching and deadbolts turning.

Will peeked out around the safety chain. "Cassie?"

I resisted the urge to look over my shoulder at Cassady and said, "Yes."

Will opened the door to admit us. Walls had been knocked down to create more of a loft space but the light was awful. Nobody painted in here. Not even their walls, which looked like cheap wallpaper had been stripped off and discarded, but further redecorating had been delayed. Cleaning had been going on, though. The whole place smelled of bleach.

Despite the bad light, the far corner of the room had been draped and lit as a basic backdrop for photography. I wondered if Will had taken the picture for the ad himself. The camera equipment looked pretty expensive. No wonder he had no decorating budget.

There was another work area in the other corner of the room, a couple of tables covered with large soft cloths with tools and cardboard boxes resting on them. I wanted to go take a peek, but knew I had to choose my moment.

"These are my associates," I said, groping for cover names, "Marcia and Cindy."

"So shouldn't you be Jan?" Will asked with a sly smile. I was so busy scoping out the room, I hadn't taken a good look at him until now. He looked to be in his late 20s, tall, muscular, his wavy hair more auburn and less red than Alicia's, with compelling brown eyes. But with all the practice I'd had ignoring Edwards' eyes, I was ready for Will's.

"Oh, she is, believe me," Cassady answered.

"We get that a lot," Tricia pitched in.

Will shifted nervously from foot to foot. "So how can I help you? You didn't say much on the phone and I haven't been able to get a hold of Alicia to ask her."

Good girl, Alicia, thank you. "We're designing a new line of scarves and we need a really splashy ad to help us launch the company."

"You're just starting out?"

I nodded, figuring if I could mold our "story" along the lines of what Gretchen had told me about the shoe jewelry people, I might appeal to the same instincts that had gotten him to work with them while he was doing whatever he was doing with Teddy and Yvonne and parties yet to be uncovered.

He nodded back. "I know how tough that can be. I'm in a similar situation myself."

"Maybe you have some tips on lining up capital that you'd like to share," Cassady suggested.

Will turned to her suddenly. He didn't seem to like that idea at all, but he quickly covered his reaction with a laugh. "I was about to ask you the same thing."

"Such a pain when you have to be the creative one and raise the money, too," I said, and he turned back to me with a nod. The three of us were slowly dispersing across the room and it seemed to bother Will that he couldn't watch all of us at once. He was a man with something hidden. Or, perhaps, something he wished was better hidden than it was.

"So we were looking for something simple but dramatic. Maybe a great picture of one of our scarves . . ." I gestured grandly, my hands moving through the air like a scarf floating to the ground. I should have picked something more dynamic than a scarf.

Will nodded, wheels turning, getting into the idea. "Where are you placing the ad?"

"We're aiming for like *Marie Claire, Zeitgeist*, we'd so love to get into *Vogue*," I said, pretending not to notice the way he perked up when I said *Zeitgeist*. Tricia and Cassady drifted through the room behind him. He kept glancing at Cassady, surprise, surprise. Using only an eyebrow, I pointed Tricia toward the worktables. I'm not sure what I was hoping she'd find, but the simple fact that the tables were covered up was intriguing. Tricia understood what my eyebrow was trying to say and drifted that way.

Will glanced back to me. "That's serious cash."

"Yeah, we're going to have to choose one, go with a single insertion."

"Even then."

"We're hoping someone will give us a break."

He nodded briskly. "You know anyone at any of those magazines?"

"Don't I wish. Do you?" I put an eager spin on it, trying to build a bridge between our supposedly common plights. It's the easiest way to get people to confide in you, that recognition of a kindred spirit.

He paused a little too long before saying, "Kind of a friend of a friend deal maybe, but nothing we've been able to make work yet." He was hiding something, I just had to figure out what.

"Really? Where?"

Connections are currency in New York. Just look at Tricia and Jasmine. Most people look for an opportunity to brag about whom they know at cool places like magazines, galleries, publishing houses. The fact that Will was again hesitant to speak made me gleeful. Now, if only what he was hiding was something I needed to know and I could find a way to pry it out of him . . .

"*Zeitgeist*," he admitted.

Oh. My. God. "Really? Who?" I asked with a fake smile. Please, God, let him be our missing piece of the puzzle.

He backtracked instantly. "Like I said, a friend of a friend, I mean, I know some of the people on the ad staff, but I'm not in tight enough to help you—"

"Oh, no, no, I'm not asking you to." Brady? One of the account managers? Or had he known Teddy and he was being smart enough not to refer to him in the past tense?

"These are beautiful," Tricia enthused from the far corner. Will whipped around to see Tricia holding up a heel jewel like the one I'd seen in Will's ad. She'd pulled back the cloths to reveal a jeweler's workbench with a number of heel jewels in various stages of completion. "What are they?"

Will hurried over and gently but emphatically removed the piece from her hand. "It's shoe jewelry. You slide this up the heel and change the whole look and feel of your shoes. The way you might change earrings after work, you slide these on and office pumps become nightclub shoes."

"Is this one of your clients?" Cassady asked.

Again, Will debated his answer first. "I actually have an interest in the company."

"It's such a fun idea. Are they in stores? Where can I get some?" Tricia enthused.

"We're trying to get them in some boutiques, but we wanted to start web-based because of capital but the website's still under construction and we haven't placed the ad.

Yet." A dark thought crossed his face and he pulled the covers back over the work. "We've hit some funding snags."

Which is why the ad that he'd essentially made for himself wasn't paid for. But how did that tie in to Teddy and Yvonne? If one of them was his connection at the magazine, what else had gone wrong that they wound up dead?

"Have you shown these to your magazine connections, the friend of a friend at *Zeitgeist*?"

That was that. I pushed too far. Will went to a dark place and it didn't look like he was going to come back any time soon. "I think you should leave."

"But we haven't talked about our ad—"

"I'll call you."

"But we've got a deadline and you said you did, too."

Will gave us all a quick and scathing once-over. "I've got problems of my own and I really can't afford to spend time with midtown dilettantes pretending to be entrepreneurs. You need to leave now."

Cassady was offended just on principle. "Will, you're making a huge mistake."

"Wouldn't be the first time. Wouldn't even be the first time this week. Good-bye, ladies." He marched to his door, flung it open, and gestured for us to exit.

"We could pay for the ad up front if it would help your situation—" I offered, not completely sure where we'd get the money, but trying to keep us in the room with Will.

He wavered for a micro-moment, then shook his head. "I don't know that anything can help my situation. Good-bye."

I would have loved to have pulled an Agatha Christie "let me explain it all to you" on him, but I didn't have it all strung together yet. We had no choice but to leave.

At the bottom of the stairs, I had a thought. "Thirsty, anyone?"

We ducked into Vinnie's, a dingy but pleasant neighborhood joint complete with red and white vinyl tablecloths and insufficient lighting. We bought iced teas and sat at a table at one of the front windows, so oily and pitted with age that it slightly warped our view of the street. But sure enough, moments after we sat down, Will came pounding out onto the sidewalk and raced around the corner. We left our drinks on the table and hurried to follow him.

The key to tailing someone is, I'm sure, maintaining a low profile yourself. We weren't dressed for it, we were certainly in the wrong shoes for it, and there were three of us. Not ideal conditions. But we did round the corner onto West 14th in time to see Will disappear into a cab.

"Follow that cab!" Tricia yelled, not that we were anywhere near a cab of our own.

Cassady sighed. "Must you?"

"It seemed appropriate. And I've never been in a circumstance where it seemed appropriate before."

"What a shame." Cassady swung her disapproving look to me. "You don't mean to follow him, do you?"

"We've already lost him. But we should get back."

I had to get back to the office and confirm some facts on that end. Cassady and Tricia dropped me off with plans to meet again for dinner and compare notes.

The office was still subdued, but how much of that was mourning Yvonne and how much of it was just Yvonne's absence, I couldn't be sure.

Gretchen had finally given in to everyone's advice that

she go home, so I stuck my head in Brady's office, having put on the most casual expression I could manage at this point. "Hey, Brady?"

He was hunched over an overflowing desk, our own Bob Cratchit. He looked up and seemed relieved that I wasn't bringing him work. "Hey, Molly."

"Did you ever get that Nachtmusik situation worked out?"

He jerked upright in his chair and his eyes widened in panic. "Damn. Gretchen was taking care of that and I let her go home."

"Which was the right thing to do. With everything that's happened, I'm sure Monday will be plenty of time to get it resolved. I was just being nosy anyway."

Brady wasn't convinced, but he nodded and returned to his work. I went further down the hall to Accounting, to be nosy with Wendy, Sophie's assistant. I'm fascinated by Wendy's presence in Accounting; she seems to have difficulty getting her breasts to balance in the demi-cup bras and baby tees she favors, so I can't imagine she can balance a spreadsheet. But the rumor is she spreads other things for a friend of The Publisher, so we all have to live with it.

I asked her about Nachtmusik and the missing payment and she stared at me blankly for a moment. I repeated the question and she cut me off halfway through. "Gimme a minute to think."

I refrained from pointing out that a minute probably wasn't going to help and did my best to be patient.

"That's the one Brady's all worked up about, right?"

I nodded, not wanting to editorialize about Brady and his capacity for getting worked up and thereby run the risk of nudging Wendy from the slender thread of thought she was spinning.

"Yeah, I got it, but so what?"

"So the problem's solved," I suggested, surprised to find myself disappointed by this turn of events. The check showing up didn't fit with my theory.

"No, 'cause it was a bad check."

"It was?" Okay now. That could fit.

"Gretchen found the stupid thing yesterday, in the wrong file in Teddy's office or something. I had to call the bank and make sure on the spot it was good 'cause we're so close to the issue closing."

"And it wasn't."

"No way. I got more money in the bank than that silly little company, whoever they are. Anyway, Gretchen was pretty bummed and asked me not to tell Brady."

"Why not tell Brady?"

"Something about Teddy being a man of his word and if his word lost value, everything lost value, some crap like that." It was apparently a concept that baffled Wendy, so I didn't waste my time trying to explain it. I just thanked her and left.

Teddy was a man of his word. That meant Teddy had promised someone—either Will or Will's friend—that the ad would run. More than that, he'd apparently promised that the ad would be paid for by a third party. But the third party clearly hadn't ponied up. So how to find that third party? I was going to have to get Gretchen to stop playing gatekeeper to Teddy's sacred memory and start dishing some dirt.

I went back to my desk and called Gretchen's apartment, but I got the answering machine. For her sake, I hoped she was doped up and snoring. I hated bothering her, but I had to. "Gretchen, it's Molly. I'm sorry to do this, but we have got to talk. Soon." I left her my cell and home numbers and hoped that she'd wake up before tomorrow.

After a couple of hours of staring at letters, I went home to get ready for dinner. I took a long, hot shower because I usually get really good ideas in the shower, but brilliance eluded me tonight.

I really wanted to bury myself in a big cowl sweater and flannel slacks, but it wasn't quite that cold yet and Tricia would make me change anyway, so I moderated to my black leather skirt and matching cropped jacket with a silk tee. It actually cheered me up in a vain, superficial sort of way, but I was willing to take what I could get at this point.

Cassady and Tricia buzzed from the lobby and I told them to save their strength and wait for me down there. As I joined them in the lobby, I congratulated myself for my clothing choice: They were both pretty swanked up. Cassady was the one in D&G now—sleek black pants with a tuxedo-esque jacket—and Tricia had traded to a Prada confection with a fitted jacket and a flighty skirt. We were all trying to cheer ourselves up.

The thing is, all I really need for cheering up is the two of them. I haven't been pulled down into a hole yet that the sight of the two of them or even the sound of them on the phone hasn't been able to pull me out of. New York can be a brutal city or it can be immense fun. You just have to share it with the right people.

And you have to be lucky enough that when someone shoots at you on a beautiful fall night in the Big Apple, you raise your arm to hail a cab at just the right moment so that the bullet hits your shoulder, ruining your leather jacket but missing your heart.

17

At least that's what Cassady and Tricia told me when I
woke up in the St. Clare's ER. That was too many saints,
too many ER's, in too short a time for me. I vaguely re-
called a freight train crashing into my shoulder, and falling
to the sidewalk. I sort of remembered Cassady screaming
and Tricia screaming, but everything got pretty fuzzy after
that. It also went black and white. What fragments of
memory I could assemble of paramedics and policemen,
but mostly of Cassady and Tricia, were all in black and
white. It was weird, but it was comforting, too. I don't
think I wanted to confront it all in living color quite yet.

The bullet wrecked my jacket and tore up my arm pretty
good, too, but there was no arterial damage. Tricia paged
a plastic surgeon she knew from her parents' social circle
and made him come do the stitches. I've never been happy
with my upper arms, but now I was going to have a good
reason to keep them covered.

Two detectives came to talk to me, but I couldn't tell
them much. I had secretly hoped it would be Edwards and
Lipscomb, but it was a very severe female detective named
Andrews and a fireplug of a guy named Ortiz. Cassady told
them the "incident" was related to the Teddy Reynolds and

Yvonne Hamilton homicides and that they needed to get Detectives Edwards and Lipscomb on the phone immediately. They said they'd consult with Edwards and Lipscomb and be in touch. They gave me their cards and asked me to call if I remembered anything else, but I told them I hoped I wouldn't, no offense.

The detectives left and that's when the real questioning started.

"What do you mean, you want to go home?" Tricia began.

"You want her to stay here, with God knows who coming and going at all hours of the night?" Cassady asked.

"You don't think whoever did this would come into the hospital, do you?"

"If they want her dead, you think they care where it happens?"

"Can you guys stop?" I managed. Cassady's question made me feel faint, but I didn't want to pass out in front of the doctors. No way they'd let me go home if I did that. And I had to go home. I needed the security of my own place. My own bed. With my own covers pulled up over my own head while quick, clever police officers stood watch outside. "I want to go home."

I'm not sure if I conveyed sincerity or desperation, but it persuaded Tricia and Cassady to end their debate and use their powers for good to try to convince the doctors to spring me. Okay, so maybe badgering and intimidating don't really qualify as noble, but they got me released. I'd lost all sense of time, but Tricia said we'd been there about four hours.

"You guys need dinner," I told them as they walked me gingerly out to the sidewalk.

"Are you kidding? I need sedatives," Tricia said.

Cassady shook the pharmacy bag the doctor had given me. "What kind of candy does Molly have and is she going to share?"

"I think he said it was Vicodin. I'm not sure I like how it makes you feel." I had to concentrate to get the words to come out straight and that was the feeling I liked least of all.

"Honey, it's being shot you don't like, not being drugged," Cassady corrected.

"I think she has every right in the world to not like either," Tricia countered.

They eased me into a cab. I let my head drop back onto the seat and licked my lips to make sure they were there. They felt puffy and tingly, but present. The drive was oddly relaxing, but maybe that was the Vicodin. I thought it would be so nice to drift off to sleep in the back seat, then have someone carry me upstairs and tuck me in like when I was little. But the image of Cassady and Tricia trying to lift me out of the cab, much less carry me anywhere, was amusing enough to keep me awake.

The questioning resumed as we got out of the cab. Were they both going to spend the night? If so, who was going to sleep where? Were we all going to pile into my bed or were they going to jury-rig the couch and chairs or what?

"Tricia, you need to get a good night's sleep. You have an event tomorrow," Cassady reminded her.

"Oh, Teddy's service," Tricia gasped.

"You can help me get her upstairs, but then you can go home and I'll stay with her," Cassady suggested. She held open the lobby door and Tricia guided me inside, like a child easing a helium balloon into the house.

Danny, our sweet little bald doorman, came rushing forward to assist. "Ms. Forrester, it's so good to know you're okay."

I had to force myself not to reach out and pat his shiny head. The Vicodin buzz was shifting from sleepy to giddy. "Sorry for all the excitement, Danny."

"It's fine, it's fine, I'm just glad you're fine, you have a visitor."

He ran it together like it was all one thought, so it took me a minute to register what he'd said. He pointed and we looked to see Detective Edwards sitting on the lobby couch, his jacket open and his tie undone. Did that mean he was off duty? He was on his cell, which he now hung up and pocketed. He stood up, straightening his tie and buttoning his jacket. Maybe not.

"Ms. Forrester, Ms. Lynch," he said, but he was only looking at me. Or was that the Vicodin?

"Ms. Vincent," Tricia supplied for herself. He nodded, but still without looking away from me.

"Detective Edwards," Cassady replied for us all. "I'm glad to see you. I told the detectives at the hospital—"

"Yes, I know," he said with that same quiet authority that had so befuddled Peter the other night. It didn't befuddle Cassady, but she did stop talking. "Let's get her upstairs."

He stepped forward and took my healthy arm, walking me to the elevator. Cassady and Tricia followed. There was an awkward silence as we went up to my apartment. Detective Edwards seemed to have a plan, but none of us could figure out what it was. Was he going to stand guard over us all night? Did he have more questions? There was no way he could still have suspicions about me unless he'd decided that I'd had a falling out with my fellow felons and they were willing to rub me out to keep things neat and tidy, which is what I had figured had happened to Yvonne anyway, so it wasn't really all that much of a stretch, but the guy had to realize that I was an innocent in all this, didn't he? Or was that the Vicodin?

Once inside my apartment, Cassady helped me change into a sweater and jeans while Tricia bustled around, fluffing pillows, brewing a pot of tea, and generally fretting. I could hear her trying to get some information, some response out of Edwards, but she wasn't having much luck.

Cassady asked me, "Why do you think he's here?"

"He's got questions. He's just biding his time."

Cassady shook her head. "He's worried about you."

"Good. I'm worried about me, too."

Cassady kissed me on the cheek and gave me half a hug, carefully avoiding my wounded arm. "We're going to take good care of you."

Not according to Detective Edwards. Cassady brought me out and she and Tricia ensconced me on the couch with pillows and a comforter, everything but a pipe and slippers. Detective Edwards stood by and watched without comment. But when they were done and about to sit down next to me themselves, Edwards said, "Thank you very much."

Cassady frowned at him. "That sounds like a dismissal."

"I'll watch over Ms. Forrester tonight. Thank you very much."

I don't know which of the three of us was more shocked. Was he saying he was spending the night? Whose idea was this? Was it a good idea? Was it an official idea? Was I ready for this? Where was my Vicodin?

Cassady wasn't sold on this either, but Tricia almost bounded to her feet. "I think it's wonderful. I for one will sleep much better knowing that you're here with Molly, Detective. Come on, Cassady."

I could tell from Tricia's smile, which was struggling not to become a grin, that as our resident romantic, she'd decided Edwards was here for personal reasons and that she and Cassady needed to get out of the way. Cassady still wasn't convinced, still suspicious of Edwards' motives, which made sense since she'd rescued me from his interrogation room so recently. I had no idea what was in store, but I did want to find out. Much as I loved the notion of my friends keeping watch over me, I was excited by the prospect of Edwards taking over those duties.

"I'll be fine, Cassady," I assured her. "I'll see you in the morning for the service."

Cassady shook her head, not sold but giving in. "If you need us—"

"I know."

They each kissed me good night, nodded their farewell to Detective Edwards, and left. Cassady hesitated at the door, but Tricia pulled her out. Edwards walked over and locked the door behind them. Then he turned and stared at me for an uncomfortably long time.

I wanted to come up with the perfect Myrna Loy line for the moment, but I was suddenly wrestling with the desire to cry. Maybe this was Vicodin Phase III. What had I done? How much of this was my fault? Had I done something wrong? What was going to happen now?

"Why'd you send my lawyer away? Is this legal?" I said, having lost control of my mind and my mouth all at the same time.

"Are you medicated?"

"Of course I am. Which means I have to be very careful about what I say because I seem to be saying what I'm thinking and around you, that could be a not very good idea." I was trying to keep calm, maintain focus, but I was distracted by my inability to feel the tip of my nose.

"Why? What don't you want me to know?"

A laugh, which I belatedly recognized as my own, bounced around the room. "You're trying to trick me into telling you secrets."

"You have secrets?"

"What woman worth her salt doesn't?"

"True."

"Now, don't agree with me because you think it's going to get you somewhere."

"Maybe I just think you're right."

"Right as in 'correct' or as in 'the right one'?"

"Let's start with being correct."

"About what?"

"A lot of things."

It was like an out-of-body experience. I knew I should clam up, but I couldn't stop myself. "You think I'm right about Yvonne killing Teddy? The problem there is that now somebody killed Yvonne and tried to kill me and I think it has something to do with this ad that was supposed to be in the magazine for these really cool jewel thingies that you put on your shoes and I think Teddy promised this guy he'd help but the money disappeared because maybe—ooh, ooh, that's why Teddy and Yvonne were stealing money from the magazine or taking kickbacks or whatever and you can check their financial records and all that kind of stuff, can't you?" I looked at him expectantly, waiting for an answer but not completely sure what I had just asked him.

"We've looked at their financials but we haven't found anything."

"They're crafty. Were crafty. There's a missing connection, you know, a person that brings it all together and I keep thinking I almost have it figured out and then somebody goes and shoots at me and that makes it really hard to concentrate."

"I can imagine."

"But I'm going to figure out who it is and you're going to believe me when I do."

"I see."

"Promise."

"Why?"

"If you promise, I'll tell you my secret."

He walked over and sat down on the coffee table, his knees bracketing mine as he faced me. "I promise."

"You have the most amazing blue eyes I've ever seen."

The amazing blue eyes crinkled, but I couldn't tell if they were amused or frustrated. "That's your big secret?"

"Yes. And I shouldn't be telling you because now I'm in your power."

"I couldn't control you if I wanted to."

"Want to?"

Taking my hands in his, he said, "I went nuts when Ortiz called me. I've been so worried that something like this was going to happen."

"But I thought you suspected me."

"I can't figure you out at all. At least, I tell myself that's the reason I can't stop thinking about you."

Somewhere deep inside where the Vicodin hadn't gone yet, I found the strength to shut up a moment. I even held my breath, wanting to preserve the moment as long as possible. "I didn't do anything wrong," I finally said.

"I know. Now we have to keep you safe while we figure out who did."

"And that's why you're here tonight. To keep me safe."

His smile was lopsided and unexpected and devastating. "Guard you as closely as possible."

"My tax dollars at work?"

"Not yet." He leaned forward and kissed me, warmer and fuller and longer than the first time. I still couldn't quite feel the tip of my nose, but I could feel this. Everywhere. And for the first time since I'd found Teddy's body, the endless questions in my head went silent and all I could think about was Edwards' mouth and his hands and his arms and I didn't say a word when he picked me up and carried me into my bedroom. It seemed perfectly right.

18

You can't blame Cassady for screaming. The terror of a homicide detective pointing his gun at you can only be diminished slightly by the fact that he's wearing nothing but boxers. And you can't blame a homicide detective for reacting instinctively when he's jolted awake by an intruder.

I didn't think to tell Kyle—the detective formerly known as Edwards—that Cassady had a key to my apartment and an understanding with the doormen which meant she was capable of appearing unannounced. And there was no way for me to tell Cassady that Kyle was going to be there in the morning because I was still marveling over the fact that he was there at all when I fell asleep and didn't wake up again until Cassady started screaming.

When I heard her scream, I instinctively rolled out of bed, which was not the nicest thing to do to my wretched shoulder, and wrapped myself in a sheet. For a moment, I thought I was having another Vicodin dream, given the sight of semi-nude Kyle drawing down on Cassady who looked about ready to throw up on her exquisite Gianfranco Ferre black brocade jacket and flouncy skirt.

Kyle lowered the gun and that seemed to make Cassady

feel a little better. I sank down on the foot of the bed and that made me feel better. Kyle and Cassady both turned to me for an explanation.

"She has a key. He has a gun," was all I could come up with.

"We figured that much out ourselves," Cassady replied.

"Bet I can count on you to fill in the rest, too," I warned.

Kyle didn't say anything, he just started collecting his clothes from various points on my bedroom floor. Cassady took advantage of his turned back to waggle her eyebrows at me as lasciviously as possible. I tried not to smile, but I couldn't hold it back completely. She rolled her eyes and leaned against the doorjamb.

"Would you like some privacy, Detective Edwards?"

"I'm fine, thank you, Ms. Lynch."

"Cassady, this is Kyle. Kyle, Cassady."

"So we're *all* on a first-name basis now. How nice." Cassady rolled her eyes again and stuck out her hand, but Kyle was in the middle of pulling on his trousers and not in a position to walk across the room. He nodded to her and she settled for nodding back. "Well. This is such a nice and cozy way to start the day, I hate to spoil it. But we do have a funeral to attend."

I actually found the thought of the funeral easier to handle than the thought of getting up and getting dressed for it. My shoulder was really starting to ache, especially when I glanced at the clock radio on my bedside table. "It's only seven thirty, Cassady."

"I had no idea how slowly you'd be moving this morning, and we promised to meet Tricia early in case she needed last-minute help."

"We did?"

Cassady's eyes slid back over to Kyle. "I'm sure some things from last night are a little hazier than others."

Kyle refrained from commenting or looking at Cassady and pulled his shirt on. "I'll meet you at the church."

"You're coming to the funeral?"

"On business."

"Ooh, are we going to flush out the killer in the middle of the service?" Cassady said, only half-jesting.

"No 'we,' " Kyle replied in complete seriousness, which was somewhat undercut by his search for his shoes and socks. "Your job, Ms. . . . Cassady, is to sit on Molly and make sure she doesn't run up to the pulpit and exhort the killer to give himself up or do anything else that even smells like investigative work. My partner and I will take care of all that."

"Including the exhortation?"

"Especially the exhortation."

Cassady started to make another smart comment, but there's something about the sight of a detective slipping on his shoulder holster that subdues your drive to make jokes. "I'll take care of her," Cassady promised instead.

"Thank you." He clipped his badge on his belt and re-loaded his pockets with his wallet and change and all that junk men jingle around. He grabbed his jacket, kissed me quickly but persuasively, and said, "Be careful."

"You, too," I murmured back.

Cassady stepped out of the doorway to let him pass and he gave her a half-smile of appreciation. She smiled back and watched him leave the apartment so she could spin on me the moment the door closed behind him.

"Dish. Now."

"I need help getting ready for the funeral," I dodged, not quite ready to share yet.

"You didn't have any trouble getting naked, why do you need help getting dressed?" Cassady scoffed.

"I had help getting naked," I assured her.

"You cannot tease me and then not dish. It's not proper etiquette."

"But watching Kyle get dressed is," I countered.

She smirked. "I was captivated and couldn't turn away. He's very nice."

"Yes, he is."

"So dish."

"No."

Cassady looked at me hard, her eyes widening in surprise, which is not an expression you see on her face very often. "Oh, no. He's got potential."

"I have to take a shower." I headed for the bathroom, still wrapped in my sheet. Cassady stomped on the edge of the sheet to stop me.

"You can't get your shoulder wet."

"Then I'll take a bath. And then you can help me get dressed."

"I get to pick what you're wearing? That'll be fun." Accepting the momentary brush-off, Cassady turned to my closet. I went into the bathroom and took one of the most awkward baths of my life. I broke my wrist in PE when I was in seventh grade—a moment in which gravity tried to take control of the sport of pole vaulting and, for the moment, won—and I had to shower with a trash bag taped around my forearm for four weeks. My shoulder was a little more difficult to isolate, but I managed. Listening through the door to Cassady's scathing color commentary on my wardrobe helped.

I did have to break down and ask for Cassady's help in washing my hair. I wrapped myself in a towel and stuck

my head in the sink. My main concern was squeezing the
two of us into my tiny bathroom which really is nothing
more than a water closet, emphasis on the closet part. It
wasn't until Cassady's hands were on the back of my head,
pushing my head under the water, that I realized I had
bigger problems.

"Tell me!" she laughed.

"Amazing!" I sputtered.

"How much potential?"

"Substantial. Real."

"This is too delicious for words. Tricia will have a cow."

Tricia couldn't have a cow if you paid her. It's not part
of her genetic makeup. Tricia is someone who has kittens.
And right there on the church steps, she had kittens as
Cassady described with great vigor walking in on Kyle and
me.

"Oh. Oh. Oh," Tricia squeaked.

"What's more," Cassady said, "she says he has *real potential.*"

"I knew it!" Tricia exclaimed triumphantly. "Oh, how
wonderful. This is so exciting!" She hugged me, swerving
away from the injured shoulder at the last second, a gesture
I appreciated since I had chosen to forgo my morning Vicodin in the interest of staying sharp at the funeral and
reception. "Not to minimize the shock and horror of your
being shot, Molly, but I'm very happy for you."

"Thanks."

"I take it there's been no progress on that front?"

"The wheels of justice turn more slowly than the wheels
of romance," Cassady suggested.

"Don't we have a funeral to go to?" I asked.

In our darkest moments, don't we all wonder about the
crowd our funerals will draw? In my episodes of bleakness,

I lean toward about fourteen people in metal folding chairs with flaking paint in a church basement with bad fluorescent lighting and exposed pipes.

It would never occur to me to imagine the epic scene that was unfolding for Teddy's service. For starters, St. Aidan's is a great old stone church, a classic Gothic church, with vaulted ceilings, elegant lighting, and solid wood pews. It probably even has a nice, warm, beautifully appointed basement.

Then there were the people. Tricia had gone up to the choir loft to check on the musicians, but Cassady and I tucked ourselves into a niche in the narthex, close to the open front doors, to watch everyone arrive.

We were just this side of a theater premiere, with town cars and limos disgorging movers and shakers dressed in elegant black outfits, ranging from business suits to cocktail dresses. I don't think many people in this crowd had dressed with church in mind; everyone was thinking about the reception.

People paused to hug or air-kiss on the church steps, then made their way through the narthex for more relatively quiet greetings, then into the sanctuary. There were presidents of ad agencies, reps from our biggest advertisers, editors and advertising directors from other magazines, newspaper people, fixtures on the charity circuit, and a couple of overwhelmed and unfamiliar folks who were probably members of Helen's or Teddy's families. It was a fascinating parade of predominantly powerful people, but I kept watching all of them thinking, which ones did he sleep with and which one killed him?

Which brought me back to Yvonne. It seemed odd to be doing this without Yvonne. It seemed odd to consider doing this again in a week for Yvonne. I bowed my head and dashed off a quick prayer of thanks that no one had to do it for me. This week.

Cassady nudged me. "You all right?" she hissed.

I lifted my head. "I'm praying," I hissed back.

Cassady blinked slowly. "Tell Him you'll call back. It's time to sit down."

We walked down the side aisle and found seats not far from a little knot of *Zeitgeist* people. I caught Kendall's eye and waved discreetly. Kendall tapped Gretchen and Fred, on each side of her, to get them to turn and acknowledge me. Fred looked doped up and Gretchen looked ill. I couldn't blame either one.

Helen was the essence of dignity when she rose to address the congregation. She didn't weep, but you could tell she was working hard not to. I glanced around to see if Kyle and Lipscomb had arrived yet. This was sincere, not a performance, and I wanted to be sure they saw it, but I couldn't spot them in the crowd.

I turned my attention back to the service. I tried to appreciate the music, to absorb all the lovely things that were being said about Teddy, to ignore The Publisher's hideous tie while he made his remarks, but I couldn't concentrate. My mind kept going back to Kyle and the night before, but I couldn't think about that in church. That was asking for lightning to strike me. Or maybe I just didn't want to analyze it at all when the thrill of it was still so fresh that I could feel it.

I forced my mind in a different direction and it started spinning, turning the puzzle pieces over and over, looking for the one that would make it all fit together. Teddy. Teddy and Yvonne. Teddy and Yvonne and me. And money. And Camille. And Alicia. And Will. Will didn't seem capable of killing, but I would have said the same about Yvonne two weeks ago. If Yvonne killed Teddy, had Will killed Yvonne because some deal had ruptured? Had all his eggs been in the Teddy basket and when the bottom had fallen out, he'd blamed Yvonne? But then how had he come to take a shot at me? Maybe I hadn't been as subtle about my investigation as I thought I'd been, but I hadn't exactly strewn bread crumbs from MePa to my front door. Was Will the key to all this? Had I been wrong about Yvonne? Had I been out of my mind to think I could figure this out at all? No. This was going to make sense.

I still hadn't figured it out when we reached the Essex House. I let Cassady steer me to the Grand Salon. The room was stunning, just enough solemnity in the flowers and linens to convey the seriousness of the occasion, but not so much that it was depressing. Tricia had done a spectacular job of getting the room dressed beautifully with such little notice, and if I managed to see her in the course of the proceedings, which I doubted, I would have to tell her so.

Cassady pushed me through the crowd, which was growing louder and looser by the moment. Give them all a drink and someone would start the game of "Remember the time that Teddy . . ." and there would be a lot of forced laughter and melancholy merriment and then we could all go home. Parking me in a fairly central spot in the room, Cassady told me to stay put while she went and got us drinks.

As wonderful a job as Tricia had done, there was still something about the Art Deco setting and its overly rich, autumnal colors that gave the proceedings a staged quality, or more precisely, a nightmarish quality of bent reality and crumbling facades. I should have taken another Vicodin and let things be even more warped, but I could feel the answer nibbling around the edges of my brain and I didn't want to do anything to startle it away.

That task fell to Peter. I was trying to build my house of cards with Will as my centerpiece when a voice in my ear intoned, "Man is the only animal that contemplates its own death. And then throws a party to celebrate it."

I turned to face him, surprised. "I didn't remember seeing you on the guest list."

"Nice to see you, too," he replied. He offered me a mimosa and I took it automatically. "I'm here on behalf of the staff of *Jazzed*."

"Thanks for pinch-hitting."

"It's as much out of a desire to see you as to pay my respects to Teddy. Are you okay?"

I wasn't sure how much he knew. I would have shrugged, but I figured that would hurt too much. "It's been a long week."

"The cops still hassling you?"

"Not since I got shot." I couldn't resist. I just had to see the look on his face, that look of sheer shock that a guy who spends all his time trying to be one up on the next guy doesn't get much practice using.

"What?"

"Someone took a shot at me last night. I figure somebody put a hit on the whole magazine and is picking us off one by one. We should have a staff retreat at a deserted summer camp in the Poconos and make it easier on the poor psycho. Or maybe The Publisher is just trying to cut down on overhead."

"The police think this is connected to Yvonne's and Teddy's deaths?"

"Leaning in that direction."

"Molly, this is amazing. What happened?" The final nail

in the coffin. Excepting Kyle, that is. No more misgivings. A guy who really cared about you would say, "This is terrible," or "I'm worried about you," right? This guy flips open the reporter's mental notebook and starts taking notes.

Cassady saved the moment by returning with more mimosas. "Hello, Peter. Pleasure to mourn with you." She indicated the entrance with a toss of the head. "Kyle and his friend are here."

We all turned to look and saw Kyle and Detective Lipscomb moving along the perimeter of the crowd. Peter looked back at me quickly. "Kyle?"

"Detective Edwards from Homicide," I said, deliberately misunderstanding his tone. "The one who questioned me yesterday." Was that really only yesterday? Amazing.

Peter was looking at me hard with that pinched brow look guys get when they're trying to decide how much dignity they can bear to part with in order to get the information they want. Peter wanted to know about Edwards' transformation to "Kyle" but he didn't want to make himself vulnerable by asking. I looked around the room to give him a moment to finish the struggle.

Helen was standing across the room with a knot of people including her sister Candy and a male version of Candy who could only be their brother. People drifted up to Helen, hugged her or shook her hand, exchanged the proper statements of sorrow or comfort and moved on. It looked like it was sucking the lifeblood out of Helen ten cc's at a time. I wondered when I should go over and decided to wait, even though it would have given me a good reason to walk away from Peter.

There was a knot of *Zeitgeist* people near Helen—Fred, Kendall, and Brady with some of the editorial staff. I was surprised not to see Gretchen with Fred and Kendall since they had seemed to be propping her up as they walked down the aisle after the service. Maybe she'd gone to the bar.

I scanned the room, half-looking for Kyle again, and I spotted Gretchen. She wasn't getting drinks, she was talking to a group of women. One I recognized as Hilary Abraham, a fashion account manager at *Femme*. I didn't recognize the others. But I recognized what they were all looking at. Gretchen was wearing the shoe jewels from the Nocturne ad and the women were all exclaiming over them.

The freight train that had hit me when I got shot hit me again, but this time it was pure emotion. The pure emotion of watching the bars fall into place as a slot machine rings up a jackpot. Gretchen was wearing the shoe jewels. Gretchen knew about the shoe jewels. So Gretchen knew Will. Maybe Gretchen was even Will's girlfriend. And as a devoted assistant, she had approached Teddy and asked him to help them out and he'd said no, so she'd killed him. I wasn't sure how that led to Yvonne getting killed or my getting shot, but I was certainly going to find out.

I started to walk away and Peter, who had been talking about something while I hadn't been listening, grabbed my arm to stop me. Fortunately, it was my left arm, but I still got him to let go with one withering glance. I handed my champagne glass to Cassady and said, "I'll be right back." Then I took Peter's face in both my hands, kissed him good-bye and said, "It's been fun. I hope you meet someone wonderful this afternoon," and walked over to Gretchen.

The group was so involved in Gretchen's explanation of how the shoe jewels were made and how they could be fitted to almost any pair of high heels that they didn't see me coming. I walked right up to them and tapped Gretchen on the shoulder. "Excuse me, but I need to ask you a quick question," I said. Gretchen threw a glance at her captivated audience. "Won't take a second," I told them. "Don't go away, you can have her right back."

I stepped back three paces and Gretchen came with me, less than willing. "What do you need?" she asked curtly, impatient to get back to what I'm sure she considered a bevy of potential customers.

"I need to know why you shot me."

I've never experienced anything like it. I could see in her eyes that I was right and the thrill that it sent through me was akin to great sex, but there was a vindication element to it that made it completely different. It was intoxicating and could be, I sensed, highly addictive.

"I . . . didn't . . ." Gretchen faltered.

"Isn't that interesting. You didn't go for the innocent, 'I don't know what you're talking about, Molly,' because you do know I was shot. You're going straight to the basic denial, which I think translates to—"

"Excuse us, please," Kyle said as he grabbed my arm and walked me away from Gretchen without warning.

"No!" I protested.

He pulled me close so he could speak quietly. "What're you doing kissing Crew Boy?"

"I was dumping him!" I turned back, but Gretchen was already melting into the crowd. "Stop her!" I called, but the room was loud and no one paid attention. I turned back to Kyle. "Gretchen did it. Did at least me. She's getting away. Let's go."

"What?"

I shook my arm out of his grasp and plunged into the crowd. I figured she'd have to try to run, which meant she'd head for the main entrance. I kept my head down, avoiding eye contact and trying not to stomp on feet. I could hear Kyle behind me, calling my name and trying to get me to stop, but I couldn't. I had to catch Gretchen.

Kyle caught up with me as I raced for the front door of the hotel. Scanning the lobby on the run, I explained, "It's Gretchen. Teddy's assistant. She's the missing piece. She did it. All of it, probably. It wasn't passion, it was business. I don't have it all laid out yet, but we have to stop her."

Kyle looked at me hard, then listened to some inner voice and nodded. "Okay."

Problem was, no one at the front door had seen anyone matching Gretchen's description in the last few minutes. Kyle said that meant she could still be in the hotel. "You go back into the reception and stay there. Lipscomb and I will look for her."

"I need to talk to her," I insisted.

"You need to stay out of harm's way," he said, marching me back toward the Grand Salon.

"I can help," I promised.

"Molly, please. Let me do my job. You've already done enough." I wasn't sure whether the last comment was a compliment or a complaint, but decided this was not the time to ask for clarification.

We got back to the Grand Salon and found Cassady and Tricia, who had been looking for me, and Lipscomb, who had been looking for Kyle. Kyle gave Lipscomb a quick rundown and they took off to try and find Gretchen elsewhere in the hotel. His parting words to me were, "Stay here."

"So are you staying here?" Cassady asked as soon as the detectives were out of sight.

"Of course not," I replied.

"Molly, you can't do this," Tricia pleaded. "You have a nice detective and a nice bullet wound which all makes for a nice article. Quit while you're ahead."

"Yeah, right."

Tricia sighed and looked at Cassady. "I had to try."

Cassady kissed Tricia on the cheek. "I know. You stay here and take care of the event. I'll go with her."

"Oh, that's nice. Expect me to stay here and work while I worry about both of you."

"Just try to cover our tracks, I don't know who else from the magazine might be involved," I told her, starting to back away toward the front doors.

"Where are you going?"

"Back to Will's. We'll call you," I said with a casual tone that surprised me.

"What about Kyle?"

"He'll only tell me no. I'll call him from there."

Cassady and I ran as best you can run in three-inch heels, which is basically that hideous locked-elbow, sway-backed mincing run made famous by high school cheerleaders, all the way across the lobby and into the first available cab.

"I can see how some might find this fun," Cassady said when she caught her breath.

All I could wish for was, "Let's hope it stays that way."

19

I *figured the cab* ride to Will's apartment would be long enough for me to develop some clever plan to trap Gretchen and get her to confess to me, rat out everyone involved, and have it all make sense by the time I got her back to Kyle. I could've used a couple more red lights.

Cassady and I told the cab to let us off around the corner, but other than the fact that it was imprinted on my consciousness from the Quinn Martin television series of my childhood, I'm not sure why. The theory was, any element of surprise would be helpful, I suppose.

But I'm not sure who was more surprised when we collided on the sidewalk—Will or us. Will was dressed for travel, with a distressed leather jacket over jeans and a sweater. He was wearing Doc Martens and carrying a duffel bag and a smaller leather satchel. His jeweler's tools, probably.

He blanched when he recognized us and tried to push past us, but Cassady took a self-defense class last year and enjoyed it a little too much. She grabbed his shoulders, kneed him in the groin, and dropped him like a sack of mulch. The duffel and the satchel went down with him. The satchel clanged, confirming my suspicions of its contents. It took him a moment to catch his breath, but as soon as he could vocalize, he groaned, "None of this was my idea."

Cassady groaned. "You gotta love a man who goes the distance."

"Where's Gretchen?" I asked.

"Upstairs. Packing."

"What?"

"She came home from the reception and said you'd figured it all out and we had to pack quickly and run. So I threw a bunch of stuff together, but she's up there folding stuff and taking her time, so I say we gotta go and she says she's hurrying and I say I'm outta here, but now we're totally screwed."

We watched him curl up into the fetal position and give up. "You okay with him?" I asked Cassady.

"Sure. I still have another knee, but he's all outta nuts," she assured me.

I tossed her my cell phone. "You should probably call Kyle. And Tricia."

"I won't tell Tricia she was second."

I started for the stairs, then stopped as a crucial question occurred to me. "Will, does she still have the gun?"

"I threw it in the sewer. Not that I had anything to do with it. She just told me what she did and showed me the gun and I freaked and threw it in the sewer."

Cassady looked like she was considering kicking Will while he was down. She leaned down to make sure he could see the disgust on her face. "Look at what she's done for you—killed two people, tried to kill a third—and this is how you repay her? You're the worst excuse for a boyfriend I've seen in the history of mankind."

I left Will in Cassady's capable hands and ran up the

stairs. At the top, I wondered if there were other weapons I should have asked about, but it was pretty much too late now. I prayed for the second time that day and tried the door. It was open.

Gretchen was at the bed and what appeared to be all her worldly possessions were on it. She was folding garments carefully and laying them into suitcases, sorting and matching separates as she went along. When she was in a prison jumpsuit, this was going to seem like even more of a waste of time than it did right now.

"Will, I need the—" She stopped when she turned and saw I wasn't Will. The silk blouse she was trying to fold slid out of her hands and heaped onto the pile on the bed. "Get out."

"I'm sorry we got interrupted, Gretchen. You were about to explain to me why you shot me."

"I didn't." Her eyes were moving around the room, maybe looking for weapons. At least that meant she didn't have one handy. I had to keep her cornered and distracted.

"Yes, you did."

"Will did it."

"No, he didn't, Gretchen. He's down there on the sidewalk, weeping like a little baby and giving you up so fast. And he's only talking to Cassady. Wait till the cops get here."

"Oh, God, they're coming?"

"Yes, so tell me what happened and I'll help you with them."

"Are you sleeping with that detective?"

"Why?"

"Why else would you think they'd listen to you?"

"I'll do what I can, Gretchen."

She shifted her weight back and forth anxiously, her

mind speeding through alternatives. If she didn't have a weapon handy, there weren't that many. Her fingers idly stroked the clothes on the bed, then she made a sudden run at the door. I lunged for her, pulling something in my injured shoulder that was going to hurt for a very long time, but managing to intercept her and knock her down. This Gracie ju jitsu instructor I dated briefly was all about leverage—emotional as well as physical, which is why it was brief—and I remembered his big thing was always taking your opponent's feet out from under him. We rolled around on the floor in finest catfight fashion, smacking my bad shoulder on the floor a time or two which made me see stars, but I managed to pin her on her stomach, then put my heel in the small of her back for emphasis.

She struggled to regain her composure. "If you don't know why I did it, then you're not as smart as I thought you were and I didn't need to bother," she spat.

I rose to the bait, not because she'd gotten to me but because I wanted her to think she was in control of the situation so she didn't develop the need to shoot at me again. "I figured out part of it. You and Will are a couple."

"Oh, bravo," Gretchen responded, "since the fact that I'm in his apartment packing my clothes has so many other explanations."

"You wanted to go into business together. The shoe jewels. Which are a killer idea, by the way, pardon the expression." I pulled the shoes off her feet and got off her, hoping that in her winded and barefoot condition she wouldn't try to run again. "And Teddy said he'd help you."

"That bastard." She sat up, brushing herself off as much as possible.

"I always thought you kinda had a crush on him." I sat down across from her, trying to keep this low key.

Tears sprang into Gretchen's eyes. I was right, but something had changed. "I told him I'd do anything if he'd help us get our business started. We just needed a little boost. Do you know how many people see an ad that appears in *Zeitgeist*? Half a million people."

"But you didn't have the twenty grand. So what did Teddy want in return?"

Gretchen flushed crimson. In spite of everything I knew, my heart sank for her momentarily. The oldest currency in the world. Complicated by the fact that she'd had a crush on the guy. "You slept with him?"

Her flush deepened. "That's just for the models and the executives. He just wanted me to . . . service him."

"And you did it?" I asked, in confirmation, not in judgment.

She nodded, tears spilling over now. "Every time he asked."

"And in return, he was going to pay for your ad."

She nodded. "But the issue was getting ready to close and he hadn't done it yet and I confronted him. And he laughed at me. He told me what I'd given him wasn't worth twenty thousand dollars, so he wanted part of the company, too." She dissolved into gulping sobs.

I could see it playing out a little too clearly for comfort. "That was Monday night?"

She nodded, pushing to her feet. I nervously rose with her, but she went to the small table in the kitchen area, grabbed the box of tissues, and blew her nose loudly.

"Okay. I get Teddy, but why Yvonne?"

She blew her nose again before replying. "It was stupid, especially because you were so sure Yvonne had killed Teddy. I should've let you just screw her up. But Will said we had to get the ad in or it was all over, we were out of money, out of time, everything. I tried to kite a check, but it didn't work, thanks to Wendy, that bitch." She pulled another tissue out of the box for the sole purpose of shredding it. "So I asked Yvonne to stake us or I'd tell Helen about the affair and maybe tell the police, too."

"This was during your supposed shopping trip to Chelsea?"

"I brought her here, so she could meet Will and see our work for herself."

"But she said no."

Gretchen's face twisted horribly. "Are you kidding? Why would she just say no when she could be wretched and hateful instead? She told me that I was insane to think that I could run a business, have an influence. She said I was never going to be anything more than an assistant and not a very good one at that."

I'd heard Yvonne say as much to Gretchen, so I knew Gretchen wasn't exaggerating. And I remembered the smell of bleach when Tricia, Cassady, and I came to the apartment. They'd done their best to clean up, then Will had dropped Yvonne's body and Gretchen, deliberately bruised, over in Chelsea and ditched the car somewhere. It was all adding up, but I still had trouble accepting it.

"But how did killing Yvonne help you? Brady still wouldn't let the ad go through."

"I didn't exactly think it through, okay? I was taking it one step at a time. And that bitch was asking for it anyway."

"Okay, Gretchen, she was a bitch, but that's no reason to kill—"

"How could you understand? You're doing what you want to do. People don't treat you like office furniture."

"There are a lot of people at the magazine who like you, Gretchen," I attempted.

"That's why I had to beg you to go shopping with me."

"I had other things on my mind," I offered, knowing it was lame even if it was true.

"You're as bad as the rest of them. Did you ever suspect me of Teddy's murder? No. I had access, I had opportunity, but you never even thought about me."

"Are you complaining?" I asked, trying to keep my voice even.

She went toward the sink to throw away her tissues and it took me a moment to realize what she had in her hand when she turned back around. It wasn't a huge knife, but it didn't need to be, given how angry and twisted Gretchen was.

"I could've killed you last night," she said. I wasn't sure if she was justifying her miss or sincerely explaining it because I wasn't listening all that carefully, the knife proving to be a major distraction. "I should have."

"I think it's really important that you didn't," I told her, backing toward the door. "It'll show the jury that you have the capacity for mercy. And remorse." Not that that was going to do much for two counts of murder, but we didn't need to get into that at the moment.

Gretchen wasn't buying it anyway. "Yeah, right," she said and ran at me, full force. I tried to scramble back to the door and get out, but I didn't have time. I threw my hands up instinctively, not thinking about how much it was going to hurt my shoulder and forgetting until the moment that the knife sliced down into them that I was still holding Gretchen's shoes. The knife buried itself in the left shoe and wouldn't come free. I used the leverage to yank the knife out of Gretchen's hand, then swung the other shoe as hard as I could and pump-slapped her in the side of the head. I knocked her off her feet and literally sat on her until the front door banged open and Kyle ran in, gun in hand.

Even though my shoulder felt like it was about to fall off, I held up the shoe with the knife sticking out of it. "Such a shame. They were great shoes."

20

Dear Molly, I recently went through an experience—well, a series of experiences that were pretty traumatic. But they were pretty exciting, too. The problem is, I'm not sure what to do now that they're over. And I'm not sure how to separate my feelings about what happened from my feelings about the people I met during them and vice versa. Truthfully, I'm worried that the feelings might go away now that the experience is over. Or maybe I'm more worried that they won't. What's the best way to clear my head and figure out what comes next? Signed, Still Spinning

Cassady raised her glass in the air. "If I may quote Dorothy Parker, 'Three be the things I shall never attain, envy, content, and sufficient champagne,' " she proclaimed, charging our glasses with more bubbly.

It was Sunday, just after noon, and Tricia, Cassady, and I were having brunch at Sarabeth's on the Upper West Side. The restaurant is decorated like an old country inn and that, combined with the eons you spend in line waiting to get in, really makes you feel like you've gotten away from the city for a moment. It wasn't so much that I wanted to be far away, I just wanted to be distracted for a while, get a little emotional distance at least.

Tricia had wanted to round up all of our friends and

have a big party to celebrate my "capture" of Gretchen, but it was too soon and I wasn't sure it was something I wanted to celebrate anyway. I felt immense satisfaction, but no joy. The whole thing was far more tragic than I had ever imagined it would be when I first stumbled over Teddy. As exhilarating as it was, it had been exhausting, too. So a champagne brunch with my two best friends seemed the perfect way to mark the day. The day after, to be precise.

"What a week," Cassady sighed.

"Thank God it's over," I admitted. "My therapist is in for a big surprise tomorrow."

"You're going to write such an amazing article," Tricia enthused.

I nodded slowly. I was looking forward to writing the article, but I was also looking forward to having more champagne and not thinking about anything else for the rest of the afternoon.

"I'm sorry to interrupt," a voice said, and we all turned in surprise to find Kyle standing beside us. He was carrying a plain white-handled shopping bag that I found intriguing and incongruous.

I hadn't seen much of him after he burst into Will and Gretchen's apartment the day before. He'd had work to do and I'd had to give a statement and it all got very crazy and not very pleasant as the reality of it all settled in, so I went home and took my belated Vicodin, turned the bell off on the phone, and shut the world out as long as possible. Since Cassady and Tricia both have keys, that wasn't as long as it might have been. But I hadn't seen Kyle again until now.

"How'd you find us?" Cassady asked.

He shook his head. "No more trade secrets. Not until the next case."

"The next case?" Tricia asked, looking at me.

"He doesn't mean it," I told her and turned back to Kyle. "Are you just dropping by?"

He lifted the shopping bag slightly. "I have something for you."

"Join us," I suggested, gesturing to our empty fourth chair.

"I can't stay," he said with a guarded look, and I realized I knew very little about him—what his obligations might be, who else was in his life other than his fish, any of it. This had not been the best-thought-out relationship, if in fact it was even a relationship. He gestured for me to come with him. I glanced at Tricia and Cassady, who were glaring at me to get up and go with him quickly. Guess I was the only one in this foursome who was nervous about what had happened between Kyle and me.

"Excuse us a minute," he said to Tricia and Cassady as he walked me away from them. He led me to a little corner by the pastry case, shielding me with his body from all the people going back and forth.

"How are you today?" he asked.

"Still a little lightheaded."

"The shoulder?"

"It hurts."

"Will for a while." He nodded as though he'd answered some question of his own. "A lot's happened this week. It's going to take some sorting out."

I knew he was talking about us as much as he was about the case. "Everything happened so fast."

"Maybe too fast?"

"I don't know yet."

"You should take some time and see if it's something you really want to get into, or whether once was enough."

"Maybe it's something we could talk through."

"Absolutely."

There was a pause, but it wasn't nearly as awkward as I would have thought. I did need to take a step back, clear my head, figure out what I was doing. And he got major points for seeing that, even if—especially if—he was feeling the same way.

"I wanted to bring you these," he said after a moment and handed me the shopping bag. I reached in and took out a shoebox. I opened the shoebox and nestled inside were a brand-new pair of Jimmy Choo Cats, the shoes I'd been wearing when I found Teddy. I tried not to think of how painful a purchase they were on a detective's salary.

"Kyle, I don't know what to say."

"We have to keep your other shoes until the trial and it didn't seem fair to deprive you. And I don't think the blood's going to come out, anyway," he explained. "If you do want to get together and talk, that'd give you an excuse to wear these."

I gently put the lid back on the box. "I'd like that."

"You have my number."

"I know it by heart."

"Then I'll talk to you." He leaned in and we kissed, the most tender and tentative kiss of our whole crazed, accelerated, ridiculous, wonderful relationship. So far. Would there be more? I wasn't sure. But since I was looking at a guy who knew when to be quiet, when to be forceful, and when to buy a girl a new pair of shoes, I was going to give it serious thought.

"Tell your friends I said good-bye," he said and walked

away. I stood there, holding the shoebox, so he'd have something to see when he turned around and looked back at the door. He waved, I waved, and then I went back to drink champagne with my two best friends and revel in having made my mark—at least on Manhattan.